THE AVRAM DAVIDSON SCIENCE FICTION & FANTASY MEGAPACK®

THE AVRAM DAVIDSON

SCIENCE FICTION
& FANTASY
MEGAPACK®

AVRAM DAVIDSON

WILDSIDE PRESS

* * * *

"What Strange Stars and Skies" was originally published in *The Magazine of Fantasy & Science Fiction*, December 1963. "The Unknown Law" was originally published in *The Magazine of Fantasy & Science Fiction*, June 1964. "The Teeth of Despair" (written with Sidney Klein) was originally published in *The Magazine of Fantasy & Science Fiction*, May 1961. "The Singular Events Which Occurred in the Hovel on the Alley Off of Eye Street" was originally published in *The Magazine of Fantasy & Science Fiction*, February 1962. "The Lineaments of Gratified Desire" originally appeared in *Ellery Queen's Mystery Magazine*, December 1963. "The Golem" was originally published in *The Magazine of Fantasy & Science Fiction*, March, 1955. "The Cost of Kent Castwell" was originally published in *Alfred Hitchcock's Mystery Magazine*, July 1961. "The Bounty Hunter" was originally published in *Fantastic Universe*, March 1958. "Present for Lona" was originally published in *Alfred Hitchcock's Mystery Magazine*, March 1958. "Now Let Us Sleep" was originally published in *Venture Science Fiction Magazine*, September 1957. "Now Let Us Sleep" was originally published in *Venture Science Fiction Magazine*, September 1957. "Mr. Stilwell's Stage" was originally published in *The Magazine of Fantasy & Science Fiction*, September 1957. "Miss Buttermouth" was originally published in *The Magazine of Fantasy & Science Fiction*, May 1962. "Love Called This Thing" (written with Laura Goforth) was originally published in *Galaxy Magazine*, April 1959. "Jury-Rig" was originally published in *Venture Science Fiction Magazine*, November 1957. "I Did Not Hear You, Sir" was originally published in *The Magazine of Fantasy & Science Fiction*, February 1958. "Fair Trade" was originally published in *The Magazine of Fantasy & Science Fiction*, July 1960. "Faed-Out" was originally published in *The Magazine of Fantasy & Science Fiction*, October 1963. "Death Of A Damned Good Man" was originally published in *Isaac Asimov's Science Fiction Magazine*, January, 1991. "Where Do You Live, Queen Esther?" was originally published in *Ellery Queen's Mystery Magazine*, March 1961.

Published by Wildside Press LLC.
www.wildsidebooks.com

CONTENTS

WHAT STRANGE STARS AND SKIES

Originally published in *The Magazine of Fantasy
& Science Fiction*, December 1963.

The terrible affair of Dame Phillipa Garreck, which struck horror in all
who knew of her noble life and mysterious disappearance, arose in large
measure from her inordinate confidence in her fellow-creatures—particularly such of them as she might, from time to time, in those nocturnal
wanderings which so alarmed her family and friends, encounter in circumstances more than commonly distressed. This greathearted and misfortunate woman would be, we may be sure, the first to deplore any lessening
of philanthropy, any diminution of charity or even of charitable feelings,
resultant from her own dreadfully sudden and all but inexplicable fate; yet,
one feels, such a result is inevitable. I am not aware that Dame Phillipa ever
made use of any heraldic devices or mottoes, but, had she done so, *Do what
is right, come what may*, would have been eminently appropriate.

It is not any especial sense of competence on my part which has caused
me to resolve that a record of the matter should and must be made. Miss
Mothermer, Dame Phillipa's faithful secretary-companion, to say nothing
of her cousin, Lord FitzMorris Banstock, would each—under ordinary
circumstances, of course—be far more capable than I of delineating the
events in question. But the circumstances, of course, are as far from being
"ordinary" as they can possibly be. Miss Mothermer has, for the past six
months next Monday fortnight, been in seclusion at Doctor Hardesty's establishment near Sutton Ho; and, whilst I can state quite certainly the false-
hood of the rumor that her affairs have been placed in charge of the Master
in Lunacy, nevertheless, Doctor Hardesty is adamant that the few visitors
she is permitted to receive must make no reference whatsoever to the affairs
of last Guy Fawkes Day, the man with the false nose, or the unspeakably
evil Eurasian Motilal Smith. As for Lord FitzMorris-Banstock, though I am
aware that he has the heart of a lion and nerves of steel, his extreme shyness
(in no small measure the result of his unfortunate physical condition) must
advertise to all who know him the unlikelihood of his undertaking the task.

It falls to me, therefore, and no one else, to proceed forthwith in setting
down the chronicle of those untoward and unhappy events.

Visitors to Argyll Court, which abuts onto Primrose Alley (one of that maze of noisome passages off the Commercial Road which the zeal and conscience of the London County Council cannot much longer suffer to remain untouched), visitors to Argyll Court will have noticed the large signboard affixed to the left-hand door as one enters. Reading, *If The Lord Will, His Word Shall Be Preached Here Each Lord's Day At Seven O'Clock In The Evening. All Welcome*, it gives notice of the Sabbath activities of Major Bohun, whose weekdays are devoted to his sacred labors with The Strict Baptist Tram-Car and Omnibus Tract Society (the name of which appears on a small brass plate under the sign). Had the major been present that Fifth of November, a different story it would be which I have to tell; but he had gone to attend at an Anti-Papistical sermon given to mark the day at the Putney Tabernacle.

The fetid reek of the Court, which has overwhelmed more than one less delicately bred than Dame Phillipa, bears—besides the effluvia of un-washed beds and bodies emanating from the so-called Seaman's Lodging House of Evan-bach Llewellyn, the rotting refuse of the back part of a cookshop of the lowest sort, bad drains, and the putrid odors of Sampson Stone's wool-pullery—tainted breath of the filthy Thames itself, whose clotted waters ebb and flow not far off.

On many an evening when the lowering sun burned dully in the dirty sky and the soiled swans squatted like pigs in the mudbanks of London River, the tall figure of Dame Phillipa would turn (for the time being) from the waterfront, and make her way, by any one of a variety of routes, towards the quickening traffic of the Commercial Road and Goodman Fields; proceeding not infrequently through Salem Yard, Primrose Alley, and Argyll Court. The fashionable and sweet-smelling ladies of the West End, as well as their wretched and garishly bedaubed fallen sisters, smell-ing of cheap "scent" and sweetened gin, just at this hour beginning those peregrinations of the East End's mean and squalid streets for which those less tender than Dame Phillipa might think them dead to all shame; were wearing, with fashion's license, their skirts higher than they had ever been before: but Dame Phillipa (though she never criticized the choice of others) still wore hers long, and sometimes with one hand she would lift them an inch or two to avoid the foul pavements—though she never drew back from contact, neither an inch or an instant, with any human being, however filthy or diseased.

Sometimes Miss Mothermer's bird-like little figure was with her friend and employer, perhaps assuming for the moment the burden of the famous Army kit-bag; sometimes—and such times Dame Phillipa walked more slowly—Lord FitzMorris-Banstock accompanied her; but usually only quite late at night, and along the less-frequented thoroughfares, where such people whom they were likely to meet were too preoccupied with their own unhappy concerns, or too brutalized and too calloused, to stare at the muscular but misshapen peer for more than a second or two.

The kit-bag had been the gift of Piggott, bat-man to Dame Phillipa's brother, the late Lt.-Colonel Sir Chiddiock Garrett, when she had sent him out to the Transvaal in hopes that that Province's warmer and dryer air would be kindlier to his gas-ruined lungs than the filthy fogs and sweats of England. The kit-bag usually contained, to my own knowledge, on an average evening, the following:

Five to ten pounds in coins, as well as several ten-shilling notes folded quite small. Two sets of singlets and drawers, two shirts, and two pairs of stockings—none of them new, but all clean and mended. A dozen slices of bread and margarine, wrapped in packets of two. Ten or twenty copies of a pamphlet-sized edition of the Gospel of St. John in various languages. A brittania-metal pint flask of a good French brandy. A quantity of hard-cooked eggs and an equal supply of salt and pepper in small screws of paper. Four cotton handkerchiefs. First-aid equipment. Two reels of cotton, with needles. A packet of mixed toffees. A Book of Common Prayer. Fifteen packets of five Woodbine cigarettes, into each of which she had thrust six wooden matches. One pocket-mirror. A complete change of infant's clothing. Several small cakes of soap. Several pocket-combs. A pair of scissors.

And three picture-postcards of the Royal Family.

All this arranged with maximum efficiency in minimum space, but not packed so tightly that Dame Phillipa's fingers could not instantly produce the requisite article. It will be observed that she was prepared to deal with a wide variety of occasions.

Tragic, infinitely tragic though it is, not even a person of Dame Phillipa's great experience among what a late American author termed, not infelicitously, The People of the Abyss, could have been prepared either to expect or to deal with such persons as the man wearing the false nose, the woman who offered the antimacassars, and the hideously, the unspeakably evil Eurasian, Motilal Smith.

* * * *

The night of that Fifth of November found the unfortunates among whom this great lady pursued her noble work no more inclined than in other years to celebrate the delivery from Gunpowder Plot of King James VI and I and his English Parliament. Here and there, to be sure, in the glare of the gin-palaces of the main thoroughfares, a group of grimy and tattered children had gotten up an even more unsavory Guy; for them Dame Phillipa had provided herself with a large supply of pennies. But that night as on most other nights there was little enough evidence of innocent gaiety.

There are multitudes, literally multitudes, in this vast labyrinth of London for whom the normal institutions of a human society seem barely to exist. There are physicians in the East End, hospitals, and dispensaries; yet numbers past counting will suffer injury and disease and creep off to die like brutes in their dim corners, or, if they are fortunate, by brute strength survive. There are public baths in every borough, and facilities for washing clothes, yet many never touch water to their skins, and wear their rags unchanged till they rot. Babes are born without benefit of any human witness to the event save their own wretched mothers, though a word to the great hospital in Whitechapel Road will bring midwife and physician without charge. And while eating places abound, from quite decent restaurants down to the dirty holes-in-the-wall offering tupenny cups of tea and sixpenny papers of breaded smelts and greasy chips, and while private and public charity arrangements guarantee that no one need quite die of hunger who will ask to be fed, no day goes by without its toll from famine of those who—having their hoards of copper and silver—are disabled by their madness from spending either tuppence or shilling; or who find it much, much easier to die like dogs in their secluded kennels than come forward and declare their needs.

As the pigeons in Trafalgar Square have learned when and where the old man with the bag of breadcrumbs will appear, as the ownerless cats near Billingsgate can tell what time and in what place to scavenge for the scraps of fish the dustmen miss, as the rats in the sewers beneath Smithfield know without error the manner in which "they seek their meet from God"; just so, from this stinking alley and from that crumbling tenement, here from underneath a dripping archway and there from a disused warehouse, slinking and creeping and peering fearfully and furtively and sidling with their ragged backs pressed against ragged walls, there appeared by one and by one cast-offs—one must call them "humans," for what other name is theirs?—the self-exiled, the utterly incapable, to take in their quick reptilian grasp the things Dame Phillipa had for them. She knew, knew by instinct and knew by practice, which ones would benefit by a shilling and which by half-a-crown; she knew those to whom money was of no more use than cowry-shells but who would relish the meat of a hard-cooked egg and the savor of the tiny scrap of seasoning which went with it; knew those who would be hopelessly baffled by the labor of cracking the shell but who could manage to rip the paper off a packet of bread and margarine (huddled and crouched in the rank, familiar darkness of their burrows, tearing the soft food with their toothless gums); knew those who would fight, squealing or wordlessly, fight like cornered stoats rather than surrender a single one of the unspeakably filthy rags into which their unspeakably filthy bodies were sewn; and those who would strip by some forgotten water-tap and wash themselves and put on the clean things she provided—but only if provided them, having no longer in many cases the ability to provide either soap or singlets for themselves. She also knew who could be coaxed another foot or two up the path to self-respect by the tempting bait of mirror and comb, the subtle appeal such things made to the ravaged remnants of pride. And she knew when even a handful of toffee or a small picture of the charismatic King and Queen could brighten a dim corner of an eroded mind.

And often (though not always) with her on this humble and saintly mission went her faithful secretary-companion, Miss Mothermer, though by herself Miss Mothermer would have died a thousand dreadful deaths in such places; and sometimes Dame Phillipa was accompanied by her unhappy and unfortunate cousin, Lord FitzMorris-Banstock, though usually he shunned the company of any but his few, familiar servants.

* * * *

On this particular night, Mawhinney, his chauffeur-foot-man, had been obliged by a Guy Fawkes bonfire and its attendant crowd to drive the heavily curtained Rolls motorcar by a different and less familiar route; hence he arrived later at the usual place of rendezvous. Miss Mothermer and Dame Phillipa, tall figure and tiny one, picture-hat and turban, had come by and, as was the unspoken understanding, had not tarried. So many considerations affected the presence or absence of Lord FitzMorris-Banstock: was he engaged in a conversation particularly interesting by means of his amateur wireless radio equipment, was he in more pain than a certain degree, was he in less pain than a certain degree, was the moon too bright—for one or more of these reasons the star-curs't noble lord might not come despite his having said he might.

The obedient Mawhinney did not turn his head as his master slowly and awkwardly crept from the vehicle, inch by inch over the black silk upholstery. Nor, well-trained, did he suggest leaving the car in a garage and coming with his master. He waited a few moments after the door closed, then he drove straightway to Banstock House, where he stayed for precisely three hours, turning the Tarot cards over and over again with old Gules, the butler, and Mrs. Ox, the cook. On this Fifth of November night they observed that the Priestess, the Fool, and the Hanged Man turned up with more than their common frequency; and were much exercized to conjecture what, if anything, this might portend: and for whom.

And at the conclusion of three hours he put on his cap and coat and drove back to the place set.

Besides those nameless (and all but formless) figures from the silent world, of whom I had spoken above, there were others who awaited and welcomed Dame Phillipa's presence; and among them were women with names like Flossie and Jewel and Our Rose, Clarabel and Princess Mick and Jenny the Hen, Two-Bob Betty and Opaline and Queeny-Kate. She spoke to every one of them, gave them (if they required it, or thought they might: or if Dame Phillipa thought they might) the money needed to make up the sum demanded by their "friends" or "protectors"; the money for rent or food or what it might be, if they had passed the stage where their earnings could possibly be enough to concern the swine who had earlier lived on them. She tended to their cuts and bruises the poor wretches received in the way of business, and which they were too ashamed to bring before the very proper nurses and the young, lightheartedly cruel, interns.

Sometimes she interceded for them with the police, and sometimes she summoned the police to their assistance; her manner of doing this was to direct Miss Mothermer to blow upon the police whistle she wore upon a lanyard, Dame Phillipa not liking the vibration this made on her lips.

Those to whom Dame Phillipa may have seemed but a tall, gaunt eccentric woman, given to wearing old-fashioned dresses, and hats which ill became her, would do well to recollect that she was among the very first to be honored with the title of *dame*; and that His Majesty's Government did not take this step exclusively in recognition of her work prior to her retirement as an educationist, or on behalf of the Woman's Sufferage Movement through entirely legal methods.

It was close to midnight when the two ladies arrived in Primrose Alley and Dame Phillipa rapped lightly with her walking-stick upon the window of a woman in whose maternity she had interested herself: actually persuading the young woman, who was not over-bright, to accept medical attention, eat something resembling proper food, and have the child christened in the nearby and unfortunately ill-attended Church of St. Gustave Widdershins. She rapped a second time—loud enough (she hoped) to wake the mother, but not loud enough to wake the child. As it happened it was the father she woke, a young man who circulated among three or four women in a sort of tandem polygamy; and who informed the lady that the baby had been sent to its mother's people in Wales, and who begged her, not altogether disdainfully, for sweet Christ's sake to bugger off and let him get back to sleep again.

Dame Phillipa left him to his feculent slumbers in absolute but resigned certainty that this time next year she would again be called upon to swaddle, victual, and renounce by proxy the World, the Flesh, and the Devil, on behalf of another squalling token of his vigor—unless the young woman should perhaps miscarry, as she had done twice before, or carry out her own suggestion of dropping the child in the River, by accident, like.

It was as she turned from the window, then, that Dame Phillipa first clearly observed the man wearing the false nose—as she thought, because of the Guy Fawkes festivities; though it appears Miss Mothermer instantly suspected that he did so by way of disguise—although she had been aware, without giving consideration to the matter, that there had been footsteps behind her. All inquiries as to this man's identity or motive have failed, but the singularity of his appearance is such that, unless he has been secretly conveyed out of the Kingdom, he cannot long continue to evade the vigilance of the police.

Thinking nothing further of the matter, as we may assume, Dame Phillipa and her companion continued their way into Argyll Court. The sound of voices, and the odor of hot gin and lemon, both proceeding from a bow-window greatly resembling in carving and overhang the forecastle of an ancient sailing-ship, directed her attention to the gas-jet which burned redly in the close air, illuminating the sign of the seaman's lodging-house. In times gone bye, Evan-bach Llewellyn had been a notorious crimp. Board regulations, closely attended to, had almost put a stop to this, as far as vessels of British register were concerned. It was widely said, however, and widely believed, that the masters of foreign vessels putting into London with cargoes of coffee, copra, palm oil, fuel oil, hardwood and pulpwood; and finding members of their crew swallowed up by The Smoke, often appealed to the giant Welshman (he sang bass in the choir of Capel Cymrig) for replacements; and did not appeal in vain. Protests entered by surprised seamen, whose heads cleared of chloral in the Bay of Biscay, when they found themselves on board of strange vessels whose language they often did not recognize, would in the general course of things prove quite bootless.

As Dame Phillipa's attention was distracted to the window, where she saw the familiar-enough silhouette of Sampson Stone, the wool-puller, who was a close crony of the crimp, smoking the churchwarden he affected when at leisure; two men, who must have been huddled silently at the other side of the court, came suddenly towards the two ladies, reeling and cursing, striking fiercely at one another, and giving off the fumes of that poisonous mixture of methylated spirits and cheap port wine commonly called *red biddy*. The ladies took a few steps in confusion, not knowing precisely what course to take, nor having much time to consider it: they could not go forward, because of the two men fighting, and it seemed that when they attempted to walk to the side, the bruisers were there, cutting off their way, too.

Dame Phillipa therefore turned quickly, leading Miss Mothermer in the same direction, but stopped short, as out of Primrose Alley, whence they had just issued, darted the man who had been wearing the false nose. He made a curious sound as he did so; if he spoke words is not certain; what *is* certain is that he had plucked the false pasteboard from his face—it was hideously pockmarked—and that the flesh underneath was a mere convoluted hollow, like some gross navel, but nothing like a human nose.

Miss Mothermer gave a stifled cry, and drew back, but Dame Phillipa, though certainly no less startled, placed a reassuring hand on her companion's arm, and courteously awaited what this unfortunate might have to say or to ask. He beckoned, he gestured, he mewled and gibbered. Murmuring to Miss Mothermer that he evidently stood in need of some assistance, and that they were bound to endeavor to find what it was, Dame Phillipa stepped forward to follow him. For an instant only Miss Mothermer hesitated—but the two larrikins menaced from behind, she was too shy to demand assistance of Sampson Stone (who seemed unaware of their presence), and she was too fearful for herself and for Dame Phillipa to allow her to go on alone; perforce she followed. She followed into a door which stood open as if waiting.

If her testimony (and if one may give so succinct a name to confused and diffused ramblings noted down by Doctor Hardesty over a period of several months) may be relied on, the door lay but a few paces into Primrose Alley. The facts, however, are that no such door exists. The upper part of the Alley contains the tenements officially designated as Gubbinses' Buildings and called, commonly, "the Jakes"; entrance is through a covered archway twenty feet long which divides into two shallow flights of steps from each of which a hallway leads to the individual apartments. It was in one of these, the window and not the door of which faced the Alley, that the young parents of Dame Phillipa Garreck's godchild were lodging. The lower part of the Alley on the same side is occupied by the blind bulk of the back of the old flour warehouse. The opposite side is lined with the infamous Archways, wherein there are no doors at all. There are, it is true, two doors of sorts in the warehouse itself, but one is bricked up and the other is both rusted shut and locked from the inside. A search of the premises via the main gate failed to show any signs that it had been opened in recent years—or, indeed, that it could have been.

* * * *

It was shortly after one o'clock on the morning of the sixth of November that Lord FitzMorris-Banstock, toiling painfully through Thirza Street, in the direction of Devonport Passage, received (or perhaps I should say, became aware of) an impression that he should retrace his steps and then head north. There is no need to suggest telepathy and certainly none to mention the supranormal in conjunction with this impression: Miss Mothermer was blowing the police-whistle, blowing it with lips which trembled in terror, and so weak and feeble was the sound produced that no police constable had heard it. On the conscious level of his mind Lord FitzMorris did not hear it, either. But there are sensual perceptions of which the normal senses are not aware, and it was these, which there can be no doubt that he (perhaps in compensation, perhaps sharpened by suffering, perhaps by both) possesses to an unusual degree, which heard the sound and translated it. He obeyed the impulse, walking as fast as he could, and as he walked he was aware of the usual noises and movements in the darkness—rustlings and shufflings and whispers, breathings and mutterings—which betokened the presence of various of Dame Phillipa Garreck's charges. It seemed to him that they were of a different frequency, as he put it to himself, accustomed to think in wireless terms, this night. That they were uncommonly uneasy. It seemed to him that he could sense their terror.

And as he turned the corner into Salem Yard he saw something glitter, he saw something flash, and he knew in that instant that it was the famous Negrohead opal, which he had seen that one time before when his lady cousin occasioned the assistance of the Metropolitan Police to rescue the girl Bessie Lovejoy, then in process of being purchased for the Khowadja of Al-Khebur by the ineffably evil Motilal Smith.

It glittered and flashed in the cold and the darkness, and then it was gone.

Fenugreek Close is long and narrow and ill-lit, its western and longest extremity (where the Lascar, Bin-Ali, perished with the cold on the night of St. Sylvester) being a *cul-de-sac* inhabited—when it is inhabited at all—by Oriental seamen who club together and rest the premises whilst they await a ship. But there were none such that night. It was there, pressed against the blank and filthy wall, pressing feebly as if her wren-like little body might obtain entry and safety and sanctuary, sobbing in almost incoherent terror, that Lord FitzMorris-Banstock found the crouching form of Miss Mothermer. The police-whistle was subsequently found in the infamous Archways, and Miss Mothermer has insisted that, although she would have sounded it, she did not, for (she says) she could not find it; although she remembers Dame Phillipa pressing it into her hand. On this point she is quite vehement, yet one is no more apt to credit it than her statement about the open door towards which they were led by the man without a nose: for as Miss Mothermer did not blow upon the whistle, who did?

The noble and misfortunate lord did not waste breath inquiring of his cousin's companion if she were all right, it being patent that she was not. He demanded, instead, what had become of Dame Phillipa; and upon hearing the name, Miss Mothermer became first quite hysterical and then unconscious. Lord FitzMorris lifted her up and carried her to the place of rendezvous where, exactly on time, Mawhinney, his chauffeur-footman, had just arrived with the Rolls motorcar. They drove immediately to Banstock

House where she was given brandy and put to bed by Mrs. Ox, the cook, whilst Lord FitzMorris summoned the police.

An alarm had already been given, or, at any rate, an alarm of sorts. One of the wretchedly miserable folk to whose succor Dame Phillipa devoted so much of her time, having somehow learned that she was in danger, had informed Police-Sergeant L. Robinson to this effect. This man's name is not known. He is, or at any event was, called by the curious nickname of "Tea and Two Slices," these being the only words which he was usually heard to utter, and then only in a sort of whisper when ordering the only items he was known to eat. His age, background, residence, and present whereabouts are equally unknown. He had apparently an absolute honor of well-lighted and much-frequented places and an utter terror of policemen, one cannot tell why, and it may be hard to imagine what agonies and efforts it must have cost him to make his way to the police-station and inform Sergeant Robinson that he must go at once and "help the lady." Unfortunately and for unknown reasons, he chose to make his way to the police-station in Whitechapel instead of to the nearer one in Shadwell. His testimony would be of the utmost importance, but it cannot now be obtained, for, after giving the alarm, he scurried forth into the night again and has not since been seen.

The matter is otherwise with the testimony of the seaman, Greenbriar. It is available, it is copious, it fits in with that of Miss Mothermer, it is unfortunate that it is quite unbelievable. Unbelievable, that it, unless one is willing to cast aside every conceivable limit of credulity and to accept that on the night of Guy Fawkes Day in this year of our sovereign lord King George V the great and ancient city of London was the scene of a visitation more horrible than any in its previous history.

* * * *

Albert Edward Greenbriar, Able-Bodied Seaman, is thirty-one years of age, and except for two occasions on which he was fined, respectively, £2 and £2.10, for being drunk and disorderly, has never been in any trouble with the authorities. On the first of November he landed at St. Katherine Docks aboard the merchant vessel *Salem Tower*, from the Straits Settlements with a cargo of rubber, copra, and tinned pine-apples. Neither the *Salem Tower* nor Greenbriar had been in the United Kingdom for the space of eleven months, and, consequently, when paid off, he was in possession of a considerable sum of money. In the course of one week he had, with the assistance of several women who are probably prostitutes, dissipated the entire sum. On discovering this, the women, who share a communal flat in Poplar, asked him to leave.

It was Greenbriar's intention to obtain another ship, but in this endeavor he was unsuccessful. He managed to obtain a loan of half-a-crown from a casual acquaintance and spent the night at a bed-and-breakfast place in Ropemakers Fields, Limehouse. The following evening, footsore and hungry, save for a single sixpence, penniless, he found himself in the Commercial Road, where he entered a cookshop whose signboard announced that good tea, bread, smelts and chips were obtainable for that sum. Obtainable they were, good they were not, but he was in no position to object. Having finished, he inquired the way to the convenience, and there retired. On emerging he observed that he was next to the back door which opened onto Argyll Court, although he did not know that was its name, and on looking out he espied a sign.

The sign is still there; in white calligraphy of a fine Spencerian sort, up on a black background it reads,

> *Seamen's Lodging House*
> *Good Beds*
> *E. Llewellyn, Prop.*

Albert Edward Greenbriar entered, rang the bell for the governor, and, upon the instant, saw a panel open in the wall, through which a face looked at him. It was the face of a gigantic cherub, white and dimpled and bland, surmounted by a poll of curly hair; in short, it was the face of Evan-bach Llewellyn. Greenbriar in a few words stated his situation and offered to give over his seaman's papers as a surety until such time as he might obtain a ship, in return for bed and board. The governor thrust forth a huge, pale hand, took the documents, slid shut the panel, and presently appeared to beckon Greenbriar down a corridor, at the end of which was a dimly lit dormitory. He gave him a thin blanket which was all in all not quite so filthy as it might have been, informed him that gaming and novel-reading were not permitted on the premises, invited him to take any bed he chose, and forthwith withdrew.

Greenbriar found an empty pallet, under the head of which he placed his shoes, not so much as a pillow as a precaution, drew the cover about him and fell instantly asleep. He was awakened several times by the entry of other men, some of whom appeared to have been flung rather than escorted into the room, and once he was awakened by the sound of the proprietor playing upon a small patent organ a hymn of his own composition on the subject of the Priesthood of Melchisedec. Greenbriar gazed at the tiny blue tip of the night-light as it burned tremulously on the twisted jet and on the odd and grotesque shadows cast upon the stained and damp-streaked walls by the tossings and turnings of the lodgers, and listened to the no less odd nor grotesque noises made by them. It was only by the start he gave upon being awakened that he realized that he had gone to sleep again.

Who awakened him he did not know, but, although the light was no brighter, there was a stir in the dormitory and men were getting to their feet and he heard the word "scoff" repeated several times. He dashed water on his face and moved with the others into what was evidently the main kitchen of the establishment. To his surprise he observed that the clock there read eleven o'clock. It was too dark to be morning. Evidently he had slept only a few hours or else he had slept round the clock and a bit more. It seemed an odd hour for victuals but he was beginning to conceive the idea that this was an odd place.

Broiled bloaters, fried sausage, potatoes, cabbage and sprouts were being turned out of pots and pans and dumped higgeldy-piggeldy onto cracked and not over-clean plates; and tea was steaming in coarse crockery cups. No one ventured to eat or drink, however, until Evan-bach Llewellyn had pronounced a grace in the Cymric tongue and immediately after the Amen imparted a piece of information, *videlicet* that he had got a ship for them. It was a good ship, too, he said; they would all be very pleased with it; it was not one of their dirty old English tubs but a fine modern vessel: he urged them all to eat hearty of the scoff, or victuals, so that no time need be lost in getting aboard, and he then produced a large bottle of gin and proceeded to pour a generous portion into each cup, with many assurances that it was free and would come out of his own commission.

No sooner had he given the signal, with a wave of his pale and dimpled paw, than the men fell to like so many ravening wolves, cramming the hot food into their mouths and gulping down the gin and lemon tea. Greenbriar concedes that the aliment was savory, and, finding himself hungrier than he had thought, took but a hasty swallow of the drink before addressing himself at length to the solids. A furtive movement at his elbow caused him to cease, abruptly. The man to his right, a hulking fellow with red hair and an exceedingly dirty face, was emptying his mug and looking at him out of the corner of his eye. It took but a second to ascertain that the wretched fellow had all but drained his own supply and then switched cups and was now doing away with Greenbriar's, who contented himself with stealing a link of the man's sausage whilst the latter was elaborately gazing elsewhere. Steeling himself to meet this man's resentment, he was dumbfounded to observe the fellow fall upon his face into the mashed potatoes and sprouts on his plate.

Within a matter of seconds, almost as if it were one of the contagious seizures which takes hold at times of the unfortunate patients of an institution for the epileptic—within a matter of seconds, then, all the others at the table sank down into unconsciousness, and Greenbriar, following suit, knew no more.

* * * *

He awoke to a scene of more than Gothic horror.

He lay with his head against the silent form of another man; he could feel the weight of another on his legs, and others lay like dead men all about. They were not dead, he knew, for he could hear them breathing. The room where they lay was walled and floored and roofed in stone and at regular intervals were carvings in bas-relief of a strange and totally unfamilar kind. Paraffin lamps were set into niches here and there. There was a humming noise whose origin was not visible to him. Very slowly, so as not to attract attention (for he could hear voices), Greenbriar turned his head. As he did so he felt that there was a rope tied round his neck, and a sudden and quite involuntary convulsive movement which he gave upon this discovery disclosed to him that his hands took a quite long time in shifting his position so as to obtain some intelligence of his surroundings. If what he had seen before was strange and uneasy enough, what he saw now was sufficient to deprive him for the moment of the use of his limbs altogether.

Off to one side, bound and linked arms to arms and necks to necks like a prostrate caffle of slaves, and to all appearances also unconscious, were the bodies of a number of women; how many, he could not say, but evidently less than the number of the men. This, however, and however shocking even to the sensibilities of a seafarer, this was nothing—

Directly in front of his gaze, which was at an angle, and seated upon a sort of altar, was a figure as it were out of eastern clime: red bronze in color, hideous of visage, and with six arms. Bowing low before it was, as Greenbriar then thought, a man, who addressed it in placatory tones and with many fawning gestures.

No other thought occurred to the British sailor at that moment but that he was in some sort of clandestine Hindu temple and that he and all his other companions would presently be sacrificed before this idol; not being aware that such is not the nature or character of the Hindu religion, which contains, despite numerous errors and not a few gross impostures, many sublime and lofty thoughts. But be that as it may; the red-bronze-colored figure proceeded to move its limbs, the torso stirred, the entire body leaned forward. The figure spoke, and as it spoke, it seized the man with four of its limbs and struck him with the other two. Then it dropped him. As he scrambled to his feet his face was turned so that the sailor could see it, and he saw that it had no nose.

Greenbriar must once again have passed into unconsciousness. When again he awoke he could not see the "idol," the altar was empty, but he could hear its voice. It was speaking in anger, and as one used to command. Another voice began when this one (deep, hollow, dreadful) had ceased;

the new voice was a thin one, and it took a moment for him to realize that, despite its curious snuffling quality, it was speaking a sort of English. Two other voices replied to it, also in English; one was that of Evan-bach Llewellyn, the other one he did not know. By his description of both speech and speaker, for in a moment the latter moved into view, it is apparent that this was no other than the inhuman and unconscionable Eurasian Motilal Smith.

The countenance of Motilal Smith, once observed, is not one likely ever to be forgotten, and proves a singular and disturbing exception to the rule that Eurasians are generally of a comely appearance; it being broad and frog-like in its flatness, protuberance of the eyes (which are green and wet-looking), reverse U-shaped mouth, and profusion of warts or wart-like swellings. Most striking of all, however, is the air of slyness, malevolence, of hostility both overt and covert, towards everything which is kindly and decent and, in a word, human.

Motilal Smith has since his first appearance in the United Kingdom been the subject of unremitting police attention, and for some time now has gained the sinister distinction of being mentioned more often in the Annual Report of the League of Nations Commission on the Traffic in Women and Children than any other resident of London. He has often been arrested and detained on suspicion, but the impossibility of bringing witnesses to testify against him has invariably resulted in his release. Evidences of his nefarious commerce have come from places so far distant as the Province of Santa Cruz in the Republic of Bolivia and the Native Indian States of Patiala and Cooch Behar, as well as two of the Trucial Sheikdoms, the Free City of Danzig, and Deaf Smith County in the Commonwealth of Texas; none of which, it must be regretted, is admissible in proceedings at the Old Bailey. As he is a British subject by birth, he can be neither deported nor denied admission on his return from frequent trips abroad. He is known to be always ready to purchase, he is entirely eclectic as to the nature of the merchandise, and he pays well and he pays in gold.

It is necessary only to add that, offered any obstacle, affront, or rebuff, he is in unremitting in his hostility, which combines the industry of the West with the patience of the East. Smith occupies both sides of the semi-detached villa in Maida Vale of which he owns the freehold; its interior is crammed with opulent furnishings from all round the world, and stinks of stale beer, spilt gin, incense, curry, raw fish, the foul breaths and bodies of those he deals with, and chips fried in ghee.

His long, lank, and clotted hair is covered in scented grease, and on his fingers are rings of rubies, diamonds, pearls and other famous precious stones worth with their settings a prince's ransom. Add only the Negrohead opal worn in his stained silk four-in-hand, (and for which Second Officer

Smollet of the *Cutty Sark* is said to have strangled Mrs. Pigler), and there you have the creature Motilal Smith in all his repulsive essence.

Something, it seemed, was "not enough." There was an insufficiency of…something. This it was which occasioned the wrath of the person or creature with the six arms. And he was also in great concern because of a shortage of time. All four—the creature with six arms, the man without a nose, Smith and Llewellyn—kept moving about. Presently there was the scrape of wood and then a thud and then the wet and dirty odor of the River. The thought occurred to Greenbriar that they might be thrown into the Thames, which was then at high tide, he reflected that (in common with a great many seamen) he had never learned to swim; and then, for a third time, he fainted.

When he awoke he could hear someone singing the Doxology, and he thought—so he says—that he had died and was now in Heaven. One glance as he opened his eyes was enough to undeceive him. He lay where he had before and everything was as it was before, save that there were two people present who he is certain were not there before, and by his description of them they were clearly Dame Phillipa Garreck and her secretary-companion, Miss Mothermer.

Miss Mothermer was crouched down with her hands over her eyes, whether in prayer or terror or not inconceivably both, he could not say. Dame Phillipa however, was otherwise engaged, for she moved from insensate figure to insensate figure and the light gleamed upon the scissors with which she was severing their bonds. She spoke to each, shook them, but was able to elicit no response. At this, Greenbriar regained his voice and entreated her help. She proceeded to cut the ropes which bound him, and left off her singing of the Doxology to inquire of him if he had any knowledge as to why they were all of them being detained, and what was intended to be done with them.

He was assuring her that he did not know, when a door opened and Miss Mothermer began to scream.

That a fight ensued is certain. Greenbriar was badly cut about and Miss Mothermer received bruises which were a long time in vanishing, though in this I refer only to bruises of the flesh; those of the spirit are still, alas, with her. But he can provide us with few details of the conflict. Certain, it is, that he escaped; equally certain, so did Miss Mothermer. Dame Phillipa plainly did not. Greenbriar was discovered at about three in the morning wandering in a daze in the vicinity of the Mile End Road by a very conscientious alien named Grebowski or Grebowsky, who summoned medical attention and the police. Little or no attention would or could have been paid to Greenbriar's account, had it not been for his description of the two ladies. His relation, dovetailing as it did with that of Miss Mothermer, left the police no choice but to cause a search to be made of the area of Argyll Court, in one corner of which a false nose was found.

Acting on the information received and under authority of a warrant, Superintendant Sneeth, together with a police-sergeant and a number of constables, entered Llewellyn's premises, which they found completely deserted. Soundings of the walls and floors indicated the presence of passageways and rooms which could have had no place in a properly-conducted establishment licensed under the Common Lodging-Houses Act, and these were broken into. A cap belonging to Greenbriar was found, as was part of the lanyard of Dame Phillipa's police-whistle, in one of these corridors. There was a perfect maze or rabbit-warren of them, and, on the lowest level, there was discovered that chamber, the existence of which was previously publicly unknown, and which Professor Singleton of the University of London has pronounced to be a genuine Mithrarium of the reign of Marcus Aurelius, or, perhaps, Nerva; and which was used by the unscrupulous Llewellyn for the illicit portion of his professional activity. It would have been here that the captives were assembled, if Greenbriar's account is to be believed. What is, as a first premise, obvious, is that it cannot possibly be believed.

That Lord FitzMorris-Banstock has chosen to believe it is, I am constrained to say, a greater testimony to the powers of his imagination than to any inherently credible elements in the story. The man Greenbriar now forms part of the staff of Banstock House; this is entirely the affair of Lord FitzMorris himself, and requires no comment on my own part, nor shall it obtain any. It may, however, be just as well to include some opinions and observations which are the fruits of Lord FitzMorris's very understandably deep concern in this tragic and intensely puzzling affair.

He has collected a number of reports of some sort of aquatic disturbance moving downstream from London River early in the morning of the sixth of November just about the time of the turning of the tide. To this he compares a report of the Astronomer Royal's concerning an arc of light which appeared off the Nore immediately subsequent. These have led him to the opinion that a craft of unknown origin and nature moved underwater from London to the sea and then rose not only above the surface of the water but into the air itself. This craft or vessel was captained by the creature with the six arms, and the man without a nose would have been an inferior officer aboard of her. Somehow this vessel became short of personnel and applied to Evan-bach Llewellyn to make up the shortage by crimping or shanghaiing the requisite number. For reasons which cannot be known and concerning which I, for one, would rather not speculate, several women were also required (Lord FitzMorris is of the opinion that they were required only for such duties as members of their sex commonly fulfill in the mercantile navies of various foreign nations, such as service in the steward's branch). This being out of Llewellyn's line of business, an appeal was made by him to the notorious and wicked Eurasian, Motilal Smith, who is known to have left his headquarters at the semi-detached villa in Maida Vale on the Fifth of November, whither he never returned.

Lord FitzMorris suggests two possible provenances for this curious and hypothetical vessel. Suppose, he suggests, the being with the six arms to have been the original of the many East Indian and Buddhist myths depicting such creatures. It is likely then, that the ship or submarine-airplane emanated from the vast and unexplored regions in the mountains which ring round the northern plateau of Tibet, the inhabitants of which have for centuries been rumored to possess knowledge far surpassing ours, and which they jealously guard from the mundane world. The other possibility is even less likely, and is reminiscent of I fear, far more of the romances associated with the pen of Mr. Herbert G. Wells, a journalist of radical tendencies, than with proper scientific attitudes. Do not the discoveries of Professor Schiaparelli, establishing that there are canals upon the planet Mars, demonstrate that the inhabitants thereof must be given to agricultural pursuits? In which case, how unlikely that they should engage themselves in filibustering or blackbirding expeditions to, of all conceivable places, the civilized capital city of the British Empire!

Lord FitzMorris: thinks that this theoretical craft of his must have carried off the unscrupulous Evan Llewellyn in order to make up the tally of captives; how much more likely it is that this wicked man has merely fled to escape detection, prosecution, and punishment—perhaps to the mountains of wild Wales, where the King's writ runneth scarcely more than it does in the mountains of Tibet.

Concerning the present whereabouts of Motilal Smith, we are on firmer ground. That he intended to devise harm to Dame Phillipa, who had on far more than one occasion interfered with him in his nefarious traffickings, we need not doubt. The close search of Superintendant Sneeth of the premises on and about Argyll Court, Primrose Alley, Fenugreek Close and Salem Yard uncovered a sodden mass of human clay lying part in and part out of a pool of muck far under the notorious Archways. It was the drowned body of Motilal Smith himself; both from the evidence of his own powerful physique and the presence of many footprints thereabouts, it is clear that a number of persons were required, and were found, to force him into that fatal submersion. The friends—silent though they are to the world, dumb by virtue of their affliction and suffering—the friends of Dame Phillipa Garreck, the so-called and by no means ill-named People of the Abyss, whom she so constantly and so assiduously attended upon, had avenged their one friend and sole protector. It must now, one fears, go ill with them.

The body of this unspeakably evil man, as well as his entire and vast estate (except the famous Negrohead opal, which was never found), was at once claimed by his half-brother, Mr. Krishna Bannerjee. The body was removed to Benares, and there subjected at the Burning Ghauts to that incomplete process of combustion peculiar to the Hindu persuasion; and has long since become the prey of the wandering crocodiles which scavenge perpetually up and down the sacred waters of the River Gunga.

As I commence my last words for the present on the subject of this entire tragic affair I must confess myself baffled. Inacceptable as are Lord FitzMorris's theories, there are really no others that I can offer in their place. All is uncertainty. All, that is, save my conviction that Dame Phillipa's noble and humanitarian labors still continue, no matter under what strange stars and skies.

THE UNKNOWN LAW

Originally published in *The Magazine of
Fantasy & Science Fiction*, June 1964.

"Then you would say, sir, that the United States has no plans for occupying any of the asteroids at all?"

"The United States has no plans for occupying any of the asteroids at
all, at the present time. By that I do not mean to say that we have plans for
occupation at any future time. Our action, our policy, in this regard, remains
fluid. What we intend to do must continue to take notice of the intentions of
the other Space Powers and the decisions of the United Nations."

There was a pause. The President faced the assembled reporters. Then,
"Thank you, Mr. President—" The reporters stood up to applaud politely.
They faded from view as the 3D wall went blank. A faint bell sounded
and a tiny light went on, set in a hood in a far corner of his desk. He lifted
the hood and took up a cup of the famous green tea which was almost a
trademark of his, steaming hot as he liked it. Prior to the campaign, "In
public—coffee," his advisors had said. But then came the ugly business
in Brazil, followed by Colombia coffee pricing itself off the market and
other supplies inadequate, followed by the popular *coup d'état* in Formosa,
which had, for the moment, scarcely any thing to sell—except green tea!
Formosa was popular, Dave Smith was popular, coffee wasn't, Byers continued to drink coffee. It wasn't that that elected Smith, anymore than it
was hard cider elected Harrison, almost a century and a half earlier. It had
helped, though.

Now he sat, in the privacy of his White House office and sipped his
cup, watching the wall come alive again, this time with open circuit 3D—
Steven Senty's bland face and voice giving the inconsequentia of the news.

"—and, apropos of the President's comments on the asteroid question, it is agreed that the other as yet unfilled cabinet position will go to
millionaire moon-estate operator Hartley Gordon, though as yet official
confirmation is lacking. Gordon's readiness to bail the party out of the hole
the last campaign left it in hasn't been forgotten. Gordon, however, sees
himself as an organizer, not an administrator; privately tells friends he will
resign after clearing up the 'mess' the Space Department is now in. Likely

successors include ex-diplomat Charles Salem Smith, no relation—" The newscaster smiled; the President made a rude noise. "And Party Stalwart J. T. Macdonald, who gave up a shoo-in chance at his father's old seat in the House to direct President Smith's campaign in the Southeast. Those in the real know say that his chances are better than might be expected."

Roger David Smith made a rude noise again, followed it by a ruder word, drank tea.

"A small but time-honored tradition gets in its once-every-four-years airing this afternoon when three major minor—or minor major, ha, ha, officeholders pay their traditional call to greet the new president in person. Personal visits with a president have become increasingly rare, partly because of security problems: how dangerous they can be was demonstrated by the assassination of President Kennedy and the attempted assassination of President Byers: and partly because of the perfection and improvement of the 3D system. No official basis for this ceremony exists, but old-time residents of the District like to tell how it originated. Back in George Washington's time, it seems that—"

The wall went blank, the President took another mouthful of unfermented tea, and reflected sourly just how much he hated the "like to tell" locution. Did the faces of old-time residents of the District light up when they had the opportunity to tell? Did they chuckle, set up the occasion or opportunity, did—Oh, well. He looked at his watch. It was just exactly time. He touched his fingertip to the *Ready* button. A bell chimed, some rooms away. Pleased, smiling, he repeated this, then three times, fast. Then he frowned in self-reproof, withdrew his hand.

Roger David Smith was thirty-five years old, just past the minimum age the Constitution sets for the presidency, and had occupied the office for exactly three days and two hours. His dark, rugged face, marked with the scars of the shrapnel he had picked up in Sumatra, showed no trace inevitable to the time and place. The new president had not even been born when Warren Gamaliel Harding was playing hide-and-go-seek with his teen-age mistress in the presidential cloakroom; nor when John Calvin Coolidge took two-hour naps every afternoon on the sofa in his office.

Some recollection of this may have been in the President's mind; just before the press conference he had made a teleview call (untapped—the presidential circuit was said to be untappable: he hoped so, but had taken care to keep the conversation innocuous,), and a woman's face was still in his eyes and a woman's voice still in his ears—would always be, it seemed—and although poor Harding had managed to hide his own cheap amour, the light which beat unceasingly down on whoever held the office was now almost intolerable.

Smith got up from the desk and faced the door just as it opened, just as the Chief Usher's voice announced the callers. He frowned again, slightly, trying to remember just exactly what it was the retiring president had said to him three days ago; quickly erased the frown and let the thought fade. He smiled politely. The smile was not returned.

The three minor major, or major minor officeholders entered, and there was the usual brief see-sawing before the order in which they approached the president was decided. Anderson, the Federal Armorer, was first; a square-shaped, ruddy man, with crispy gray hair. After him, the Sergeant-Secretary of the Cabinet, Lovel, tall and bony and pale. Both wore the plaids which were, with their short capes, fashionable for formal but unceremonial occasions. Dressed in the lime-green which psycho-dynamicists included among the preferred shades for work clothes was Gabrielli, Civil Provost of the Capital, elf-small and moving soundlessly; the President knew that he held the Medal of Honor for his part in the assault on Telukbetung.

Not one of them smiled.

The door closed behind them, and, after a second or two, the silence was broken by the small noise of the door in the outer office being shut.

"Gentlemen," said Roger David Smith, keeping up the little smile, though with a little difficulty. He extended his hand. Each of the callers took it in turn; still, none smiled. A feeling of unease settled on the President, not great, but definite. Thoughts of other times he had felt it came to him in quick-rushing reflection. There was the time he had been summoned to see his CO, in Sumatra, near The Rice Paddy, that dreadful summer, expecting to be court-martialed for exceeding his orders; instead he had been commended for quick thinking. There was the time six Party leaders had called on him in his hotel room at the Convention, to tell him (he had been thinking) that he stood no chance after all of being offered the vice-presidential nomination; instead they had asked him to allow his name to go forward for the presidency. And there was the third time, in between the other two, when he had first met the woman to whom he had earlier this afternoon spoken to on the teleview. *She doesn't like me*, was his instant thought then. But she had become his mistress after all.

She could not become his wife.

"Mr. President," said Anderson, "we have come to ask you to accept our felicitations on your selection as Chief Magistrate of the Republic, and to assure you that we stand, as always, ready to assist you in maintaining the integrity of our national confederation."

In the silence which followed this declaration Smith had time to reflect that it all seemed damned odd. He started to say, "Thank you," but Anderson was already speaking.

"We'll be as brief as we can, sir," he said. "We've made this same declaration to other presidents, in happier times, in unhappier times, and in times equally unhappy. I've done it on five occasions—I'm acting as spokesman because of seniority in office—Lovel and Gabrielli have done it four times each."

The President of the United States said, "I don't really know—"

"You don't really know what this is all about, sir, do you?" Roger David Smith shook his head. The Federal Armorer nodded, unsurprised. "Except—well, I remember now, just before we left for the inauguration, President Byers told me…let's see…he did tell me you would come here today to tell me something. And he said, 'You'd better believe them, too.' I remember now. I was a little surprised, but there were so many other things on my mind right then…. And besides that, only what I've seen in the newspapers and 3D: very little." This was all *damned* odd, he thought. He thought also of his appointments schedule—tire Ambassador of the great (and sole remaining) neutral power of the Nether Orient, two western state governors eager to see what they could do about mustering regional support for the president's program (and even more eager to see what they could do about mustering presidential support for their own putative senatorial campaigns), the American Representative to the U.N.—who, of course, should have been scheduled before the governors, but politics had to go on as usual, no matter what. Even if the "what" be the ever-shaky Condominium of the Moon, the threat of the South American Civil War spreading into Central America, the looming rocketry strike, and—not once and again, but again and again—the matter of the asteroids… Still, his appointments secretary had allotted fifteen minutes to these three men. So—

"As I understand it, this tradition began when the first three men to hold your office saved George Washington from an assassination attempt," said President Smith. "And that he promised them that they would have the power to nominate their own successors and to greet every new president on the third day of his term. Isn't that—?"

Anderson asked, "Correct? Not quite, Mr. President."

Smith caught a fleeting resemblance, in the older man's face, to his own father's. Quickly, the thought brought others: his father's insistence, gentle but insistent, when young Dave Smith had failed to make the Space Academy, that he go to law school rather than Paris; then Sumatra, cutting short his legal career before it had really begun; the entry into politics via a local "reform" club; Sarra—

For ten years, almost, everything had been Sarra. Jim, too, of course, but mainly Sarra. The state legislature, the race for the House seat, getting Jim's father to use his great popularity and influence… And how had he, Roger David Smith, repaid the old man? By putting horns on his son.

Fortunately, the old man never knew. But Jim knew—Jim *must* know. He just didn't care. So—Roger David ("Dave") Smith, here he was: the high school teacher's son, the youngest man ever to sit in the White House. Jefferson, Jackson, Lincoln, the two Roosevelts… Kennedy and now Dave Smith. And it was all Sarra. She would have made a damned vigorous president herself, he thought, not for the first time. Only she would never do it, even if it were possible; she'd rather have Jim be elected, had the chance existed, and rule through him. Rule? *Reign!*

And, sighing, without being aware that he was sighing, his eye fell on the new asteroid chart they had installed only this morning. White lights for the U.N., blue for the U.S.A., red for the U.S.S.R., and yellow for the disputed ones—ones which were, in American eyes, disputed: the Russians, of course, had a different listing.

His eyes came back to Anderson, his mind recalled Anderson's last comment. "'Not quite correct?' Your jobs aren't civil service and they're not on the patronage list, either. So—

Lovel said nothing, bent his long gaunt face a few inches toward his senior, who caught the movement, nodded, and said, "That's true enough, sir, about our being traditionally allowed to nominate our successors. Not exactly true about the assassination thing. Not the *whole* truth."

The whole truth, Anderson went on to say, standing on the rug which a Persian ambassador had given Mrs. Grover Cleveland; the whole truth was that during Washington's first Administration, at a time when New York was still the Capital, a great danger towards the nation had arisen, arisen in secret—a cabal, as it was then called. A plot to seize power, to force the new president to follow the direction of a group of men who, alarmed by the radical ideas then emanating from France, intended a more rigorous system of government.

There was evidence, oh, there was evidence in plenty. But it was not evidence that you could bring to court, on which you could base a hope that the matter would be settled swiftly and peacefully.

Delay meant either a successful *coup d'état* and an oligarchy like that of the Venetian Republic—rule by the heads of the great families, secret police, dungeons, and everything hateful and dangerous to liberty-loving Americans—or else full civil war. The nation was new, the nation was young and weak, operating under a constitution barely tried and largely suspect. British troops still maintained bases on American soil, Spanish armies ringed our Southern and Western borders, French navies were on the seas; and the Indians, still powerful, were everywhere…

"I've never heard a word of it," Smith declared. "I'm not sure I believe it. Although—" memory flashed—"is this what President Byers meant when he said I'd better believe you? Because—"

"It's all true, sir," Anderson said. "Great names were involved. Conway's Cabal was nothing in comparison to it. Three men came and brought the evidence before President Washington—they'd served under him in the War of the Revolution—they presented him with the evidence on his third day in office. One was the Federal Armorer, William Dickensheet."

"One was the Sergeant-Secretary of the cabinet, Richard Main," said Lovel.

"The third was Simon Stavers, Civil Provost of the Capital," Gabrielli said.

President Smith stared at them. It hardly seemed possible to remain in doubt of these three men, known to be honorable career men, sober, stable and loyal. But surely they had not come to give him a history lesson? "Go on," he said.

Those three, Anderson continued, discussed the matter a whole night through with President Washington. They debated as to what the right course would be. Speed—as it was counted in those days of slow and difficult transport and communication—speed was essential, if the country was to be spared either a tyranny whose end no man could foresee, or a bloody domestic war. *Wars*, perhaps, and perhaps ending in invasion and conquest and an end to national independence.

Despite the teleview, the luminescents, the model on his desk of the latest moonship, Roger Smith felt something of that evening so far back— he believed it now, he did believe; it was impossible to doubt those three good men any longer: the archaic formula of their greeting to him ("...*our felicitations on your selection as Chief Magistrate...we stand, as always, ready to assist you in maintaining the integrity of our national confederation*")—that long-distant night when the Father of his Country, no doubt with his wig set aside and perhaps his famous painful and ill-fitting false teeth as well, debated what move to make and make fast...and the candles guttered in the dimness. President Smith had his own problems, the United States of America under the First Administration of President Roger David Smith had its own problems. They were heavy, grave and great, and no one now spoke of or scarcely dared dream of any "return to normalcy." (The Harding note again!)

He leaned forward, caught up in this account (unaccountably, till now, concealed from him) of the Nation's first crisis under its Constitution. "What did they decide to do?" he asked.

"Immediate contact was made," Anderson said, in the same steady tones he had used throughout, "with those members of the Government who were then in town." He paused. His colleagues nodded slowly, gazing steadfastly at the President. "The leader of the cabal was known, his whereabouts were known. It was also known that if he were removed, the scheme would collapse. It was agreed that the welfare of the Nation depended upon—demanded—his removal.

"He was, accordingly, removed."

"*How?*"

"The decision was, by pistoling."

Smith half-turned his back and struck his fist on his desk.

"Are you trying to tell me," he cried, "that *George Washington* ordered the murder of a man he couldn't convict on a fair trial?" And swung around to face them again.

But they wouldn't admit the word, *murder*. Execution was not *murder*. The slaying of an enemy was not *murder* in time of war. Nor did "war" depend upon a formal declaration. The welfare of the Nation had to be the paramount thing in the eyes of its Chief. The enjoyment of private scruples was a luxury with which he had no right to indulge himself in his official capacity.

"Go on," said Smith.

Could anyone looking back, Anderson went on, doubt that the original decision was the best one? It was obvious beyond doubt even at the time. It had been obvious also that similar situations would arise again—and again and again. It was inevitable. So there grew up a law, he said—and the nods of his colleagues' assents confirmed his words, a law unwritten, but, unlike the so-called "Unwritten law" justifying a husband's killing his wife's lover, it was an unknown law—unknown except to the fewest possible people—the men who held these three offices, their predecessors, the President, and the ex-Presidents—but a *law*, nonetheless, authorizing a President to order the death of any person in the country whose existence constituted what was later to be called a "clear and present danger" to the welfare of the Nation.

"My G-d!" said Roger Smith. Then—a sudden rush of interest overcoming his shock—he asked, "How in the Hell did they miss Aaron Burr?"

"He skipped the country too soon. And by the time he came back he wasn't dangerous."

"I see. Well—"

"There have to be limits, of course, Mr. President," the Federal Armorer explained. "The President has to declare his intention to us. And he can only do it once. Once in each term of office, that is. Because there have to be limits. There *have* to be—" His voice, for the first time, rose just a trifle.

After a moment, "I see," said the President. "How often—"

"In the country's history? Seventeen times. Who carries out the decision? One of us. How chosen? By lot. Is there any danger of detection? Almost none. Over the course of almost two hundred years," said Anderson, "certain techniques have been developed. Effective ones. How often during our own tenures of office? Once."

President Smith swallowed. "Who is the man who was…killed?"

"That question, sir, is not answered."

"I see. I'm sorry. Of course not. Well, which one of you—"

"And *that* question, sir, is not even asked."

There was silence. "*You'd better believe them,*" the ex-President Byers had said. Was there something of a deeper, personal knowledge in Byers' voice when saying it? Smith could not now remember, the Inauguration, only moments away, had driven anything but bare reception of the words from his mind. He searched his memory; who had died—suddenly—during the previous Administration, whose death might have…? No name occurred to him. He glanced at the clock set into his desk-top at a slant. The fifteen minutes were up. During that fifteen minutes anything might have occurred. Panama invaded by the Continentalists ("South America ends at the northern boundary of Mexico," Lopez-Cardoso was said to have said; he was dead now, could neither confirm nor deny it; but his slogan of "One Continent, One People, One Faith, One Destiny" was certainly very much alive), the friendly but unstable Colored government of the Free Cape State overthrown by either Black or White intransigents, another "incident" unfavorably affecting the Lunar Condominium—nothing, it seemed, could affect it favorably any more, further troubles in the still-vex'd Asteroids: any or even all of these could have occurred in the quarter-hour he'd just spent chittering over ancient history.

"Have you anything else to tell me?" he asked, starting forward.

"Only that at least one of us will remain in the District at all times, in case of, well, immediate need, let's say… No, sir, nothing else to tell you."

Smith nodded. Anderson glanced at his colleagues. Gabrielli, the most junior of the three in office, spoke for the first time. "Mr. President, we tender you our renewed assurances that we stand, as always, ready to assist you in maintaining the integrity of our national confederation. And we ask your permission to withdraw." He was elf-small and some people found his voice amusing, but the President knew that he held the Congressional Medal of Honor for his part in the assault on Telukbetung.

* * * *

After those three came the ambassador of the great neutral power of the Nether Orient, equally full of his grave misgivings about American space policy and his grave insistence upon increased American financial aid to his own country, both couched in the most mellifluous English, and after him came one of the Western American state governors, slyly awkward or awkwardly sly, not even knowing the name of the diplomat who had preceded him but knowing just what to offer and just what to demand in the way of political horse-trading. Neither of these two were present in person, of course. And after him—

"What are you doing here, Jim?" the President demanded, frowning. "Governor Millard was supposed to be next; you're not down for an appointment until tomorrow afternoon." He was brusque, not so much because he gave a damn about that as because he had been wondering—tired, disgusted, knowing that his impending interview with the American representative to the U.N. would bring new problems which neither weariness nor disgust could ignore—had been wondering if there were any chance of his being with Sarra that night. There was, he had finally realized, no chance at all. A President of the United States might sell his country down the river or let it drift down by incompetence, but he could never under any circumstances let it be hinted that he had a mistress. Perhaps ten years ago he might have gotten away with it, so far had the pendulum swung from the old morality. But there had been one, or perhaps two, scandals too many; now the pendulum was on the far swing again.

James Thackeray Macdonald smiled, waved his hand; Smith fancied he could smell the familiar odor of the man's cigar, but of course it was only fancy—the 3D hadn't gotten that far yet, despite continual efforts. There was not the slightest chance in the world of Jim's being any sort of menace in his physical person, but—protocol was protocol. "The day I can't persuade Millard or a thousand yokels like him to trade appointments with me, that's the day I'll close the store and go fishing," Jim said, his ruddy face glowing and cheerful as usual.

"What did you promise him? Off-shore oil rights on the Moon?"

Macdonald leaned back in the chair which he had taken, unbidden, and laughed. It was the famous Macdonald laugh, with rich echoes of his famous father, and, despite everything, Roger Smith found himself smiling faintly. Jim had charm, if nothing else. And there was damned little else between the charm and the nothing else.

"Well, come on, Jim, what the Hell do you want?"

J.T. Macdonald smiled indulgently. "Yes, I *know*, Rog: okay, I'll make it brief, and then you can let Nick Mason tell you his latest hard luck story about the Rooshians and the Prooshians. Okay. I spoke to Harley Gordon just a few minutes ago, and he told me that he definitely will not stay in office more than three months, not if you offered him Manhattan Island for a nickel. So what I want to know is, how about my taking an undersecretariat now, so I'll be able to step into his shoes without any trouble when he quits?"

The faint smile on the President's face had slipped easily into a frown. Macdonald's appointment to a Cabinet position had been suggested—once, and not by the President, either. J.T.'s name had been, was being frequently mentioned by the media in this connection, however; but speculation of this sort was too common for the President to think it seemed worth even an unofficial denial. He had assumed it would die down. But Jim seemed to be taking it seriously.

"Have you talked about this with Sarra?" Smith asked.

Now the frown was Macdonald's, as faint as the President's smile had been. "Dammit, Rog, I don't have to talk over every little thing with Sarra. I have a mind of my own, you know."

"A Cabinet appointment is no little thing, Jim. I never—no, don't interrupt me—I never promised it to you, I never even suggested it. I know Sarra did mention it, but I never thought you'd think she meant it seriously. Who it was that leaked the fact of your name having been proposed at all I don't know, but I can't be committed by a *leak*, dammit! You have no right, none whatsoever, to treat a lighthearted remark of Sarra's as if it were a promise from me. I am not to be cornered that way. The Secretariat is *out*. And that means, so is an undersecretariat." Macdonald was still trying to speak, but the President swept on over him. "Besides, as far as I'm concerned, it's been definite for some time now that you would take a position on my personal staff here. Hasn't it? I value your talents, Jim, especially with meeting people face to face, and—"

But Jim wasn't taking the compliment. Thanks for nothing, was his attitude. He had no intention of becoming the Presidential Grover Whalen, he said, pinning carnations on visiting dignitaries' wives, and glad-handing prominent Rotarians and Exempt Spacemen from the Middle West, taking them on personally conducted tours of the White House.

"I deserve better than that," he said, stormily. "If you hadn't won in the Southeast you wouldn't be here—"

"Yes, you're a good man for smoke-filled rooms and rostrums, Jim, just as I've just told you: the personal touch. But listen—the Southeast? Don't let's kid ourselves. The strategy there wasn't yours anymore than it was mine. It was Sarra's, all the way."   Macdonald uttered a short, ugly word. Roger Smith's head snapped back. "You're talking to the President of the United States," he said.

Macdonald laughed. "No, I'm not. I'm talking to the guy who sleeps with my wife."

Smith stared at him, bleakly.

Then he said, "I'm turning you off. You get out of here."

But Macdonald shook his head. "You talk to me or I talk to the press. Okay?" Smith said nothing, continued staring at him. "Okay," Macdonald muttered. What he was going to do, he said, leaning back, and taking out a cigar, was to give Rog a little history lesson, free... His expression, as he lit his cigar, raised his eyebrows, darted little glances at the grim-faced man viewing him, and gazed at the smoke as it came swirling from his own pursed lips, was that of an actor in a classical "B movie"—a heavy, who has just announced that he is "going to enjoy this, very much."

"Go ahead," Smith said. "But just remember that while you are getting this off your chest, or wherever the hell you've been keeping it, that the job I have is the most difficult one in the world, and that the world isn't going to stand still for either of us. Now, go ahead."

Jim, who had waved his hand, lightly, at mention of difficulty, now nodded, puffed at his cigar. After a moment he said, "You've heard, I suppose, of Charles Stewart Parnell."

"Parnell? Parnell? The Irish—"

"*That's* the one. Home rule for dear old Ireland. The 1880's, 90's. Well, Parnell had a friend named Captain O'Shea—Willie O'Shea. Ever heard of him? No? Doesn't matter. O'Shea, you see, was useful to Parnell, acted as his confidential agent, took care of difficult matters for him, let his own political career languish in order to help Parnell's…. And Parnell appreciated it. In fact, he appreciated it so much that he determined to keep O'Shea happy. That is, not exactly *Captain* O'Shea, but *Mrs*. O'Shea. The beautiful Kitty O'Shea. Willie wasn't good enough for her, it would seem. Whether he lacked *looks*, or *glamour*, or whether she couldn't twist him quite so far around her finger as she'd've liked to, who knows. Anyway, whatever it was that Willie didn't have, Smith—oops, sorry—Parnell had it."

He grinned, lifting his upper lip in front, and glancing sideways at the other man.

"Did Willie know about it? Oh, you bet your life Willie knew about it. He was nobody's fool. Of *course* he knew about it. Almost right from the start. Why didn't he do anything?" Jim considered his own question, shrugged. "Might be any one of a number of reasons. Maybe Willie didn't think that something was necessarily wrong just because an old book said it was. Maybe Willie *liked* Parnell—maybe he even *loved* Parnell, hmm?— so much that he just didn't *care*. Or…maybe even…maybe Kitty was the kind of woman that no one man could satisfy, hey? Oh, I don't just mean sexually. Maybe she had other desires—power, say. A lust for intrigue, for action, for—And maybe Willie figured that, if there had to be another man, well, he'd rather it was Parnell than anyone else. Could've been *any* of those reasons. Or all of them. Hey, Rog?"

Roger David Smith continued to stare at him, said nothing. Now and then he raised a hand and stroked the tiny scars on his face. Macdonald took another fleeting look at him, resumed.

"Well, where were we? *Oh*, yes—'*And the song he sang / Was, "Old Ireland free."*" Well, Home Rule. It was almost all wrapped up, you see.

Gladstone was all for it. Ireland was to have its own government at last, with Parnell as Prime Minister. Now, Willie had worked as hard for the cause as any man. And he felt it was time that he had his reward. It was a modest one—a place in Parnell's Cabinet."

After all, what difference did it make who held what Cabinet post? The actual work was always done by underlings, career men, drudges who delighted in details and red tape and hard work...

"Do you see the point, Rog?"

The President nodded. "I see it. And the answer is still 'No.'"

For the first time something like uncertainty flickered across Macdonald's face. "Ah, come on, Rog," he said, almost pleadingly. "You know something? I wouldn't make the worst Space Secretary in the world. I've followed things closely, damned closely. I've read up on it very, ver-ry carefully. I've got ideas which go beyond re-organizing the bookkeeping system, which is about all that Harley Gordon has in mind, or just sitting tight and hoping that the bogeymen will go away, which is all that Salem Smith has in mind."

"*You've* got ideas?"

Evidently stung by the tone of the questioning voice, Macdonald went from ruddy to red. "Yes, I've got ideas," he said. "And a lot of other important people have the same ideas—people whose support you'll damned well be needing." His eyes left the President's face and rested on something in the White House room behind the President; met the President's eyes as he returned his gaze; for an instant, fell; then faced him squarely and defiantly. Smith turned his head. There it was—the white, blue, red and yellow lights of the newly-installed Asteroid chart.

The President snorted. What would Macdonald do? he demanded. Occupy the Asteroids? Was that one of his ideas?

Yes, it was. It certainly was. The USA was tied hand and foot in one big Gordian knot, he said. The Condominium of the Moon, just look at it? The Russians did just as they damned well pleased, and in return for being let alone they raised every kind of hell imaginable with what the United States was doing. Whenever the United States *did* anything, that is; which was damned seldom...too damned seldom. And Mars? The U.S. had one station on Mars, count them, one; the British had one; the U.N. had two; and the Russians had *four*! The same as everyone else put together. And yet there were people claiming that the single American Mars station was costing too much.

"In a way they're *right*, Rog," Jim said, confidently now, almost cockily. "For a weather bureau, which is about all we use it for, it *is* costing too much. But Rog, if we occupied the Asteroids, then Mars Station could be busier than New York! And—rocketry strike? Hell, there'd be so much doing, we could double, triple their pay—the 'teers would be so busy making money they wouldn't have *time* to strike!"

"Uh-huh. And which ones would you occupy? Just the ones we claim? The ones the Russians claim, too? Any unclaimed ones we fancy? Or the whole works, maybe?"

For a moment Macdonald's face hung askew. Then something hateful and ugly entered it. Then he caught control of himself once more.

"How much longer are the American people going to sit still and let the Russians get away with insisting that everything they've already claimed is theirs and that everything they haven't claimed belongs to the U.N.? Where does that leave *us*? The American people—"

Smith got up abruptly, so abruptly that Macdonald jumped.

"I don't know who put you up to this—"

"Nobody put me—"

"I could make a good guess. You can tell them that they picked the wrong cat to try the chestnut game. 'The American people?' Listen, little Jimmy, the American people showed last November what they wanted in the way of leadership, and it wasn't *your* hand that went on the Bible three days ago."

"You—"

"*Me.* That's right. And I'll tell you something else, I'll give it to you right between the eyes, fellow—even if you didn't have these dangerous ideas you still wouldn't stand a chance at the job. Not a pip in a snow-hole. Because without Sarra you're not worth a—"

Scarlet, his cigar fallen unnoticed from his hand, Macdonald on his feet gestured and yammered in incoherent rage.

"My appointing *you*, if you hadn't so obviously sold yourself out, would have meant that *she'd* be the brains of the post. And I don't need her there, I don't want her there."

Now silence fell. Outside, the wet gray afternoon vanished as the exterior lights went on.

"Then it's 'No,'" Macdonald said, very softly. He looked older, he looked genuinely stricken, he looked a little sick.

"It's 'No,' Jim."

Jim nodded. "I'll wait… I'll wait until tomorrow. Just the same. Because… 'history lesson.' Parnell said 'No' to Captain Willie O'Shea, too, you see. And then Willie sued Kitty for divorce, naming Parnell as correspondent. He got the divorce. And Parnell got the axe. His party kicked him out. Gladstone backed off on Home Rule. Parnell died of a broken heart. And Ireland drowned in blood."

He paused in turning to go, did not look back.

"But I'll wait till tomorrow, anyway," he said.

Nicholas Mason, the American Representative to the U.N., his face noble and haggard, thanked the President again for having asked him to continue in office. Then, in a low voice, he told his latest tale of defeats, struggles, major setbacks, and minor victories.

Smith interrupted him, "What in your opinion, Mr. Ambassador—in your personal and confidential opinion—would be the effect of a scandal, an open and notorious and unsavory scandal, concerning the personal life of the President?"

Mason brought his mind to bear upon this abrupt question with visible difficulty. Slowly he raised his eyes and looked at Smith. Then a tremor ran over his face. "I can hardly suppose…that this question is hypothetical, Mr. President?" The President shook his head. In a voice still lower, Mason asked, "Could this…scandal of which you speak be averted? Is it possible? Then—"

"Averted only at great cost to the welfare of the Nation, and possibly, probably, involving dangers to its prestige, its proper functioning, and perhaps even its peace."

Mason slowly raised his hand and laid the palm against his face. "I may at least hope that the danger could not be that great. Even so, it would then be a matter of balancing dangers…costs. I need hardly tell you—I need hardly tell you—at this juncture, anything which would divide the country might well destroy the country. And then—you spoke of our prestige—it's none too high as it now is… I…" His voice died into a whisper.

Smith muttered, "I could resign, I suppose."

Mason snapped straight. "No President of the United States has *ever* resigned! *Mr. President*! Had you forgotten who would succeed you? If the present Vice-President were put in charge of a chickenyard, my money would be on the hawks and the weasels!"

Smith's face twisted.

"You have been a soldier, Mr. President," Mason continued. "I have not. But I know, and you surely know, that there is more than one way to win a battle. It is up to you to decide which way it has to be now. And… need I say…if I can in any way…?"

The President shook his head.

* * * *

Left alone, he got up and went to the windows. It was miserable weather. Only three days ago he had been inaugurated, on a crisp and sparkling afternoon. Despite all he knew of the world scene, the day had seemed flecked with gold. He had caught sight of Sarra, face shining with triumph, dressed in a gray robe which had appeared to his eyes then as brighter than scarlet or crimson. Now the dying sun broke through the clouds briefly and turned the wet walks and puddles red: yet his mood was gray, grayer than it had ever been before in his life. Sarra's voice rang in his ears, her face was before his eyes, and for the first time he failed to draw comfort from either. Could she deal with Jim at this late stage? Persuade him to do nothing? Could he be trusted to remain persuaded?

Or should he, the President, give the man the office he coveted, oblige him to live up to his own first picture of it, a sinecure in which the actual work was done by others? And depend upon the tight reign of the President from there on?

But would Jim remain content? Might he not have more "ideas"? His own, or others, it might not even matter—ideas, policies, plans, purposes, ambitions? Where would it stop? James Thackeray Macdonald, red-faced little politician, the Secret President of the United States!

But where, where had he gotten the *nerve*? Why—and how—after all these years, had he brought himself to defy his wife? Except in those easy cajoleries which came so naturally to him, and which had made politics his natural field; except in these shallows he had scarcely ever seemed to have a mind of his own or an ambition which was not Sarra's. Why, after all these years, had the worm turned?

For a long time, in the lowering dusk, the President of the United States stayed at the window, deep in thought. Then he drew the curtains and went to the teleview.

* * * *

He had thought that the three men might ask many questions—or, rather, bring forth cautions and disagreements disguised as questions—but they asked only two, after all.

Anderson, this time, was silent. It was Lovel who spoke first.

"Mr. President," he began, "have you concluded that in order to maintain the integrity of our national confederation it is imperative for you to invoke the unknown law?"

"I have," said Roger David Smith.

Lovel's face was impassive, but the skin seemed suddenly tighter upon the almost fleshless bones.

"What is his name?" he asked.

Softly, almost gently, the President corrected him.

"*Her* name," he said.

THE TEETH OF DESPAIR

written with Sidney Klein

Originally published in *The Magazine of Fantasy & Science Fiction*, **May 1961.**

The full import of the singular series of events involving the groves of academe with the jungles of television, and culminating, perhaps significantly, on a certain April Fool's Day not so very long ago, has remained until now unknown to the American public. From a nation which went into something resembling a state of shock following the disclosure of corruption, nepotism, and anarcho-syndicalist infiltrations into one of its most cherished institutions, much, of necessity, had to be concealed.

It is only now that we are able to disclose this piece of history which, unknown to the protagonists themselves at the time, was eventually to result in the application to transtellurian satellite communications of that revolutionary principle whose name is now known to all the world. But at the beginning…

It was on a Sunday night in late February. The family of Dr. Thomas Grew, Professor of Physics at Ryland University, had some hours ago finished a supper consisting of the remains of the previous day's hamburger, hashed with potatoes. The meal had been eaten thoroughly, if not enthusiastically. After doing the dishes, Mrs. Grew and her elder daughter, Juanita, went out baby-sitting—not together—as they did several evenings a week. By this means they contrived to earn enough to buy Juanita's clothes. What Juanita discarded her mother wore, and after that they were cut down and passed into a second avatar for the use of Isabel, the younger Grew daughter. Isabel, an ungainly child with acne, ill-adjusted to her peer-group, objected stridently to this arrangement, which was the best that could be managed on her father's salary.

For some weeks, fortunately, Isabel had contented herself with being merely sullen, and at eight o'clock that evening she joined her brother Dudley, the Grew's only son, in fitting bobby-pins onto fan-shaped cards—an arrangement, in violation of child-labor laws, connived at by a Mr. Caiman, a drugs-and-sundries wholesaler in a small way of business, whose establishment was located on the ground floor of the run-down apartment house in which the Grews lived. Kindly Mr. Caiman paid seventy-five cents per hundred cards, and supplied all materials. The children were allowed by their parents to keep the money in lieu of allowance.

Dr. Grew had recently been replaced in his part-time job as busboy in a chow-mein restaurant, owing to the arrival from Hong Kong (on a fraudulently obtained passport) of the proprietor's third cousin, a former Lt. Colonel in the Nationalist Army who had been living very quietly since the fall of Canton. As he had not yet been able to secure other employ, and as he had marked all his class papers that morning during the hour or so respite afforded by the attendance of his children at an Ethical Society Sunday school, Dr. Thomas Grew found himself momentarily with some spare time. He employed it in tinkering with a piece of electronic equipment he had pieced together for his amusement over a period of years by smuggling out a resistor here, a capacitor there, from the University lab. The fingers of his children dipped mechanically into the box of bobby pins. Their eyes were fixed immovably to the screen of the television set.

The presence of a television was absolutely against every principle which Dr. Grew held culturally dear, and its cost was astronomically beyond his own means. But it had been presented to them, second-hand, with much flourish, by the wealthy widow of a master plumber, a friend of his mother-in-law's. Dr. Grew did not wish to offend this woman, a Mrs. Novack, because she turned over to him the boxes of cigars which still came her way as gifts from various plumbing equipment manufacturers (she retained an interest in the business); and these cigars he traded off to Mr. Caiman for a cheaper brand at the rate of one for one-and-a-half, shredding them and smoking them in his pipe. He had been unable to afford pipe tobacco proper since his marriage, which had occurred during the latter part of the vice-presidency of John Nance Gamer.

First the children spent half an hour in flaccid delight watching a mixed bag of trained dogs, ventriloquists, acrobats, and fancy roller-skaters; then they watched a patriotic drama concerning the actions of a heroic female Confederate spy against the foul ploys of an evil and lecherous Union general. From time to time Grew said, "Please make that a weeny bit softer, kiddies"; but they paid him no mind, nor did he expect they would. After a while he ceased to notice the noise as he tenderly soldered in place the diode which was his latest acquisition.

And then, finally, it was time for *Get It While You Can*, a program during which even Dr. Grew attended carefully, only pretending from time to time to make a ritual and face-saving clatter with his wire-stripper.

Last week Robby Rheinhart, the loveable M.C., had faced the cameras with a little girl in a wheel chair, and the week before that it had been a war veteran on crutches. *This* week, however, he had with him a sturdy old man with a white cane, as the shapely female assistants, beaming vacantly, wheeled out a table on which were two huge bowls filled with large, opaque capsules. After the applause died down, Robby introduced This Week's Guest of Honor, Mr. Edward Palumbo of the Calabrese Home For the Blind. Then there was a commercial. Mr. Palumbo was induced to say a few words and answer a few questions. Then there was another commercial, in which a wistful young man in a bath towel sprayed his armpits with something from a squeeze bottle. Then they dollied in once more on the oleaginous Rheinhart and on honest, rugged old Palumbo. While the orchestra played the theme music, the old guy took off his coat, rolled up his sleeves, held up both hands. The music played slower, he dipped his hand in the starboard goldfish bowl, and pulled out a capsule.

The music stopped.

"Inside this capsule which our dear old Pal, Eddie Palumbo, has just selected at random," Robby said, breathlessly, "is inscribed the name of one of our wonderful *stoodio* audience. Every one of their names, as you all know, is inside one of those capsules, but only one at a time can be chosen. And NOW." He broke open the capsule, stared at the slip of paper. The cameras played over the faces in the audience, some tense, some picking their noses, some breaking into shy gestures as they caught their faces in the monitor. Robby milked the moment, then, in a high, breathless voice, declaimed, "Mis-ter… Herman… GRACKL!"

The camera panned in on the name on the slip, then a view of the audience again, finally focusing on someone who had just realized that *he* was Mr. Herman Grackl. Hesitantly, and in sections, like a telescope, he rose in his seat.

"Mr. Grackl?" burbled Robby, "Well, for gosh sakes, aren't *you* the lucky one! Come on up *here*, time's a-wasting, and—*Get it while you can!*"

The lucky man shambled forward, smirking and blinking and mumbling his jaws, while the music played a rapid tempo. After he had shaken hands with the M.C. and been turned—by main force—*away* from the shapely female assistants, and *towards* the audience, he played with the buttons on his shabby coat while Robby asked him a few questions. "Where are you *from*, Mr. Grackl?"

"Uh, I live right here in town."

"*Right here in town!* And what do you do for a living, Herman?"

"Uh, I'm retired."

"Retired! Well, aren't *you* the lucky one! I wish I were—What am I *saying?*" Robby Rheinhart screamed, clutching his own throat with both hands and bulging his eyes. "The *sponsor* may be listening!" The audience roared. "Well. What did you *used* to do for a living, Herm?"

"I git socia' securidy," said Herm, sucking in his lips and cheeks, then expelling them.

The Grew children giggled. "Dope," said Isabel. "Dope yourself," Dudley said, promptly. Isabel dropped her card of bobby-pins and struck at him. Their screams finally attracted the attention of their father, to whom had suddenly occurred a solution to the problem of proper RF shielding. It was a full minute before he succeeded in wedging the kids apart and getting them reasonably quiet again. With a few deft twists of his long-nose pliers he then made the necessary adjustments.

"—in nineteen thirty-six?!" Robby Rheinhart was screaming. "*And out of oatmeal boxes*! Well, isn't *that* something? Isn't that *some*-thing?"

"There, see," muttered Isabel petulantly, "and we missed what he said."

Perhaps the possibility again occurred to the M.C. that his *padrone* might be watching—conceivably with a stopwatch—because he suddenly became less strident and more businesslike. Old Mr. Palumbo, in return for $500 which the sponsors (Robby had already announced four times) were going to donate to the Calabrese Home For the Blind, thrust his big, gnarled hand into the other glass bowl and came up with another capsule, which Robby took from him and opened with pinch-lipped concentration. A glance at the contents and he had another fit of convulsions, combined with renewed manifestation of exophthalmia.

"Thirty-three hundred *dollars*!" he screamed, holding up the slip for the camera. "Every question that you answer correctly will be worth *thir-ty three hun*-dred *dol*-lars! *How about that!*"

Professor Grew groaned. The butcher who supplied his family with hamburger (the only meat they could afford) was becoming importunate. An increase in faculty salaries was, as the President of Ryland had pointed out only a month earlier, quite impossible at this time. Owing to the lousy season at football, alumni contributions had dropped to almost zero.

Glumly he watched Herman Grackl, shambling and blinking and mumbling his jaws, being escorted up the thirty-steps to the throne from which he would answer—or fail to answer—the questions. A curtain parted on the studio stage, revealing a huge vault. Two presidents of well-known banks came forward and, one after the other, concealing the combinations, twirled dials. The door swung open, revealing another door. Two presidents of theological seminaries, followed by the national directors of two veterans' organizations, proceeded in turn to open four more doors by means of keys in their possession and in their possession only. Finally, in the innermost recess of the vault was revealed an envelope approximately the length and width of an Ispahani rug, and sealed with seven seals.

"Are you ready, Herm?" Robby, once again serious, asked.

Herm sucked in his cheeks, thrust out his lower lip, pulled it in again, nodded. "Ee-yup. Ready," he said, and gave an imbecile grin.

Robby Rheinhart broke the seven seals solemnly.

"Very well. And here is your first question. For $3300, tell us—*who designed the Brooklyn Bridge?*"

Mr. Grackl's grin faded. He rolled his eyes, breathed noisily into the microphone, and wiped his brow on his coat-sleeve.

"You have twenty seconds in which to answer. It's worth three thousand dollars—*so-o-o—Get it while you can!*"

Professor Grew said, "George Washington Roebling, if I'm not mistaken."

"George Washington Roebling, if I'm not mistaken," said Mr. Grackl.

Professor Grew, hearing his very words repeated, smiled. Deadpan, Robby Rheinhart asked, "Is that your answer?"

"Of course it is. Certainly," said Grew.

"Of course it is. Certainly," said Grackl.

Professor Grew smiled—somewhat uncertainly, this time. Robby Rheinhart leaped into the air, clicked his heels, flung wide his arms, and shrieked, "*You're RIGHT! For thir-ty three hundred dol-lars!*" The audience burst into applause, and the band into music. Herman Grackl clasped his hands above his head and beamed. ("Silly ass," said Grew. Grackl's face fell. So did his hands.)

"Will you go for a second thirty-three hundred dollars, Herm?" the M.C. asked, when the noise died down. Herm hesitated, gazed all around him, chewed his lips.

"Go ahead," urged Grew. "You'll never get another chance like this."

"I-I think I'll go ahead," said Herman Grackl. A swallowing movement was clearly visible the length of his long neck. "I'll never get another chance like this"

During the applause, and the commercial that followed, Grew bit his fingernails and pondered. Three times—oh, there wasn't any doubt about it—the contestant, Mr. Herman Grackl, had repeated the words of Thomas Grew. Could it be a coincidence? Could (here almost automatically, he laughed scornfully) could that fellow Rhine be right? Telepathy? "Well, we'll see," he said.

He saw soon enough.

"Our next question," announced Robby, solemn as a Senate investigator, "deals with a man who was a great man in his own right and whose *father* was also a great man Now, Herm, for sixty-three hundred dollars, tell us: *Who* was Secretary of War in the Cabinet of President Garfield, and *who* was his father?"

The music played. "Oh, Christ," muttered Dr. Grew "Oh, Oh. Oh. *Ahhh*!" In a flash, the Paraclete descending, it came to him. History wasn't, never had been, his strong point; after all, he was a physicist, damn it! but this he'd learned somewhere, and-

The music stopped. Robby repeated the question. Determining to play it slow, play it cool, find out for certain—sure, Grew said, "In the cabinet of President James A. Garfield—"

"In the Cabinet of President James A. Garfield—" said Herman Grackl.

"James *Abram* Garfield," Grew said.

"James *Abram* Garfield," Grackl said. The audience laughed a little bit. The M.C. picked it up, put on a wry grin of admiring surprise.

"The son of the Great Emancipator—" Grew's voice trembled.

"The son of the Great Emancipator—" Grackl's voice didn't. Grew could stand it no longer.

"Robert-Todd-Lincoln!" he said, very rapidly. "Robert-Todd-Lincoln!" shot out Grackl.

Robby Rheinhart took a quick gander at his paper, then another one off stage, then his face cleared. "Well, you got the middle name slightly wrong but we'll accept it—you're RIGHT! For six-ty six hun-dred DOL-lars!"

It wasn't till the band stopped its victory blast that Grew found his voice again. "Listen, you better not take any more on tonight," he said. "I don't think I can do it again right now. Tell him you'll come back next week. I'll be in touch with you after the show."

This is just what Herman did. His expression, as the two shapely female assistants led him away, was dazed, pleased, and haunted.

Everbright, the Professor of Zoroastrian Philology, was a small, scrannel man with rufous eyes. For the past twenty odd years (tap-tap on his little bench, like Dr. Manet), he had made and mended not only his only shoes and those of his wife, father, father-in-law, and six children, but in his cellar did clandestine cobbling for a fashionable bootmaker. "A preposterous tale, Grew," said Professor Everbright, now.

Yeoville, Professor of Provençal prose, who (being a bachelor, and feeling he could not spare from his studies the time for an outside job) lived mostly on canned spaghetti, shook his pale and pendulous cheeks. "Not to be credited, my dear Tom," he said.   Wearing the turtle-neck sweater and puffing the bull-dog pipe, both of which had been obligatory equipment for chaplains at non-denominational colleges when he had first come to Ryland in the choppy wake of the Dayton Monkey Trial, De Wet (Comparative Religion) sighed. His burning eyes and deep pallor were due not so much to ascetic zeal as to his playing a set of skins in various crowded and ill-ventilated jazz joints at non-union rates. "I don't dig this bit," he said. "Where *is* that cat? I'm buzzed for time, man, I've got a jam session in the Biblical Chaldee in an hour."

There were noises of approval from other Ryland faculty members—English, Chemistry, Teutonic Languages, (Per-Gunnar Maelstrom, the Ibsen expert, trimming his frayed cuffs with a small pair of scissors borrowed from Goldberg of Botany), and all the rest.

"Very well," said Grew. "We will demonstrate the fact as any other fact is demonstrated." He opened the door of the Faculty Lounge—cautiously, for it had only one hinge. "Herman, will you come in, please?"

Herman Grackl entered, nodding bashfully right and left. "I've told them and they don't believe me," said Professor Grew. "So suppose you tell them."

"Jeez, maybe I should of taken the money and quit, huh?" said Grackl apprehensively. "Well, I kind of like don't blame you professors. But it's a fact. Why me? Why not say a hundred other people? I dunno. Maybe it's a gift. It comes and it goes. Rudy Vallee, in the old days it use to be Rudy Vallee more than anyone else. Sometimes—whatever they had like playing at the old Steel Pier in Atlantic City. Couple a weeks ago it was a drunken woman she was takin' off alla her clothes down at—"

"What in the Hell are you talking about?" demanded Pighafetti, the biochemist, the envy of all the rest: kept all his family rosy-cheeked and warmly clad on his after-school hours earnings as a pizza-baker. The strain told, however, in the deep circles under his eyes.

Herman Grackl made haste to oblige. "First of all, as a result of an industrial accident incurred at sea during the Prohibition Era, I got like a plate in my head and it comes down—" he traced its descent with a large finger, "—in ta the jore, right around *here*." He paused. Dr. Grew nodded encouragement. "But nothing happen as a result a that, except I use to get a headache, off and on. Until I got this now pyorrhea condition and I lose haffa my teeth. There was a dennis in them days, maybe you heard o him? Dr. Goldpepper? Dr. Morris Goldpepper? Well, he made me this plate and he told me it had no less than two different metallic substances in it—"

Professor Everbright raised a thin, semi-transparent hand. "One moment," he said, in a voice like the rustle of falling leaves at Vallambrosa. "Are we to understand that you receive communications through your false teeth via the Marconi waves?"

"Your technical terms are a little archaic, Elmer," said Dr. Grew; "but in substance—well, yes."

"You stick to your Department and I'll stick to mine," Everbright said, with unexpected fire. "I'd like to see how *you'd* make out on a Pahlevi palimpsest with Kufic superscriptions all over it!"

Grew hastily signaled to Grackl, who had been listening with mingled incomprehension and respect, to continue. "So that's it," said Herm. "*How* it happens, Ida know. *When* it's going to happen, I never use to be able to predick. It'd fade in—'High-ho, everybody'—fade out again. Sometimes a short interlude of organ music. Sometimes, if it's inny immediate neighborhood, I get a police call. Once inna while: TV. But I *never* got anything as what I mean *clear* until I got Professor Grew's message the other night. All them creck answers! And then, afterwards, he told me to come over to his house, so I come; he says to come here, so I'm here. And that's it."

There was a silence. Then—"Demonstration, I promised a demonstration," said Dr. Grew, bustling around with slips of torn-up examinations (the University providing no scrap paper for Faculty use) and pencils which students had from time to time imprudently left behind in class or lab. Half of the assembled savants he sent outside with Herman Grackl, the other half remained with him. And he then and there proceeded to send such messages and other data ($E=MC^2$, for example), via his little black box, through the dental prosthesis of Mr. Herman Grackl, as demonstrated conclusively the absolute truth of his account thereof.

However, there were no shouts of exultation. Dr. Yeoville sighed heavily and said, "Very well, we are convinced. Now what? Is it your intention to attempt to market this curious engine with monies raised from the Ryland Faculty? If so, here is fifty cents: I shall go without lunch for three days."

Grew smiled crookedly. He then spoke (Busztromowicz of the English Department later declared) as never man spoke to man before. With burning words that blazed and crackled in the ambient air he sketched their poverty—deep, of ancient duration, the scars of it beyond cure. He spoke of the utter contempt in which they were held; the vast sums spent annually in the United States on bubble gum, Tom Collins mixer, and pin-ball equipment, he compared with the pittances devoted to higher education...

They listened, their eyes burned hotly, they made little growling noises in their throats and chests; shuffled their cracked shoes.

Finally, "All that you say is true," acknowledged Maelstrom. "Painfully, agonizingly true. But—as my students too often ask me—'So what?'"

"So this: Colleagues, I but state a simple fact when I say that we have here among us an accumulation of knowledge in no way inferior to that possessed by the sponsors of *Get It While You Can*. It is impossible that a question should be asked which at least one of our number could not answer. We have been poor long enough. Riches now lie within our grasp."

The University Poet-in-Residence, his lungs weakened by the steamy fumes of the dog-laundry in which he toiled after hours, coughed fitfully. "Your proposal, Dr. Grew," he said in a thin voice, "is quite obvious. It is also dishonest, unethical, and meretricious. I am in favor of accepting it."

When the applause died away one single head was seen to shake. It was gray, and belonged to the Professor of Hellenic Civilization. "I fear me," he muttered. "I fear me. Beware of *hubris*, the sin of overweening pride, lest it destroy us. Is not poverty as becoming to scholars as a scarlet bridle to a white horse?"

"If Homer said that," roared Professor Maelstrom, "no wonder they threw him off a cliff!"

An unexpected touch of color glowed in the other's cheeks.

"That was Hesiod, you Gothic oaf!" he snapped. Then the fight went out of him and he slumped in his seat, waved his hand in feeble surrender. "Yeypaod, yeypaod," he whispered. "Do what you will. I shall be with you."

The faculty made the acquaintance of Herman's lady-friend, a Mrs. Doll Moomaw, who had accompanied him and had waited in an outer room.

"Well-preserved," conceded Grew, in a whisper.

"And pneumatic," observed Everbright.

"I toll Doll that you professors are, now, trying to find me a job," said Grackl, winking ponderously over her shoulder.

"I be damned and go-to-Hell," said Doll, briskly, "if I can figure out what Herman could do at a college besides sweeping out the can, but listen, as long's he makes some money. I think he's had this same suit on since the six-day bicycle races."

"Aw, now, *Doll*," said Herman, smirking bashfully.

"The late Mr. Moomaw, rest his soul, was of a short, stocky built; otherwise—"

But here Herman grabbed a hold and pulled her out, still explaining why the deceased's suits were of no use to his successor-apparent.

Professor Yeoville shook his head and dewlaps. "That woman worries me," he said.

But Grew, sanguine, clapped him on the back. "Ho, ho, you old bachelor!" he chuckled. Yeoville winced, fell silent.

The following Sunday night the Faculty of Ryland University (excluding, of course, the Professor of Athletic Science, who was known to be a fink for the Board of Trustees and the Alumni Association, and had therefore been omitted from the cabal) assembled behind the locked doors of their Lounge. Dr. Grew, speaking into his mechanism and gazing at the television set smuggled up, said, "If you receive me okay, Herman, stroke your right cheek twice."

Herman Grackl stroked his right cheek twice. ("Hot diggety!" exclaimed an excited pedagogue—and was stricken silent by the warning glares of the others.)

That night Herman answered questions involving the tributaries of the Sepik Watershed, the more obscure poems of Fulke Greville, the Eleventh Mihir Yast, and the Presidents of the U.S. Congress under the Articles of the Confederation (in chronological order). He answered them all correctly; after which, by a show of hands, he was advised to retire until the following week. He had won, the previous week's score included, $19,800.

"Oughtn't we to have stopped right there?" the Professor of Hellenic Civilization asked.

"Why, it would come to less than a thousand dollars apiece," Grew objected.

"A thousand dollars!" repeated the Professor of Zoroastrian Philology, in tremulous tones.

"We must learn to think big," pointed out the Professor of Provençal prose. "*I* think we should wait until we have at least *two* thousand dollars apiece!"

* * * *

In the month that followed, Herman Grackl, by naming the Mayors of the Palace, twenty-three dwarf stars in order of magnitude, all the vessels involved in the Battle of Lepanto, the Dodecanese Islands with their principal cities and populations and chief exports, all the steps involved in the Activated Sludge method of sewage disposal and descriptions thereof; by explaining the systems of proportional representation obtaining in four Scandinavian countries and Switzerland, Frenet's formulas for a space curve, the Twenty-Four Traditional Measures of Welsh poetry, and the meaning of thirty-two symbols from the Popul Vuh; and by correctly identifying twelve Proto-Etruscan artifacts, paintings by Murillo, Winterhalter, and Rembrandt Peale, as well as musical pieces by Arne, Bartok, Pietro Yon, and Henry VIII…he became a national figure.

He was featured on the covers of *Time* and *Life* magazines.

The then President of the United States, being asked in press conference about a clause in the tariff bill he was urging on Congress, replied, "Well, you are informing me of something about which the precise particulars I am not aware of. After all, I am not Herman Grackl." (Laughter.)

It was a merry group of scholars which assembled in the Faculty Lounge the evening of Hermans sixth appearance of *Get It While You Can*. Dr. Grew passed around the latest box of cigars which Chromo-Bright Tube and Pipe had presented to Mrs. Novack, and she to him; as one who was shortly to cut up a kitty in excess of $957,000 (for all concerned had determined that this would be the last evening), he felt he could well afford the gesture. The Professor of Levantine Archaeology declared that he had been pricing Jaguars. The Poet-in-Residence argued the claims of the Ferrari. Dr.

Maelstrom announced a certain method he intended to recommend to the President of the University to relieve his (the Presidents) prostate condition. And then all conversation died down as they closed in to watch their protégé engage in preliminary banter with Robby Rheinhart, the genial M.C. of the program.

"Herm, there seem to be a few changes in your appearance," Robby said.

"Hey, you know, man, he's right," observed the Professor of Comparative Religion. "Like he looks different, somehow." Herman Grackl smirked. "Well, Robby, when you're in love, it *does* make a change."

Robby did a double-take. "Did you say—*in love*?"

Another smirk. "Ee-yup. T'tell the truth—I'm engaged!"

Grew exclaimed, "He didn't say anything to us about—But I suppose it was inevitable—"

Robby inquired, "Well, Herm, is your fiancée by any chance *here* tonight?"

With a dip of his knees and a bob of his head, Herm allowed as how she was, and, with much palaver, coyness, applause, laughter, and hoo-hah, the camera showed the fiancée to all America. Mrs. Moomaw, beamed, bowed, bridled, and displayed her superabundant charms to the ambient air.

"—so she says, 'Honey,' she says, 'the whole country is lookin at you so why don't you get yerself fancied up?' So I says, 'You are right, Doll.'"

"*That's* what's like new about him," the Professor of Comparative Religion exclaimed. "Dig those crazy threads, man!"

And, after more persiflage, the refurbished Herman mounted the steps to the throne. The ceremony of opening the vault and removing the questions was gone through, and, as Robby Rheinhart broke the seventh seal, a certain amount of tension gripped those present in the Faculty Lounge.

"*Now*. Following the death of Alexander the Great—" ("Hah!" snorted the Professor of Hellenic Civilization, rubbing his hands.) "—there arose in the East a dynasty known as the Sassanian, or New Persian, Dynasty." (The Hellenicist bit his lip and ignored the glance of ill-concealed triumph thrown his way by the Professor of Zoroastrian Philology.) "There were twenty-eight members of this dynasty. For Thirty-three hundred dollars a point, Herm, name all twenty-eight members of the Sassanian, or New Persian, Dynasty. You have already won nine hundred and fifty-seven thousand dollars. If you name all twenty-eight correctly you will win ninety-two thousand four hundred dollars, which will make a total OF—" he paused— "one *million*, forty-nine thousand…four-hundred DOLLARS! Good luck, Herm. You have twenty seconds to think of your answer. Should you miss, of course," he concluded, cheerfully, "you lose everything."

The music began to play. "All right," asked Grew, flipping the switch on his hootenanny, "what's the first one?"

"Artaxerxes I," said Professor Everbriglit.

"Artaxerxes I," repeated Grew. "Got that, Herman?"

The music stopped. "Sapor, Hormisdas, Vahrahan, Narses," mumbled Everbright, counting on his fingers.

"All right, Herm," burbled Robby. "Your twenty seconds are up."

"He actually looks worried," chuckled Maelstrom. "What an actor!"

"For three thousand, three hundred dollars, tell us the names of the first Sassanid Kings of Persia."

Herman said nothing. "Artaxerxes I," repeated Grew. Herman cast an agonized look around him.

"I'll have to call for an answer, Herm," said Robby.

"*He's not acting*!" shouted Professor Maelstrom. "He doesn't hear you! The transmitter isn't working!"

"The transmitter is in perfect order!" Grew insisted. "ARTAXERXES I!" he yelled at the top of his voice. Herman's face broke out in sweat. He suddenly clapped his hands to his mouth, then began to slap, pat, prod, and pole his pockets, one after the other. Again and again. And then the hideous truth came to Professor Grew. "He's looking for his old teeth!" he wailed. "That blowsy old bitch he shacked up with—she's hypnotized him or something—she not only made him get a new suit of clothes, but *she made him get a new set of teeth, too*!"

The Poet-In-Residence uttered a hoarse scream and fell senseless to the floor. Pandemonium raged in the Faculty Lounge, while (unheard) on tire screen Robby Rheinhart slowly shook his head.

"Hubris," whispered the Professor of Hellenic Civilization, as tears rolled down his seamed, emaciated face. "Hubris. Whom the gods would destroy—"

* * * *

The proprietor of the chow mein restaurant where Dr. Thomas Grew had formerly worked passed him on the street the week following. Having a Confucian respect for scholarship, and being struck by the Professor's threadbare condition, he rehired him on the spot as supernumerary bus-boy.

Grew works there three nights a week, and though the pay is minimal and the tips scant, he is frequently able to bring home nourishing scraps of food.

It was there one night, whilst surreptitiously slipping into his great-coat pocket the contents of a bowl of left-over won-tons which the ex-general had earmarked for his Peke, that there occurred to the foreign-devil bus-boy in a blaze of illumination the practical application of what has since become to known to all the world as the Grew-Grackl-Gold-pepper Principle of Bimetallic Coupling which has made such revolutionary changes in satellite communications.

Under the circumstances it would be pointless to cavil at the fact that the overriding needs of the national security preclude the possibility of a patent; and that, hence, none of the three men has been able to realize any financial profits whatsoever.

THE SINGULAR EVENTS WHICH OCCURRED IN THE HOVEL ON THE ALLEY OFF OF EYE STREET

Originally published in *The Magazine of Fantasy & Science Fiction*, February 1962.

In 1961, the year when the dragons were so bad, a young man named George Laine, an industrial alchemist by profession, attended the coronation of the new president in Washington. The guilds were in high favor with the president-select, John V (the first of that name since John IV C. Coolidge), who sent to each and every of their delegation, as a mark of his esteem, garments of virtue worthy of the occasion, *viz.* a silken hat, a pair of galoshes with silvern buckles, a great-coat with a collar of black samite, cuff-links enchased in gold, and a pen-and-pencil set of malachite and electrum which was guaranteed to write under water and over butter: both, as it happened, essential to the practice of industrial alchemy.

The ceremonies proceeded without any untowardness. The Supreme Justice of the Chief Court placed on the President's head the sacred beaver with the star-spangled band and declared that "Regardless of rape, crude, choler, or national ore or gin, any resemblance is purely coincidental." The Chairman of the Board of Augurs of the Federal Reserve System pronounced a curse in weirdmane and in womrath on anyone who should presume to send gold o'er the white-waved seas. The new Veep, wearing the ritual ten-gallon hat, and mounted on a palomino, cantered up and down before the Selectoral College and uttered the prescribed challenge: "Whosoever doth deny that the Honorable John V Fitz-Kenneth is the rightful Chief Executive of Thiscountry lies, and is an S.O.B." The out-going Jester raised the liturgian *hwyl* of *We want Wilkie*, and was smitten twice with a slapstick and thrice with a bladder, both wielded by his successor. The Fall River Chamber of Commerce and Horror presented the ceremonial breakfast of cold mutton soup, sliced bananas, and an axe: it was ceremoniously refused. A Boston Brahmin, clad in cutaway, *dhoti*, and sacred thread, offered a salver bearing two curried codfish balls; the new President ate both whilst the Brahmin intoned,

> *Eat it up, wear it out,*
> *Make it do, or do without;*

after which he, the B.B., hurried to wash himself in sacred 6% Charles water to remove the impurity of feeding with a lower caste.

George Laine and his fellows of the alchemists and other guilds were not forgotten even afterwards; for Prex Jax (as the news-guild had already termed him *in parvo*) sent them out great smoking helpings of buffalo hump, bear paws, caponized peacocks, pemmican, ptarmigan, succotash, and syllabub, from the high table where he was dining with his notables, including Surgeon-General Doctor Caligari, who had just been raised to Cabinet rank.

It was during these moments of revelry and mirth that George choked on a quartern of orange in an Old Fashioned Cocktail, all went black before his face, and, on awakening to find himself bound with silken cords in a hovel on an alley off of Eye Street, knew that he had been ensorceled.

There was a bim looking bemused at him with a bodkin in her bosom, and he wotted well it were for lack of wit anent her that he bode bound: for who was she but Yancey-Courtney Bellergarde, a Drum Majorette 1/c, who had been sitting in his lap that time he raised the dram-glass to his lips.

"I say, that bodkin must hurt something dreadful," he said (not having attended the N.Y. High School of Gallanterie Trades in vain): "untie me and I'll have it out for you in a trice: there's a good gel, do."

The bim smiled scornfully. Her lips were as red as the chassis of a new-model Jaguar of the first enameling. "Not on your tin-type, Cully," she said. "Rats. Nit." She spoke in the Archaic tongue of the bim-folk, which is akin to elf-talk, and cognate with 23 Skiddoo (unlawful for a man to know until he has passed his finals in The Deep School, and been awarded the right to wear the Navel Plug, with two Pips).

"Nix on the soft-soap, Charlie," she said; "I only keep the bodkin there because these, now, sorcelsacquets don't have any pockets in them, as if you didn't know. Oh you kid!" she concluded, archly. And with this she withdrew the bodkin, dipped its prickle into a pot labeled *Poyson Moste Foule*, and approached the supine young industrial alchemist with the tip of her tongue held between her teeth.

"Slip me the Formula for the Transmutation of Borox Without the Use of Cockatrice-egg," she said (speaking with some difficulty, her tongue, as we have already noted, you clod, being between her teeth), "and we'll be back in the Grand Ballroom of the Mayflower in lots of time to see Ed Finnegan made a K.T.V.; afterwards we can tiptoe up to any of the thirty-odd double rooms which my Company keeps rented at all times, and you may have your wicked will o' me without fearing the House-Dick, because I'll put a Cheese-it spell on the door, see, which it's proof against

Force, Force-Fields, Stealth, Mort-Main, Nigromancy, Mopery, and Gawk: so give, Cully, give."

A cold sneer crossed George's hot lips. "I say, what an absolutely rotten proposal!" he exclaimed. "You know perfectly well that I have sworn by the most frightful oaths to remain true in mind and deed to Alchymy, Ltd. of Canada, and to keep myself physically clean, mentally straight, and morally pure! I suppose you're one of these simply awful party girls which one hears that General Semantics, Inc., of Delaware, keeps on their payrolls to entrap, ensorcel, enviegal, enchant, anduce, endive, and endamage clean-living young chaps into betraying secrets. Well, I shan't, do you hear? Better I should die. So there!"

But the bim, far from being one whit abashed by this manly defiance, laughed as coarsely as the position of her tongue would permit. "Well, if that don't take the cake," she snickered. "Gee, what a simp!" and made feint as though she would withdraw George's Plug, two Pips or no two Pips.

"No, really, don't touch me, do you hear?" George said, stoutly, trying to roll over on his stomach. "I'm really most frightflie ticklish, and besides, without the Plug I should swell up with lint in simply no time; funny thing about me, I'm very susceptible to navel lint, always was, from a child."

But the silken cords held him fast.

"The Formula for the Transmutation of Borax Without the Use of Cockatrice-egg," she said, inexorably, making little jabs at him with the bodkin dip't in Venom.

George mimicked her: "—Uthe of Cockatwithe-egg!"

Unguardedly she laughed, releasing the tip of her tongue from between her teeth, and thus... Those who are Cupboard Certified Auditors of The Deep School will understand *thus*, and those who are *not* needn't imagine for one minute that we are going to reveal for free, secrets for which others have paid good money, no siree. Suffice it, then, to say that in a trice George had leapt out of his bonds, flung the bodkin from the bim's hands with such force that it pierced the door and hung quivering. This produced a startled cry from behind the door, which George flung open, revealing a man, a tape-recorder, and a flash-camera. The man first cringed, then assumed an expression combining both defiance and a falsely hearty air of good will.

"Weh-hell, Laine," he birbled.

"What," demanded George, sternly, "is the Assistant Director of Research for the Middle Atlantic States Division of Alchymy, Ltd., of Canada, doing cowering behind the door of a hovel on an alley off of Eye Street, with a tape-recorder and a flash-camera; what?" A question which, put like that, might make any man pause before answering.

Mr. Marcantonio Paracelcus (for such was his name) paused before answering. He swallowed. "It was a Test, you see, George."

"I fail to see."

"Well, it was a *test*. The Company is considering you for an important new job. In order to find out how you would shape up under pressure, we have tested you. I am, um, happy, to say that you have passed the Test."

George said, "Oh, good. Then I get the job. *What* job?"

Mr. Marcantonio Paracelcus seemed to find some difficulty m answering this question. Whilst he stood there, came a buzz and a clatter, and that which George had hithertofore considered to be merely a tallboy-sized TV set opened up, revealing itself to be an Observation Armoire containing a microphone, two tape-recorders, an automatic closed-circuit television camera, and Dr. Roger Bacon Buxbaum, Chief Director of Research for the Middle Atlantic States Division of Alchymy, Ltd. of Canada. Marcantonio Paracelcus, on perceiving his superior, turned ashen, livid, and pale, in that order.

"The job in question, George," said Dr. Buxbaum, "is that which until a moment ago was held by the gentleman you now see cowering behind the door; but which is no longer so held. On realizing that you were being considered for his position, he determined on this unworthy method of discrediting you: hence, the tape-recorder, on which he hoped to capture the sound of your voice as you revealed the Formula for the Transmutation of Borox without the Use of Cockatrice-egg; hence, the flash-camera with which he hoped to capture the sight of you in a—" and here tired, benign, balding Buxbaum blushed a bit, "compromising position with this young female person here. Little did he know," the urbane researcher winked, and placed his right forefinger by the right side of his nose, "that we were onto his jazz from the word Go...

"And to think that he would sully the semi-sacred season of the Coronation by his meretricious machinations: fie, sir, do you call yourself a Thicountrean? But I forbear harshness; modern science has taught us that such a one as you is really sick, and needs help. Come along now—George! Expect to see you for lunch, day after tomorrow, at the Alembic, one sharp!"

George went pink with pleasure, for what was the Alembic but the most expensive eatery favored by the upper echelons of the M.A.S.D. of Alchymy, Ltd. (Canada); and this invite betokened his full acceptance into the post previously held by his unfortunate predecessor, who even now, sniveling miserably, was being firmly guided out by the elbow. George's feelings of sorrow, which did him credit, were tempered by the reflection that, after suitable treatment at the Company's Rehabilitation Farm in North Baffin Land, the man might still prove capable of many years of devoted service; though, of course, in a minor capacity.

For a moment all was silent in the hovel on the alley off of Eye Street. George eyed the bim. The bim eyed the floor. After a while she spoke. "I suppose you hate me," she said.

"No, I—"

"I suppose you think I'm miserable and treacherous."

"No, I—"

"I suppose you think I would really have stuck you with a poysoned bodkin, don't you? Well, the jar only contained a Sophronia Finkelstein preparation for the treatment of tired skin and subcutaneous tissues; so there."

George said, "No, I fully realize that as a bim, and as a sorceress under contract to General Semantics, Inc. of Delaware, you were only carrying out your duty. And now, if you don't mind, I wonder if I might use your phone to call a taxi?"

Fancy his astonishment when she burst into tears.

"We have no phone," she wept. "I'm not a bim. I never worked for General Semantics. My parents couldn't afford to send me to Sorcery School. How I put you under that spell and brought you here, my old Auntie Eglantine was a white witch, and I picked up some little piddly old spells from her, is all. I am really just a Drum Majorette, 1/c. Oh, I wish I were dead! A hoo, hoo, hoo!"

George, at first with awkwardness, then with growing appreciation for the task, patted her hands, her shoulders, and the general area of the small of her back. "To tell you the truth, Miss Yancey-Courtney," he said, "I would just purely hate it if you were to be a bim. I mean, like those hairy *feet*? And their toenails *glow* in the dark? Why, a man couldn't hardly relish his victuals, let alone keep his mind on his Transmutations… Of course, I'm just speaking speculatively, I mean, having always kept myself physically pure, mentally clean, and morally square, according to the terms of my Triune Oath to the Company, which I have never regretted," he said, regretfully.

"Of course," she murmured, wiping her eyes on his shirt-tail.

"Listen," she said. "Do you know when it was that I first felt a revulsion I was barely able to conquer at the infamous Marcantonio Paracelcus' proposal? It was when the Veep rode in. When he gave out the Challenge I could see you clench your fists until your knuckles went what I mean *white*; as if you were just *daring* any old Recounter to challenge the Selection!"

"Hm," said George, grimly.

"I'll bet you must be awfully strong."

George, modestly, said, well, shoving all that lead and gold around, *you* know. She said that she could well imagine. There was a pause. Then he asked what time it was. She said it was 7:45, why? He said that if they hurried, they could still get to see Ed Finnegan dubbed a K.T.V. She said, yes, they could, couldn't they? She asked if he was very fond of Ed Finnegan. There was a pause. He said that as a matter of fact he couldn't stand Ed Finnegan.

"Neither can I!"

"All those trained wombats!"

"And that incessant, hearty laugh!"

There was another pause. Then, "My those are handsome galoshes!" she said.

"Gift of the President."

"Pipe the silvern buckles, will yuh?"

"Mmm."

"But don't you think you'd be more comfortable if you took them off?"

"The buckles?"

"Oh, you silly! The *galoshes*!"

"I might at that."

And he did. And he was.

Outside, the Northern Lights hissed and crackled (or, again, it might have been the dragons, which were so bad that year); outside, the noise of revelry continually rose and fell in the sheets; but inside, all was quiet in the hovel on the alley off of Eye Street.

THE LINEAMENTS OF GRATIFIED DESIRE

(aka "The Price of a Charm")

Originally appeared in *Ellery Queen's Mystery Magazine*, December 1963.

The mountain air was clear and sweet, scented with wild herbs, and although the young man had come quite a distance, he was not at all tired. The cottage—it was really little more than a hut—was just as it had been described to him; clearly, many people in the district had had occasion to visit it. At one side a tiny spring poured over a lip of rock and crossed the path beneath a rough culvert. At the other side was a row of bee-hives. A goat and her kid grazed nearby, and a small black sow ate from a heap of acorns with a meditative air.

A man with white hair got up from the bench and held out his hand. "A guest," he said. "A stranger. No matter, guest, all the same. Everyone who passes by is my guest, and the toll I charge is, I make them drink with me." He laughed, his laugh was infectious, and the young man laughed, too, though his sallow, sullen face was not that of one who laughed often.

The hand he shook was hard and calloused. "I am called Old Steven," the peasant said. "It used to be Black Steven, but that was a long time ago, even my moustache is white, now—" he stroked its length, affectionately—"except for here, in the middle. I am always smoking tobacco. Smoking and drinking, who can live without them?"

He excused himself, returned almost at once with bottle, glasses, and cigarettes.

"I do not usually—" the young visitor began, with a frown which seemed familiar to his face.

"If you do not smoke, you do not smoke. But I allow only Moslems to refuse a drink, and they do not often do so. One drinks, a mere formality."

They had one drink for formality, a second drink for friendship, and a third drink to show that they did not deny the Trinity.

Steven wiped his moustache between index finger and thumb of each hand, thrust in a cigarette, lit it, and smiled contentedly.

"A good thing, matches," he said. "When I was a boy we had to use tinderboxes—how the world does change… You came for a charm."

The young man seemed relieved, now that the preliminaries of the visit were over. "I did," he said.

"Your name?"

"Gabriel."

Old Steven repeated it, nodding, blowing out smoke. "I am, of course, well-known for my charms," he said, complacently. "I refer to those I make, not those with which Providence endowed me—although, there was a time… Well, well. My hair was black in those days. I can make quite a number of charms, although some of them are not in demand any longer. I don't remember the last time I supplied one to keep a woman safe from Turks. Before you were born, I'm sure. But, on the other hand, charms to help barren women conceive are as much called for as ever."

Gabriel said, scowling, that he was not married.

"My charges are really quite reasonable, too. I can guarantee you perfect protection against ghosts, vampires, werewolves, and the evil spirits of the hills and forests—their cloven hoofs and blood-red nails—"

"I am not afraid of those. I have my crucifix." His hand went to the neck of his open shirt.

"Very well," said Old Steven, equitably. "I've nothing to say against that.

"I also," he said, "prepare an excellent charm for success in the hunt…"

"*Ah…*"

"And an equally excellent one for success in love."

"*Yes…*"

Old Steven nodded, benignly. "That's it, then, is it? The love-charm?"

Gabriel hesitated, scowled again.

"Which one means most to you? Or, putting it another way, at which are you best? Take the charm for the other."

The young man threw out his hands. "I am good at neither! And it is important to me that I must excel in one of them."

Steven lit another cigarette. "Why only one? Take both. The price—"

But Gabriel shook his head. "It's not the price." He looked out on the wide-spread scene, the deep and dark-green valleys with their forest of oak and beech and pine, the mountains blue with distance, the silvery river. "It's not the price," he repeated.

"As far as you can see on all sides," the old man said, quietly; "in fact, farther, my reputation is known. People have come to me from across the frontier. If it is not the price, take both." He saw Gabriel shake his head, but continued to speak. "The hunt. A day like today. You take your gun and go off in the woods with a few friends. The road is dusty, but in the woods, in the shade, it is cool. Your friends want to go to the right, but you, you have the charm, you know that the way to turn is *left*. They may protest, but you are so certain that they follow. Presently you see something out of the corner of your eye. The others have not noticed it at all, or perhaps assume it is a branch of that dead tree. But you know better, your eye is clear, you turn swiftly, your arm and hand are quick as never before, the bird flushes, you fire! There it is, at your feet—a fine woodcock. Eh?"

Gabriel nodded, eyes gleaming.

"Or it might be a red doe, or a roe-buck. A fine stag! You can hardly count the points! Everyone admires you... Perhaps in the winter the peasants come to you. 'Master, a wolf. No one is such a hunter as you are. Come, save our flocks.' They have not even seen the beast when your shot brings it down. You wait while they fetch it. They drag the creature along, shouting your praise: 'Only one shot, and at that distance, too!' they cry, and kiss your hand. 'Brave one, hero,' they call you."

A dreamy smile played on Gabriel's face, and he slowly, slowly nodded.

Old Steven waited a few moments; as his visitor said no word, he went on. "Then there is love. What can compare to that? A man who does not enjoy the love of woman is only half alive—if even so much. No doubt there is a young woman on whom you have looked, often, with longing, but who never returns that look. She has long, long black hair. How it glistens, how it gleams! Her lips are soft and red, and sometimes she wets them with her red little tongue. Inside her bodice the young breasts grow, ripe and sweet as fruit..."

The young man's eyes seemed glazed. He did not stop the slow nodding of his head.

"You return, the love-charm is in your pocket, against your heart, *here*. There is a dance, you join in, so does she. Presently you come face to face. She looks at you as if she has never seen you before. How wide her eyes grow! Her mouth opens. Her teeth are small and white. You smile at her and instantly she smiles back, then looks away, shyly...but only for an instant...and you dance together...

"Soon the stars come out, and the moon rises. The old women are drowsing, the old men are drunk. You take her hand in yours and the two of you slip away. The moment you stop, she throws her arms around you and puts her mouth up to be kissed. The night is warm, the grass is soft. The night is dark and deep, and love is sweet."

Gabriel made a sound between a sigh and a groan. Slowly, he reached into his pocket, took out his purse, and began to slide its contents into his hand. "You have made up your mind?" the old man asked. "Which is it to be, then?" There was no answer. Something caught the old man's eye. "This one is a foreign coin," he said, touching it with his finger. "But never mind, I will take it—it is gold."

Gabriel's eyes fell to his hand. He picked up the coin, and an odd look came at once over his face. The dreamy, undecided expression vanished immediately. His eyelids became slits, his lips turned down in an ugly fashion, something like a sneer.

After a moment the old man said, "You have made up your mind?"

"Yes," Gabriel said. "I have made up my mind."

* * * *

There was only an old woman before him at the ticket-window. He had crossed the river just a few minutes before. The contents of his small suitcase had not engaged the attention of the customs officials for long; and from there it was only a short walk to the railroad station.

The old woman went away, and Gabriel stepped up to the window. On the wall of the tiny office, facing him, were two framed photographs, side by side. The likeness of the older man was the same one that had been on the coin which had caught Old Steven's attention; but Gabriel knew the younger man's face, too; knew it very well, indeed. Once again the odd, ugly, strangely determined expression crossed his face.

The station-agent looked up. "Yes, sir," he said, "where to?"

"One ticket, one way." Gabriel kept looking at the face in the photograph.

"Very well, sir, a one-way ticket—but, where to? Trieste, Vienna?" He was a self-important little man, his tone grew a trifle sarcastic. "Paris? Berlin? St. Petersburg?"

Slowly, Gabriel's eyes left the picture. He did not seem to have noticed the sarcasm.

"No," he said. "Just to Sarajevo."

THE GOLEM

**Originally published in *The Magazine of
Fantasy & Science Fiction*, March, 1955.**

The gray-faced person came along the street where old Mr. and Mrs.
Gumbeiner lived. It was afternoon, it was autumn, the sun was warm and
soothing to their ancient bones. Anyone who attended the movies in the
twenties or the early thirties has seen that street a thousand times. Past
these bungalows with their half-double roofs Edmund Lowe walked arm-
in-arm with Leatrice Joy and Harold Lloyd was chased by Chinamen wav-
ing hatchets. Under these squamous palm trees Laurel kicked Hardy and
Woolsey beat Wheeler upon the head with codfish. Across these pocket-
handkerchief-sized lawns the juveniles of the Our Gang Comedies pursued
one another and were pursued by angry fat men in golf knickers. On this
same street—or perhaps on some other one of five hundred streets exactly
like it.

Mrs. Gumbeiner indicated the gray-faced person to her husband.

"You think maybe he's got something the matter?" she asked. "He
walks kind of funny, to me."

"Walks like a *golem*," Mr. Gumbeiner said indifferently.

The old woman was nettled.

"Oh, I don't know," she said. "*I* think he walks like your cousin, Men-
del."

The old man pursed his mouth angrily and chewed on his pipe-stem.
The gray-faced person turned up the concrete path, walked up the steps to
the porch, sat down in a chair. Old Mr. Gumbeiner ignored him. His wife
stared at the stranger.

"Man comes in without a hello, goodbye, or how-are-you, sits himself
down and right away he's at home... The chair is comfortable?" she asked.
"Would you like maybe a glass tea?"

She turned to her husband.

"Say something, Gumbeiner!" she demanded. "What are you, made of
wood?"

The old man smiled a slow, wicked, triumphant smile. "Why should *I*
say anything?" he asked the air. "Who am I? Nothing, that's who."

The stranger spoke. His voice was harsh and monotonous. "When you learn who—or, rather, what—I am, the flesh will melt from your bones in terror." He bared porcelain teeth.

"Never mind about my bones!" the old woman cried. "You've got a lot of nerve talking about my bones!"

"You will quake with fear," said the stranger. Old Mrs. Gumbeiner said that she hoped he would live so long. She turned to her husband once again.

"Gumbeiner, when are you going to mow the lawn?"

"All mankind—" the stranger began.

"*Shah*! I'm talking to my husband... He talks *eppis* kind of funny, Gumbeiner, no?"

"Probably a foreigner," Mr. Gumbeiner said, complacently.

"You think so?" Mrs. Gumbeiner glanced fleetingly at the stranger. "He's got a very bad color in his face, *nebbish*. I suppose he came to California for his health."

"Disease, pain, sorrow, love, grief—all are nought to—"

Mr. Gumbeiner cut in on the stranger's statement.

"Gall bladder," the old man said. "Guinzburg down at the *shul* looked exactly the same before his operation. Two professors they had in for him, and a private nurse day and night."

"I am not a human being!" the stranger said loudly.

"Three thousand seven hundred fifty dollars it cost his son, Guinzburg told me. 'For you, Poppa, nothing is too expensive—only get well,' the son told him."

"*I am not a human being!*"

"Ai, is that a son for you!" the old woman said, rocking her head. "A heart of gold, pure gold." She looked at the stranger. "All right, all right, I heard you the first time. Gumbeiner! I asked you a question. When are you going to cut the lawn?"

"On Wednesday, *odder* maybe Thursday, comes the Japaneser to the neighborhood. To cut lawns is *his* profession. *My* profession is to be a glazier—retired."

"Between me and all mankind is an inevitable hatred," the stranger said. "When I tell you what I am, the flesh will melt—"

"You said, you said already," Mr. Gumbeiner interrupted.

"In Chicago where the winters were as cold and bitter as the Czar of Russia's heart," the old woman intoned, "you had strength to carry the frames with the glass together day in and day out. But in California with the golden sun to mow the lawn when your wife asks, for this you have no strength. Do I call in the Japaneser to cook for you supper?"

"Thirty years Professor Allardyce spent perfecting his theories. Electronics, neuronics—"

"Listen, how educated he talks," Mr. Gumbeiner said, admiringly. "Maybe he goes to the University here?"

"If he goes to the University, maybe he knows Bud?" his wife suggested.

"Probably they're in the same class and he came to see him about the homework, no?"

"Certainly he must be in the same class. How many classes are there? Five *in ganzen*: Bud showed me on his program card." She counted off on her fingers. "Television Appreciation and Criticism, Small Boat Building, Social Adjustment, The American Dance… The American Dance—nu, Gymbeiner—"

"Contemporary Ceramics," her husband said, relishing the syllables. "A fine boy, Bud. A pleasure to have him for a boardner."

"After thirty years spent in these studies," the stranger, who had continued to speak unnoticed, went on, "he turned from the theoretical to the pragmatic. In ten years' time he had made the most titanic discovery in history: he made mankind, *all* mankind, superfluous: he made *me*."

"What did Tillie write in her last letter?" asked the old man.

The old woman shrugged.

"What should she write? The same thing. Sidney was home from the Army, Naomi has a new boy friend—"

"He *made* ME!"

"Listen, Mr. Whatever-your-name-is," the old woman said; "maybe where you came from is different, but in this country you don't interrupt people the while they're talking… Hey. Listen—what do you mean, he *made* you? What kind of talk is that?"

The stranger bared all his teeth again, exposing the too-pink gums.

"In his library, to which I had a more complete access after his sudden and as yet undiscovered death from entirely natural causes, I found a complete collection of stories about androids, from Shelley's *Frankenstein* through Capek's *R.U.R.* to Asimov's—"

"Frankenstein?" said the old man, with interest. "There used to be Frankenstein who had the soda-*wasser* place on Halstead Street: a Litvack, *nebbish*."

"What are you talking?" Mrs. Gumbeiner demanded. "His name was Franken*thal*, and it wasn't on Halstead, it was on Roosevelt."

"—clearly shown that all mankind has an instinctive antipathy towards androids and there will be an inevitable struggle between them—"

"Of course, of course!" Old Mr. Gumbeiner clicked his teeth against his pipe. "I am always wrong, you are always right. How could you stand to be married to such a stupid person all this time?"

"I don't know," the old woman said. "Sometimes I wonder, myself. I think it must be his good looks." She began to laugh. Old Mr. Gumbeiner blinked, then began to smile, then took his wife's hand.

"Foolish old woman," the stranger said; "why do you laugh? Do you not know I have come to destroy you?"

"What!" old Mr. Gumbeiner shouted. "Close your mouth, you!" He darted from his chair and struck the stranger with the flat of his hand. The stranger's head struck against the porch pillar and bounced back.

"When you talk to my wife, talk respectable, you hear?"

Old Mrs. Gumbeiner, cheeks very pink, pushed her husband back in his chair. Then she leaned forward and examined the stranger's head. She clicked her tongue as she pulled aside the flap of gray, skin-like material.

"Gumbeiner, look! He's all springs and wires inside!"

"I *told* you he was a *golem*, but no, you wouldn't listen," the old man said.

"You said he *walked* like a *golem*."

"How could he walk like a *golem* unless he *was* one?"

"All right, all right… You broke him, so now fix him."

"My grandfather, his light shines from Paradise, told me that when MoHaRaL—Moreynu Ha-Rav Low—his memory for a blessing, made the *golem* in Prague, three hundred? four hundred years ago? he wrote on his forehead the Holy Name."

Smiling reminiscently, the old woman continued, "And the *golem* cut the rabbi's wood and brought his water and guarded the ghetto."

"And one time only he disobeyed the Rabbi Low, and Rabbi Low erased the *Shem Ha-Mephorash* from the *golem's* forehead and the *golem* fell down like a dead one. And they put him up in the attic of the *shul* and he's still there today if the Communisten haven't sent him to Moscow… This is not just a story," he said.

"*Avadda* not!" said the old woman.

"I myself have seen both the *shul* and the rabbi's grave," her husband said, conclusively.

"But I think this must be a different kind *golem*, Gumbeiner. See, on his forehead: nothing written."

"What's the matter, there's a law I can't write something there? Where is that lump clay Bud brought us from his class?"

The old man washed his hands, adjusted his little black skullcap, and slowly and carefully wrote four Hebrew letters on the gray forehead.

"Ezra the Scribe himself couldn't do better," the old woman said, admiringly. "Nothing happens," she observed, looking at the lifeless figure sprawled in the chair.

"Well, after all, am I Rabbi Low?" her husband asked, deprecatingly. "No," he answered. He leaned over and examined the exposed mechanism. "This spring goes here…this wire comes with this one…" The figure moved. "But this one goes where? And this one?"

"Let be," said his wife. The figure sat up slowly and rolled its eyes loosely.

"Listen, Reb *Golem*," the old man said, wagging his finger. "Pay attention to what I say—you understand?"

"Understand…"

"If you want to stay here, you got to do like Mr. Gumbeiner says."

"Do-like-Mr.-Gumbeiner-says…"

"*That's* the way I like to hear a *golem* talk. Malka, give here the mirror from the pocketbook. Look, you see your face? You see on the forehead, what's written? If you don't do like Mr. Gumbeiner says, he'll wipe out what's written and you'll be no more alive."

"No-more-alive…"

"*That's* right. Now, listen. Under the porch you'll find a lawnmower. Take it. And cut the lawn. Then come back. Go."

"Go…" The figure shambled down the stairs. Presently the sound of the lawnmower whirred through the quiet air in the street just like the street where Jackie Cooper shed huge tears on Wallace Beery's shirt and Chester Conklin rolled his eyes at Marie Dressier.

"So what will you write to Tillie?" old Mr. Gumbeiner asked.

"What should I write?" old Mrs. Gumbeiner shrugged. "I'll write that the weather is lovely out here and that we are both, Blessed be the Name, in good health."

The old man nodded his head slowly, and they sat together on the front porch in the warm afternoon sun.

THE COST OF KENT CASTWELL

**Originally published in *Alfred Hitchcock's
Mystery Magazine*, July 1961.**

Clem Goodhue met the train with his taxi. If old Mrs. Merriman were aboard he would be sure of at least one passenger. Furthermore, old Mrs. Merriman had somehow gotten the idea that the minimum fare was a dollar. It was really seventy-five cents, but Clem had never been able to see a reason for telling her that. However, she was not aboard that morning. Sam Wells was. He was coming back from the city—been to put in a claim to have his pension increased—but Sam Wells wouldn't pay five cents to ride any distance under five miles. Clem disregarded him.

After old Sam a thin, brown-haired kid got off the train. Next came a girl, also thin and also brown-haired, who Clem thought was maybe the kid's teenage sister. Actually, it was the kid's mother.

After *that* came Kent Castwell.

Clem had seen him before, early in the summer. Strangers were not numerous in Ashby, particularly strangers who got ugly and caused commotions in bars. So Clem wouldn't forget him in a hurry. Big, husky fellow. Always seemed to be sneering at something. But the girl and the kid hadn't been with him then.

"Taxi?" Clem called.

Castwell ignored him, began to take down luggage from the train. But the young girl holding the kid by the hand turned and said, "Yes—just a minute."

"Where to?" Clem asked, when the luggage was in the taxi.

"The old Peabody place," the girl said. "You know where that is?"

"Yes. But nobody lives there any more."

"Somebody does now. Us." The big man swore as he fiddled with the handle of the right-hand door. It was tied with ropes. "Why don't you fix this thing or get a new one?"

"Costs money, Clem said. Then, "Peabody place? Have to charge you three dollars for that."

"Let's go dammit, let's go!"

After they'd started off, Castwell said, "I'm giving you two bucks. Probably twice what it's worth, anyway."

Half-turning his head, Clem protested. "I told you, mister, it was three."

"And I'm telling you, mister," Castwell mimicked the driver's New England accent, "that I'm giving you two."

Clem argued that the Peabody place was far out. He mentioned the price of gas, the bad condition of the road, the wear on the tires. The big man yawned. Then he used a word which Clem rarely used himself, and never in the presence of women and children. But this young woman and child didn't seem to notice.

"Stop off at Nickerson's Real Estate Office," Castwell said.

Levi P. Nickerson, who was also the County Tax Assessor, said, "Mr. Castwell. I assume this is Mrs. Castwell?"

"If that's your assumption, go right ahead," said Kent. And laughed.

It wasn't a pleasant laugh. The woman smiled faintly, so L.P. Nickerson allowed himself an economical chuckle. Then he cleared his throat. City people had odd ideas of what was funny. Meanwhile, though—

"Now, Mr. Castwell. About this place you're renting. I didn't realize—you didn't mention—that you had this little one, here."

Kent said, "What if I didn't mention it? It's my own business. I haven't got all *day*—"

Nickerson pointed out that the Peabody place stood all alone, isolated, with no other house for at least a mile and no other children in the neighborhood. Mrs. Castwell—if, indeed, she *was*—said that this wouldn't matter much, because Kathie would be in school most of the day.

School. Well, that's it, you see. The school bus, in the first place, will have to go three miles off what's been its regular route to pick up your little girl. And that means the road will have to be plowed regular—snow gets real deep up in these parts, you know. Up till now, with nobody living in the old Peabody place, we never had to bother with the road. Now, this means," and he began to count off on his fingers, "first, it'll cost Ed Westlake, he drives the school bus, more than he figured on when he bid for the contract; second, it'll cost the County to keep your road open. That's besides the cost of the girl's schooling, which is third."

Kent Castwell said that was tough, wasn't it? "Let's have the keys, Nick," he said.

A flicker of distaste at the familiarity crossed the real estate man's face. "You don't seem to realize that all this extra expense to the County isn't covered by the tax assessment on the Peabody place, he pointed out. "Now, it just so happens that there's a house right on the outskirts of town become available this week. Miss Sarah Beech passed on, and her sister, Miss

Lavinia, moved in with their married sister, Mrs. Calvin Adams. 'Twon't cost *you* any more, and it would save *us* considerable."

Castwell, sneering, got up. "What! Me live where some old-maid land-lady can be on my neck all the time about messing up her pretty things? Thanks a lot. No thanks." He held out his hand. "The keys, kid. Gimme the keys."

Mr. Nickerson gave him the keys. Afterwards he was to say, and to say often, that he wished he'd thrown them into Lake Amastanquit, instead.

* * * *

The income of the Castwell ménage was not large and consisted of a monthly check and a monthly money order. The check came on the fif-teenth, from a city trust company, and was assumed by some to be inherited income. Others argued in favor of its being a remittance paid by Castwell's family to keep him away. The money order was made out to Louise Cane, and signed by an army sergeant in Alaska. The young woman said this was alimony, and that Sergeant Burndall was her former husband. Tom Tally, at the grocery store, had her sign the endorsement twice, as Louise Cane and as Louise Castwell. Tom was a cautious man.

Castwell gave Louise a hard time, there was no doubt about that. If she so much as walked in between the sofa, on which he spent most of his time, and the television, he'd leap up and belt her. More than once both she and the kid had to run out of the house to get away from him. He wouldn't follow, as a rule, because he was barefooted, as a rule, and it was too much trouble to put his shoes on.

Lie on the sofa and drink beer and watch television all afternoon, and hitch into town and drink bar whiskey and watch television all evening— that was Kent Castwell's daily schedule. He got to know who drove along the road regularly, at what time, and in which direction, and he'd be there, waiting. There was more than one who could have dispensed with the plea-sure of his company, but he'd get out in the road and wave his arms and not move until the car he got in front of stopped.

What could you do about it? Put him in jail?

Sure you could.

He hadn't been living there a week before he got into a fight at the Ashby Bar.

"Disturbing the peace, using profane and abusive language, and resist-ing arrest—that will be ten dollars or ten days on each of the charges," said Judge Paltiel Bradford. "And count yourself lucky it's not more. Pay the Clerk."

But Castwell, his ugly leer in no way improved by the dirt and bruises on his face, said, "I'll take jail."

Judge Bradford's long jaw set, then loosened. "Look here, Mr. Castwell, that was just legal language on my part. The jail is closed up. Hasn't been anybody in there since July." It was then November. "It would have to be heated, and illuminated, and the water turned on, and a guard hired. To say nothing of feeding you. Now, I don't see why the County should be put to all that expense on your account. You pay the Clerk thirty dollars. You haven't got it on you, take till tomorrow. Well?"

"I'll take the jail."

"It's most inconvenient—"

"That's too bad, Your Honor."

The judge glared at him. Gamaliel Coolidge, the District Attorney, stood up. "Perhaps the Court would care to suspend sentence," he suggested. "Seeing it is the defendant's first offense."

The Court did care. But the next week Kent was back again, on the same charge. Altogether the sentence now came to sixty dollars, or sixty days. And again Castwell chose jail.

"I don t generally do this," the judge said, fuming. "But I'll let you pay your fine off in installments. Considering you have a wife and child."

"Uh-uh. I'll take jail."

"You won't like the food!" warned His Honor.

Castwell said he guessed the food would be up to the legal requirements. If it wasn't, he said, the State Board of Prison Inspectors would hear about it.

Some pains were taken to see that the food served Kent during his stay in jail was beyond the legal requirements—if not much beyond. The last time the State Board had inspected the County Jail it had cost the taxpayers two hundred dollars in repairs. It was costing them quite enough to incarcerate Kent Castwell, as it was, although the judge had reduced the cost by ordering the sentences to run concurrently.

All in all, Kent spent over a month in jail that winter, at various times. It seemed to some that whenever his money ran out he let the County support him, and let the woman and child fend for themselves. Tom Talley gave them a little credit at the store. Not much.

* * * *

Ed Westlake, when he bid again for the school bus contract, added the cost of going three miles out of his way to pick up Kathie. The County had no choice but to meet the extra charge. It was considered very thoughtless of Louise to wait till *after* the contract was signed before leaving Castwell and going back to the city with her child. The side road to the Peabody place didn't have to be plowed so often, but it still had to be plowed *some*. That extra cost, just for one man! It was maddening.

THE COST OF KENT CASTWELL | 71

It almost seemed—no, it *did* seem—as if Kent Castwell was deliberately setting himself in the face of New England respectability and thrift. The sacred words, "Eat it up, wear it out, make it do, or do without," didn't mean a thing to him. He wasn't just indifferent. He was hostile.

Ashby was not a thriving place. It had no industries. It was not a resort town, being far from sea and mountains alike, with only the shallow, muddy waters of Lake Amastanquit for a pleasure spot. Its thin-soiled farms and meager woodlots produced a scanty return for the hard labor exacted. The young people continued to leave. Kent Castwell, unfortunately, showed no signs of leaving.

All things considered, it was not surprising that Ashby had no artists' colony. It *was* rather surprising, then, that Clem Goodhue, meeting the train with his taxi, recognized Bob Laurel at once as an artist. When asked afterwards how he had known, Clem looked smug, and said that he had once been to Provincetown.

The conversation, as Clem recalled it afterwards, began with Bob Laurel's asking where he could find a house which offered low rent, peace and quiet, and a place to paint.

"So I recommended Kent Castwell," Clem said. He was talking to Sheriff Erastus Nickerson (Levi P.'s cousin) at the time.

"'Peace and *quiet?*'" the sheriff repeated. "I know Laurel's a city fellow, and an artist, but, still and all—"

They were seated in the bar of the Ashby House, drinking their weekly small glass of beer. "I looked at it this way, Erastus," the taxi-man said. "Sure, there's empty houses all around that he could rent. Suppose *he*—this artist fellow—suppose *he* picks one off on the side road with nobody else living on it? Suppose *he* comes up with a wife out of somewhere, and suppose *she* has a school-age child?"

"You're right, Clem."

"'Course I'm right. Bad enough for the County to be put to all that cost for *one* house, let alone two."

"You're right, Clem. But will he stay with Castwell?"

Clem shrugged. "That I can't say. But I did my best."

Laurel stayed with Castwell. He really had no choice. The big man agreed to take him in as lodger and to give over the front room for a studio. And, holding out offers of insulating the house, putting in another window, and who knows what else, Kent Castwell persuaded the unwary artist to pay several months' rent in advance. Needless to say, he drank up the money and did nothing at all in the way of the promised improvements.

Neither District Attorney Gamaliel Coolidge nor Sheriff Nickerson, nor, for that matter, anyone else, showed Laurel much sympathy. He had grounds for a civil suit, they said; nothing else. It should be a lesson to him not to throw his money around in the future, they said.

So the unhappy artist stayed on at the old Peabody place, buying his own food and cutting his own wood, and painting, painting, painting. And all the time he knew full well that his leering landlord only waited for him to go into town in order to help himself to both food and wood.

Laurel invited Clem to have a glass of beer with him more than once, just to have someone to tell his troubles to. Besides stealing his food and fuel, Kent Castwell, it seemed, played the TV at full blast when Laurel wanted to sleep; if it was too late for TV, he set the radio to roaring. At moments when the artist was intent on delicate brush-work, Castwell would decide to bring in stove-wood and drop it on the floor so that the whole house shook.

"He talks to himself in that loud, rough voice of his," Bob Laurel complained. "He has a filthy mouth. He makes fun of my painting. He—"

"I tell you what it is," Clem said. "Kent Castwell has no consideration for others. That's what it is. Yep."

Bets were taken in town, of a ten-cent cigar per bet, on how long Laurel would stand for it. Levi Nickerson, the County Tax Assessor, thought he'd leave as soon as his rent was up. Clem's opinion was that he'd leave sooner. "Money don't mean that much to city people," he pointed out.

Clem won.

* * * *

When he came into Nickerson's house, Levi, who was sitting close to the small fire in the kitchen stove, wordlessly handed over the cigar. Clem nodded, put it in his pocket. Mrs. Abby Nickerson sat next to her husband, wearing a man's sweater. It had belonged to her late father, whose heart had failed to survive the first re-election of Franklin D. Roosevelt, and it still had a lot of wear left in it. Abby was unraveling old socks, and winding the wool into a ball. "Waste not, want not," was her motto—as well as that of every other old-time local resident.

On the stove a kettle steamed thinly. Two piles of used envelopes were on the table. They had all been addressed to the Tax Assessor's office of the County, and had been carefully opened so as not to mutilate them. While Clem watched, Levi Nickerson removed one of the envelopes from its place on top of the uncovered kettle. The mucilage on its flaps loosened by steam, it opened out easily to Nickerson's touch. He proceeded to refold it and then reseal it so that the used outside was now inside; then he added it to the other pile.

"Saved the County eleven dollars this way last year," he observed. "Shouldn't wonder but what I don't make it twelve this year, maybe twelve-fifty." Clem gave a small appreciative grunt. "Where is he?" the Tax Assessor asked.

"Laurel? In the Ashby Bar. He's all packed. I told him to stay put. I told them to keep an eye on him, phone me here if he made a move to leave."

He took a sheet of paper out of his pocket and put it on the table. Levi looked at it, but made no move to pick it up. To his wife he said, "I'm expecting Erastus and Gam Coolidge over, Mrs. Nickerson. County business. I expect you can find something to do in the front of the house while we talk."

Mrs. Levi nodded. Even words were not wasted.

A car drove up to the house.

"That's Erastus," said his cousin. "Gam should be along—he *is* along. Might've known he wouldn't waste gasoline; came with Erastus."

The two men came into the kitchen. Mrs. Abby Nickerson arose and departed.

"Hope we can get this over with before nightfall," the sheriff said. "I don't like to drive after dark if I can help it. One of my headlights is getting dim, and they cost so darned much to replace."

Clem cleared his throat. "Well, here 'tis," he said, gesturing to the paper on the table. Laurel's confession. "'Tell the sheriff and the D.A. that I'm ready to give myself up,' he says. 'I wrote it all down here,' he says. Happened about two o'clock this afternoon, I guess. Straw that broke the camel's back. Kent Castwell, he was acting up as usual. Stomping and swearing out there at the Peabody place. Words were exchanged. Laurel left to go out back," Clem said, delicately, not needing to further comment on the Peabody place's lack of indoor plumbing. "When he come back, Castwell had taken the biggest brush he could find and smeared paint over all the pictures Laurel had been working on. Ruined them completely."

There was a moment's silence. "Castwell had no call to do that," the sheriff said. "Destroying another man's property. They tell me some of those artists get as much as a hundred dollars for a painting… What'd he do then? Laurel, I mean."

"Picked up a piece of stovewood and hit him with it. Hit him hard."

"No doubt about his being dead, I suppose?" the sheriff asked.

Clem shook his head. "There was no blood or anything on the wood," he added. "Just another piece of stove wood… But he's dead, all right."

After a moment Levi Nickerson said, "His wife will have to be notified. No reason why the County should have to pay burial expenses. Hmm. I expect she won't have any money, though. Best get in touch with those trustees who sent Castwell his money every month. *They'll* pay."

Gamaliel Coolidge asked if anyone else knew. Clem said no. Bob Laurel hadn't told anyone else. He didn't seem to want to talk.

This time there was a longer silence.

"Do you realize how much Kent Castwell cost this County, one way or the other?" Nickerson asked.

Clem said he supposed hundreds of dollars. "Hundreds and *hundreds* of dollars," Nickerson said.

"*And*," the Tax Assessor went on, "do you know what it will cost us to try this fellow—for murder in any degree or manslaughter?"

The District Attorney said it would cost thousands. "Thousands and *thousands*… and that's just the trial," he elaborated. "Suppose he's found guilty and appeals? We'd be obliged to fight the appeal. More thousands. And suppose he gets a new trial? We'd have it to pay all over again."

Levi P. Nickerson opened his mouth as though it hurt him to do so. "What it would do to the County tax-rate…" he groaned. "Kent Castwell, he said, his voice becoming crisp and definite, "is not worth it. He is just not *worth* it."

Clem took out the ten-cent cigar he'd won, sniffed it. "My opinion," he said, "it would have been much better if this fellow Laurel had just packed up and left. Anybody finding Castwell's body would assume he'd fallen and hit his head. But this confession, now—"

Sheriff Erastus Nickerson said reflectively, "I haven't read any confession. You, Gam? You, Levi? No. What you've told us, Clem, is just hearsay. Can't act on hearsay. Totally contrary to all principles of American law… Hmm. Mighty nice sunset." He arose and walked over to the window. His cousin followed him. So did District Attorney Coolidge. While they were looking at the sunset Clem Goodhue, after a single glance at their backs, took the sheet of paper from the kitchen table and thrust it into the kitchen stove. There was a flare of light. It quickly died down. Clem carefully reached his hand into the stove, took out the small corner of the paper remaining, and lit his cigar with it.

The three men turned from the window.

Levi P. Nickerson was first to speak. "Can't ask any of you to stay to supper," he said. "Just a few leftovers is all we're having. I expect you'll want to be going on your way."

The two other County officials nodded.

The taxi-man said, "I believe I'll stop by the Ashby Bar. Might be someone there wanting to catch the evening train. Night, Levi. Don't turn on the yard light for us."

"Wasn't going to," said Levi. "Turning them on and off, that's what burns them out. Night, Clem, Gam, Erastus." He closed the door after them. "Mrs. Nickerson," he called to his wife, "you can come and start supper now. We finished our business."

THE BOUNTY HUNTER

Originally published in *Fantastic Universe*, March 1958.

There was a whirring noise and a flurry and part of the snow-bank shot up at a 45-degree angle—or so it seemed—and vanished in the soft gray sky. Orel stopped and put out his arm, blocking his uncle's way.

"It's a bird…only a bird…*get* on, now, Orel," Councillor Garth said, testily. He gave his nephew a light shove. "They turn white in the wintertime. Or their feathers do. Anyway, that's what Trapper says."

They plodded ahead, Orel, partly distracted by the pleasure of seeing his breath, laughed a bit. "A bird outside of a cage…" The councillor let him get a few feet ahead, then he awkwardly compressed a handful of snow and tossed it at his nephew's face when he turned it back. The first startled cry gave way to laughter. And so they came to the trapper's door.

The old fellow peered at them, but it was only a thing he did because it was expected of him; there was nothing wrong with his eyes. Garth had known him for many years, and he was still not sure how many of his mannerisms were real, how many put on. Or for that matter, how much of the antique stuff cluttering up the cabin was actually part of the trapper's life, and how much only there for show. Not that he cared: the trapper's job was as much to be quaint and amusing as to do anything else.

Orel, even before the introductions were over, noticed the cup and saucer on the top shelf of the cabinet, but not till his two elders paused did he comment, "Look, Uncle: earthenware!"

"You've got a sharp eye, young fellow," the trapper said, approvingly. "Yes, it's real pottery. Brought over by my who-knows-how-many-times-removed grandfather from the home planet… Yes, my family, they were pretty important people on the home planet," he added, inconsequentially. He stood silent for a moment, warmed with pride, then made a series of amiable noises in his throat.

"Well, I'm glad to meet you, young fellow. Knew your uncle before he was councillor, before you were born." He went to the tiny window, touched the defroster, looked out. "Yes, your machine is safe enough." He turned around. "I'll get the fire started, if there's no objections? And put some meat on to grill? Hm?"

The councillor nodded with slow satisfaction; Orel grinned widely.

* * * *

The trapper turned off the heating unit and set the fire going. The three men gazed into the flames. The meat turned slowly on the jack. Orel tried to analyze the unfamiliar smells crowding around him—the wood itself, and the fire: no, fire had no smell, it was *smoke*; the meat, the furs and hides… he couldn't even imagine what they all were. It was different from the cities, that was sure. He turned to ask something, but his uncle Garth and Trapper weren't attending. Then he heard it—a long, drawn-out, faraway sort of noise. Then the trapper grunted and spit in the fire.

"What was it?" Orel asked.

The old fellow smiled. "Never heard it before? Not even recorded, in a nature studies course? That's one of the big varmints—the kind your uncle and the other big sportsmen come out here to hunt—in season—the kind I trap in any season." Abruptly, he turned to Councillor Garth. "No talk of their dropping the bounty, is there?" Smilingly, the councillor shook his head. Reassured, the trapper turned his attention to the meat, poked it with a long-pronged fork.

Orel compared the interior of the cabin to pictures and 3-D plays he had observed. Things looked familiar, but less—smooth, if that was the word. There was more disorder, an absence of symmetry. Hides and pelts—not too well cured, if the smell was evidence—were scattered all around, not neatly tacked up or laid in neat heaps. Traps and parts of traps sat where the old man had evidently last worked at mending them.

"Council's not in session, I take it?" the trapper asked. Orel's uncle shook his head. "But—don't tell me school's out, too? Thought they learned right through the winter."

Garth said, "I was able to persuade the Dean that our little trip was a genuine—if small—field expedition, and that Orel's absence wouldn't break the pattern of learning."

The trapper grunted. *Pattern!* Orel thought. The mention of the word annoyed him. Everything was part of a pattern: Pattern of learning, pattern of earning, pattern of pleasure… Life in the city went by patterns, deviations were few; people didn't even *want* to break the patterns. They were afraid to.

But it was obvious that the trapper didn't live by patterns. This…disorder.

"Do you have any children, Trapper?" he asked. The old man said he didn't. "Then who will carry on your work?"

The trapper waved his hand to the west. "Fellow in the next valley has two sons. When I get too old—a long time from now," he said, defiantly, "one of them will move in with me. Help me out. Split the bounties with me.

"I was married once." He gazed into the fire. "City woman. She couldn't get used to it out here. The solitude. The dangers. So we moved to the cities. *I* never got used to *that*. Got to get up at a certain time. Got to do everything a certain way. Everything has to be put in its place, neatly. All the people would look at you otherwise. Breaking the patterns? They didn't like it. Well, she died. And I moved back here as fast as I could get permission. And here I've stayed."

He took down plates, forks, knives, carved the meat. They ate with relish.

"Tastes better than something out of a factory lab, doesn't it?"

Orel's mind at once supplied him with an answer: that synthetics were seven times more nutritious than the foods they imitated. But his mouth was full and besides, it *did* taste better. Much better... After the meal there was a sort of lull. The trapper looked at Councillor Garth in an expectant sort of way. The councillor smiled. He reached over into the pocket of his hunting jacket and took out a flask. Orel, as he smelled it (even before: after all, everyone knew that the bounty-hunters drank—the flask was part of every 3-D play about them), framed a polite refusal. But none was offered him.

* * * *

"The purpose of this two-man field expedition," his uncle said, after wiping his mouth, "is to prepare a term paper for Orel's school showing how, in the disciplined present, the bounty-hunters maintain the free and rugged traditions of the past, on the Home Planet...let me have another go at the flask, Trapper."

Orel watched, somewhat disturbed. Surely his uncle knew how unhealthy...

"My family, they were pretty important people back on the Home Planet." The Old Trapper, having had another drink, began to repeat himself. Outside—the dusk had begun to set in—that wild, rather frightening, sound came again. The old man put the flask down. "Coming nearer," he said, as if to himself. He got to his feet, took up his weapon. "I won't be gone long...they don't generally come so near...but it's been a hard winter. This one sounds kind of hungry. But don't you be frightened, young fellow," he said to Orel, from the door. "There's no chance of its eating *me*."

"Uncle..." Orel said, after a while. The councillor looked up. "Don't be offended, but...does it ever strike you that we lead rather useless lives in the city—compared, I mean, to *him*?"

The councillor smiled. "Oh, come now. Next you'll be wanting to run away and join the fun. Because that's all it is, really: fun. These beasts—the big 'varmints,' as he calls them—are no menace to us any longer. Haven't been since we switched from meat to synthetics. So it's not a truly useful life the old man leads. It's only our traditional reluctance to admit things have changed which keeps us paying the bounty…" He got up and walked a few steps, stretched.

"We *could* get rid of these creatures once and for all, do it in one season's campaign. Drop poisoned bait every acre through the whole range. Wipe them out."

Orel, puzzled, asked why they didn't.

"And I'll tell you something else—but don't put it in your report. The old fellow, like all the trappers, sometimes cheats. He often releases females and cubs. He takes no chance of having his valley trapped out. 'Why don't we?' you ask—why don't we get rid of the beasts once and for all, instead of paying bounties year after year? Well, the present cost is small. And as for getting an appropriation for an all-out campaign—who'd vote for it? *I* wouldn't.

"No more hunting—no more 3-D plays about the exciting life in the wild country—no more trappers—why, it would just about take what spirit is left away from us. And we are dispirited enough—tired enough—as it is."

Orel frowned. "But why are we like that? We weren't always. A tired people could never have moved here from the Home Planet, could never have conquered this one. Why are we so—so played out?"

The councillor shrugged. "Do you realize what a tremendous effort it was to move such a mass of people such a distance? The further effort required to subdue a wild, new world? The terrible cost of the struggle against colonialism—and finally, the Civil Wars? We don't even like to think about it—we create our myths instead out of the life out here in the wilds—and all the time, we retreated farther and farther, back into our cities. We are tired. We've spent our energies, we've mortgaged them, in fact. We eat synthetics because it's easier, not because it's healthier."

* * * *

A gust of cold wind blew in on them. They whirled around. The Old Trapper came in, dragging his kill by the forelimbs. He closed the door. The two city folk came up close. The beast was a huge male, gaunt from the poor hunting which winter meant to the wild creatures.

"See here—" the trapper pointed out. "Lost two toes there. *Old* wound. Must've gnawed his way out of a trap one time. *There—got these* scars battling over a mate, I suppose. This *here's* a burn. Bad one. When was the last big forest fire we had?—one too big to outrun—" He figured with moving lips. "*That* long ago? How the time does pass… Let me have that knife there, young fellow—" Orel glanced around, located the knife, handed it to him; gazed down in fascination and revulsion. The wild life did not seem so attractive at this moment.

"Watch close, now, and I'll show you how to skin and dress a big varmint," the Old Trapper said. He made the initial incision. "Dangerous creatures, but when you know their habits as well as *I* do… Can't expect to wipe them out altogether—" He looked at the two guests. Orel wondered how much he knew or guessed of what had been said in his absence. "No. Keep their numbers down, is all you can expect to do." He tugged, grunted. "I *earn* my bounty, I can tell you." He turned the creature on its back.

Orel struck by something, turned to the councillor.

"You know, Uncle, if this beast were cleaned up and shaved and"—he laughed at the droll fancy—"and dressed in clothes, it—"

Councillor Garth finished the sentence for him. "Would bear a faint, quaint resemblance to *us*? Hm, yes…in a way…of course, but their external ears and their having only five digits on each—" He clicked his tongue and stepped aside. The Old Trapper, who didn't care how much blood he got on things or people, worked away, but the Councillor took his nephew closer to the fire to finish what he had to say.

PRESENT FOR LONA

Originally published in *Alfred Hitchcock's Mystery Magazine*, March 1958.

There was sawdust—just like in a butcher shop—on the floor of the long room where Jack Clauson stood waiting for the man he was going to kill. Whatever the man had done, Clauson did not hate him for it But he had to die, and Clauson had to kill him. Not out of hate, but for love—for love of Lona.

I won't be the only one, he kept telling himself. It won't just be me… And he has it coming to him anyway… But it was no use. He felt an unfamiliar rigidity in his throat, struggled against nausea.

Bright lights, terribly bright lights, bore down from overhead on the far end of the long room. The near end was dark. The men there shifted from foot to foot, coughing nervously. The coughing stopped abruptly as the door at the far end opened.

Clauson tensed, fighting against the impulse to drop what he held in his hands and run.

A group of people entered, but Clauson had his eyes only on the one in the open shirt. As he watched, the man—his face paper-white—blinked and ran the tip of his tongue along his lips. I can't do this… Clauson's thoughts darted around frantically, like rats cornered in a pit. I never saw him before… I won't do it; they can't hurt me if I refuse… The man walked steadily enough and his head was up and he didn't say anything. But there was suddenly the sharp fresh smell of his sweat; it was the odor of fear.

Clauson started to move. Then he remembered. I must. I have to. He'll die anyway. He deserves to die. He killed an innocent man.

The guards bound the arms of the man in the open shirt swiftly, tightly. The chaplain murmured from his little book. A target was pinned over the heart.

The man's head began to move from side to side. It was still moving when the bullets hit him.

* * * *

Jack Clauson counted his money. Twenty-five dollars. Not a lot, not for killing a man. His hand jerked suddenly at the thought Why, he could earn that much from his regular work in a single morning, and work six days a week—to say nothing of overtime. So what was twenty-five dollars?

Not much. Only a man's life. Only another man's marriage. Clauson loved his wife. Now he'd killed for her. This was the first money he'd made in over a month, and it was for just a few minutes' work too. He'd buy Lona something. Something nice. She loved to get presents. He'd make her smile; she'd come into his arms, and things would be all right between them again... Or would they?

He drove along the new road on his way back. It was really longer. There was a quicker route to reach the trailer camp, but he liked to ride along the new one. He'd helped build it. It was finished a month ago. He and Lona really should have been moving on long ago. She couldn't have much left out of the last of his earnings—the money he'd given her when everything was all right between them. But everything wasn't all right between them anymore. He was moody; she was moody; they quarreled and yelled at one another. *She* wanted to settle down and *he* wanted to keep moving; *that* was the trouble. And so they rubbed each other raw, and it had been sullen and ugly and apart that they'd spent the last week. They both knew that a split was coming, knew the other knew. It had been hell. Because he wanted her. Badly.

Jack knew he had to *do* something to show he wanted her. Words would no longer be enough. There had to be something from outside the two of them.

How the man's head had weaved from side to side! As if he was looking for an out—and knowing there wasn't any. Then the bullets, smashing into him—

Recalling it made Jack hunch over the wheel, drive faster and faster, sorry he'd taken the longer route, anxious to be back at the trailer camp, eager to show her his token of love—the present. Lona had always loved to get presents. He laughed—why, he hadn't even bought it yet! But it wouldn't take long; it was Late Closing Night at the stores in the little town. The neon signs beckoned to him as he carefully parked the car. They were mostly red. Red. The color of blood. Blood soaking into sawdust. When the bullets hit, the man didn't even yell. He just grunted. And then the blood...

Seeing the lights out in the trailer, Jack thought Lona might be asleep. If she was, he'd wake her up. He couldn't just turn in by himself, not now, not with *this* on his mind and heart. He'd done it for Lona and Lona alone could make it all right He could forget, in her arms... Maybe she was just lying awake in the dark as she sometimes did. Softly, he opened the door. "Lona?" he called, making his voice gentle. There was no answer, and his eyes, adjusting to the dark, saw she wasn't in bed. He grunted, flicked on the lights.

He jumped at the sudden flood of brightness, swore. For a moment he'd thought he'd seen a man under the lights, a man with bound arms and a bloody target on his chest. Badly frightened. Clauson stood still, waiting for his racing heart to slow down. He looked around him.

The place was a mess, clothes scattered all around, bed unmade, a paper bag of garbage spilling on the floor. Lipstick-smeared tissues and a scattering of face-powder told him that she'd gone somewhere she expected to meet people. But—he hastily checked—her things were still here. She'd be back—but he wasn't going to wait. Not alone.

"Why couldn't you be here?" he asked the empty trailer, aloud. "I wanted to give you the present I got for you." His face twisted in disappointment as he looked down at the fancy-wrapped package. The money had gone just far enough—two crisp tens and one new crisp five. Twenty for the present. A bottle of bourbon used up all but some loose change out of the remainder.

A man's life = a present + a bottle of bourbon = a happy couple and a saved marriage. Or *does* it? Because it was as close as that with them. It was as close at that...

There was an almost-empty half-pint on the table. That was something Lona had taken to again. She did that when things were bad between them. If only she'd drink *with* him—but she wouldn't, not with that black mood on her. And afterwards they were certain to quarrel, screaming at each other the empty threats that made no more sense than the rest of their quarreling.

"You like it so much here?" his own voice rang in his ears. "Then you can stay—all by your lonesome! I'm getting out!"

And her voice, shrill, "I'll kill you! I'll kill you!"

Each knowing the other didn't mean it... With a sigh, Jack went out and walked over to the Roanes' trailer. Ed and Betty Roane were the only friends they had left in the trailer camp; most of the construction workers had moved away as soon as work on the new road was over. Jack envied them; he longed for the feeling of freedom, the long trips across the state and even into a different part of the country, perhaps. But not Lona.

He sighed again.

There was a heavy weight on his chest. How much of it, he half-formed the question, was his wife—and how much of it was the man he'd helped kill?

The sounds of radio and TV, the smell of late suppers cooking, the murmur of conversation, children's voices... Maybe if they'd had children, but each had wanted to be modern and wait. Suddenly bitter, he muttered, "Wait for what?" and then he was at the Roanes' trailer, knocking.

And with each knock, he felt it was no use. It had all been for nothing. His heart sank, and he felt he was sinking with it. The gap between him and Lona was too wide by now for any gift to bridge. He'd done a terrible thing, and it was all for nothing.

* * * *

Ed and Betty never fought. They were easy-going, and it was always "Yes, dear" and all that sort of thing.

Lona was there. She smiled briefly and tightly as she saw him. He was right: it *was* too late. No—she wouldn't snap or snarl if others were present, but neither would she pretend. And old Mrs. Cheener was there too: Mrs. Cheener who owned the camp, a tiny little woman with wild white hair. Her age and position made her a privileged character and she now at once proceeded to take advantage of it.

"Well, so you finally got here, did you?" she rattled away at him. "I suppose you were boozing it up while your poor little wife sets here with us. If she takes a notion to walk out on you, nobody'd be to blame but you there, Clauson, I'm speaking to you. The way you yell and threaten her!"

Jack asked, with a forced grin, "But what about the way she threatens *me*, Mrs. Cheener?"

Lona looked up. Jack noticed that she didn't appear to be taking his remark as an affront Could it possibly be that it wasn't too late, after all?

Mrs. Cheener's bright eyes turned to the Roanes. The implication, that she didn't want to waste any more of her valuable time on Jack.

"Turn on the television," she directed, as if it were *her* place. "I want the news." Betty obeyed—reluctantly, it seemed to Jack. Ed avoided his eye.

The newscaster's face flowed into focus. "—the only State which allows such a choice or uses such a means of execution—" his voice boomed out. Betty, grimacing, hastened to soften it.

"There, we tuned in late and missed the beginning," the old lady fretted.

"—a target was pinned over the condemned man's heart and—"

"Ah, it's that no-good from down the state that killed his partner," the old woman remarked grimly.

"—the firing-squad was, as is customary, composed of paid civilian volunteers, who—"

Betty shuddered. "Oh, I'd rather not listen to this!" She screwed up her face and put her hands over her ears. She and Ed stared at each other. Mrs. Cheener gazed avidly at the screen, as if expecting it to reveal the death-event itself. Jack Clauson sat stiff, saying nothing. Then he reached across to where Lona was sitting and took her hand, held it though she did make an attempt to free it.

"Meanwhile, the death toll continues to mount in the California floods," the announcer was saying, in his smooth, rich voice, summing up the number of drownings as if he were lauding a hair tonic.

As soon as the news was over, Lona and Jack left.

* * * *

They walked to their trailer without speaking. Just wait until she sees that present, Jack told himself. Just you wait.

As soon as they got inside, still without speaking, Lona started picking up some of the stuff that littered the place, not to make order but to be doing something, absently.

He got the box in its fancy wrappings, wanted to hand it to her, but didn't know how. That she might refuse to unwrap it bothered him. So he said, "Here's something for you," and started jerking off the ribbon and the paper. He got the nightgown out ?Take a look at this, would you," he said, holding it up. And the festive quality he'd put in his voice, he didn't feel.

Lona dropped what she had in her hand and moved toward Jack—toward the black lace nightgown—as though mesmerized.

"Oh, it's *beautiful!*" Lona's face—so like a child's, he thought, for all that she was almost thirty—was wide-eyed and delighted. Her eyes explored the nightgown avidly. She touched her cheek to its softness, virtually embraced it.

"Lovely," she said. "It's lovely…"

"Glad you like it, honey," Jack said, but he was aware that Lona was still so taken up with the beauty of her present that she hadn't heard him. He wanted to kiss her. But he couldn't let her think that he was buying her affection with the present. Slowly does it, he told himself.

"How about a drink?" he asked, louder this time. They'd celebrate the end of all bad feeling. And he, in addition, would celebrate the fact that his plan had worked—the end of his fear that it wouldn't. "How about a little drink?"

Then—as suddenly as if a curtain had been pulled—the smile left Lona's face. "Will one bottle be enough?" She didn't so much ask the question as throw it at him.

"I, ah, I guess so," he answered, uncertainly. He was confused. "What do you mean, doll?" he asked.

She stood there, stiff. Her face was cold, sullen. "This lovely nightie." There was a sneer in the way she said that. She pushed the nightgown from her, glowered at it. "All this lace. The woman in me must have been carried away by it. Take the thing back. Go on, get your twenty-five dollars.

That—that ought to buy enough liquor to get you good and drunk. I know if I were you I'd never want to sober up again as long as I lived."

What *happened*? What made her change? Why had she—? Then, ringing like a bunch of jangly bells, the words—*Twenty-five dollars Twenty-five dollars Twenty-five*—He stared at her, swallowed. "How'd you know?" he asked, his voice thick. He poured whiskey into the glass, tossed it down.

"How'd I *know*?" Her voice rose shrilly. "Why, there won't be anybody around here tomorrow who won't know! Mrs. Cheener's son-in-law, the guard at the pen, called to give her the information. Did you forget about her son-in-law? He *saw* you there. Ugh!"

She looked at him with disgust and horror. He *had* forgotten. He never once thought of it "How could you *do* it?" Lona asked, her face twisted.

"I did it for *you*!" He cried his outrage aloud. "*That's* how I could do it! For us—to buy some nice present for you—to make you happy…" He moved toward her, his face hurt and baffled, his hands groping. They found the nightgown she had dropped, held it out to her in one last offering.

Lona stepped away. She shook her head. "Oh, no," she said softly, almost in a whisper. "Not for me. I wouldn't touch it. What do you think I am?" And once again she cried, incredulously, "How could you do it? *Oh*!"

His head was buzzing. The straight whiskey, no supper, the whole horrible business at the penitentiary, now this. But he had to answer her question.

"Well, uh…he had it coming to him. He killed someone. If it wasn't me, it would of been someone in my place, so what's the difference? That's the law." And, pleased with this neat summation, he cocked his head on one side and looked at her. For a moment there was silence. Then Lona moved away, began to pick up her clothes and fold them up haphazardly. She pulled a suitcase from its place. Her mouth was tight-pressed.

Jack looked at her in anguish. Ten minutes ago he'd thought hoped, that their marriage was saved. Now… He wiped his face. "Where're you—? Lona? Please!"

She spun around and screamed at him, "I'm packing up! I'm going to get out of here. And this—and this—" She pushed at the black lace nightgown which he continued to hold out to her in supplication. "Get it away from me!"

Jack dropped the frothy garment and held her shoulders.

"Oh, no, you've got to stay—you've got to wear it, Lona! I only did it for you—only for you. It was awful, horrible—and if you don't stay, then it was all for nothing. I'll have helped kill a man I never knew, never even saw before, and all for nothing. All—"

She struck away his hands from her shoulders, and—when he touched her again—she clawed at him, spitting out ugly words. Then he knew that it had indeed been all for nothing, and a fury he had never known in his life took him.

"I'll kill you!" he cried. "I'll kill you!" He hit her—once—twice. He lost count…

* * * *

There were voices outside, old Mrs. Cheener's, the Roanes', others. What was he looking for? he asked himself. A towel. There wasn't any. He knelt slowly to the floor, picked up the black lace nightgown, wet it at the sink, knelt again, began to wipe the blood away. The voices were baying outside, people pounding at the door, while he sponged his wife's face. "Lona?" he said slowly. "Lona?"

* * * *

There was sawdust on the floor of the long room, just like in a butcher shop. Bright lights, terribly bright, bore down from overhead on the far end. The near end was dark. The men there shifted from foot to foot, coughed nervously. The sound stopped abruptly as the door at the far end opened.

A group of people entered, but the men already waiting had eyes only for the one in the open shirt—the one who blinked, who ran the tip of his tongue along his lips. The man walked steadily enough and his head was up and he didn't say anything. But there was, suddenly, the sharp fresh smell of his sweat. It was the odor of fear. His face was paper-white.

The guards bound his arms, swiftly, tightly. One of them pinned a target over his heart. The chaplain murmured from his little book. These were the regular officials of the State and the State's justice and mercy. The men waiting at the far end of the room—the bright lights enabled them to see but not to be seen—were volunteers. They had driven up to the prison in their own cars. Later they would drive away, each one with twenty-five dollars in his pocket (two crisp tens and one crisp five); and many of them would drive away along the newly-built road. The road Jack Clauson had helped to build.

Jack Clauson blinked in the bright lights. The straps were very tight. His head moved from side to side—as if he was looking for an out—and knowing there wasn't any. He blinked and licked his lips and waited.

NOW LET US SLEEP

**Originally published in *Venture Science
Fiction Magazine*, September 1957.**

A pink-skinned young cadet ran past Harper, laughing and shouting
and firing his stungun. The wind veered about, throwing the thick scent of
the Yahoos into the faces of the men, who whooped loudly to show their
revulsion.

"I got three!" the chicken cadet yelped at Harper. "Did you see me pop
those two together? Boy, what a stink they have!"

Harper looked at the sweating kid, muttered, "You don't smell so sweet
yourself," but the cadet didn't wait to hear. All the men were running now,
running in a ragged semicircle with the intention of driving the Yahoos
before them, to hold them at bay at the foot of the gaunt cliff a quarter-mile
off.

The Yahoos loped awkwardly over the rough terrain, moaning and
grunting grotesquely, their naked bodies bent low. A few hundred feet
ahead one of them stumbled and fell, his arms and legs flying out as he hit
the ground, twitched, and lay still.

A bald-headed passenger laughed triumphantly, paused to kick the Yahoo, and trotted on. Harper kneeled beside the fallen primitive, felt for a
pulse in the hairy wrist. It seemed slow and feeble, but then, no one actually
knew what the normal pulse-beat should be. And—except for Harper—no
seemed to give a damn.

Maybe it was because he was the grandson of Barret Harper, the great
naturalist—back on Earth, of course. It seemed as if man could be fond of
nature only on the planet of man's origin, whose ways he knew so well.
Elsewhere, it was too strange and alien—you subdued it, or you adjusted
to it, or you were perhaps even content with it. But you almost never *cared*
about the flora or fauna of the new planets. No one had the feeling for living
things that an earth-born had.

The men were shouting more loudly now, but Harper didn't lift his
head to see why. He put his hand to the shaggy grey chest. The heart was
still beating, but very slowly and irregularly. Someone stood beside him.

"He'll come out of it in an hour or so," the voice of the purser said. "Come on—you'll miss all the fun—you should see how they act when they're cornered! They kick out and throw sand and—" he laughed at the thought—"they weep great big tears, and go, '*Oof*! *Oof*!'"

Harper said, "An ordinary man *would* come out of it in an hour or so. But I think their metabolism is different... Look at all the bones lying around."

The purser spat. "Well, don't that prove they're not human, when they won't even bury their dead?... *Oh*, oh!—look at that!" He swore.

Harper got to his feet. Cries of dismay and disappointment went up from the men.

"What's wrong?" Harper asked.

The purser pointed. The men had stopped running, were gathering together and gesturing. "Who's the damn fool who planned this drive?" the purser asked, angrily. "He picked the wrong cliff! The damned Yahoos *nest* in that one! Look at them climb, will you—" He took aim, fired the stungun. A figure scrabbling up the side of the rock threw up its arms and fell, bounding from rock to rock until it hit the ground. "*That* one will never come out of it!" the purser said, with satisfaction.

But this was the last casualty. The other Yahoos made their way to safety in the caves and crevices. No one followed them. In those narrow, stinking confines a Yahoo was as good as a man, there was no room to aim a stungun, and the Yahoos had rocks and clubs and their own sharp teeth. The men began straggling back.

"This one a she?" The purser pushed at the body with his foot, let it fall back with an annoyed grunt as soon as he determined its sex. "There'll be Hell to pay in the hold if there's more than two convicts to a she." He shook his head and swore.

Two lighters came skimming down from the big ship to load up.

"Coming back to the launch?" the purser asked. He had a red shiny face. Harper had always thought him a rather decent fellow—before. The purser had no way of knowing what was in Harper's mind; he smiled at him and said. "We might as well get on back, the fun's over now."

Harper came to a sudden decision. "What're the chances of my taking a souvenir back with me? This big fellow, here, for example?"

The purser seemed doubtful. "Well, I dunno, Mr. Harper. We're only supposed to take females aboard, and unload *them* as soon as the convicts are finished with their fun." He leered. Harper, suppressing a strong urge to hit him right in the middle of his apple-red face, put his hand in his pocket. The purser understood, looked away as Harper slipped a bill into the breast pocket of his uniform.

"I guess it can be arranged. See, the Commissioner-General on Selope III wants one for his private zoo. Tell you what: We'll take one for him and one for you—I'll tell the supercargo it's a spare. But if one croaks, the C-G has to get the other. Okay?"

At Harper's nod the purser took a tag out of his pocket, tied it around the Yahoo's wrist, waved his cap to the lighter as it came near.

"Although why anybody'd *want* one of these beats me," he said, cheerfully. "They're dirtier than animals. I mean, a pig or a horse'll use the same corner of an enclosure, but these things'll dirty anywhere. Still, if you *want* one—" He shrugged.

As soon as the lighter had picked up the limp form (the pulse was still fluttering feebly) Harper and the purser went back to the passenger launch. As they made a swift ascent to the big ship the purser gestured to the two lighters. "That's going to be a mighty slow trip *those* two craft will make back up," he remarked.

Harper innocently asked why. The purser chuckled. The coxswain laughed.

"The freight-crewmen want to make their points before the convicts. *That's* why."

The chicken cadet, his face flushed a deeper pink than usual, tried to sound knowing. "How about that, purser? Is it pretty good stuff?"

The other passengers wiped their perspiring faces, leaned forward eagerly. The purser said. "Well, rank has its privileges, but that's one I figure I can do without."

His listeners guffawed, but more than one looked down towards the lighters and then avoided other eyes when he looked back again.

* * * *

Barnum's Planet (named, as was the custom then, after the skipper who'd first sighted it) it was a total waste, economically speaking. It was almost all water and the water supported only a few repulsive-looking species of no discernible value. The only sizable piece of land—known, inevitably, as Barnumland, since no one else coveted the honor—was gaunt and bleak, devoid alike of useful minerals or arable soil. Its ecology seemed dependent on a sort of fly: A creature rather like a lizard ate the flies and the Yahoos ate the lizards. If something died at sea and washed ashore, the Yahoos ate that, too. What the flies ate no one knew, but their larvae ate the Yahoos, dead.

They were small, hairy, stunted creatures whose speech—if speech it was—seemed confined to moans and clicks and grunts. They wore no clothing, made no artifacts, did not know the use of fire. Taken away captive, they soon languished and died. Of all the Primitives discovered by man, they were the most primitive. They might have been left alone on their useless planet to kill lizards with tree branches forever—except for one thing.

Barnum's Planet lay equidistant between Coulter's System and the Selopes, and it was a long, long voyage either way. Passengers grew restless, crews grew mutinous, convicts rebellious. Gradually the practice developed of stopping on Barnum's Planet "to let off steam"—archaic expression, but although the nature of the machinery man used had changed since it was coined, man's nature hadn't.

And, of course, no one *owned* Barnum's Planet, so no one cared what happened there.

Which was just too bad for the Yahoos.

It took some time for Harper to settle the paperwork concerning his "souvenir," but finally he was given a baggage check for "One Yahoo, male, live," and hurried down to the freight deck. He hoped it would be still alive.

Pandemonium met his ears as he stepped out of the elevator. A rhythmical chanting shout came from the convict hold. "Hear that?" one of the duty officers asked him, taking the cargo chit. Harper asked what the men were yelling. "I wouldn't care to use the words," the officer said. He was a paunchy, gray-haired man, who probably loved to tell his grandchildren about his "adventures." This was one he wouldn't tell them.

"I don't like this part of the detail," the officer went on. "Never did, never will. Those creatures *seem human* to me—stupid as they are. And if they're *not* human," he asked, "then how can we sink low enough to bring their females up for the convicts?"

The lighters grated on the landing. The noise must have penetrated to the convict hold, because all semblance of words vanished from the shouting. It became a mad cry, louder and louder.

"Here's your pet," the gray-haired officer said. "Still out, I see... I'll let you have a baggage-carrier. Just give it to a steward when you're done with it." He had to raise his voice to be heard over the frenzied howling from the hold.

* * * *

The Ship's Surgeon was out having tea at the Captain's Table. The duty medical officer was annoyed. "What, another one? We're not veterinarians, you know... Well, wheel him in. My intern is working on the other one... *whew*!" He held his nose and hastily left.

The intern, a pale young man with close-cropped dark hair, looked up from the pressure-spray he had just used to give an injection to the specimen Yahoo selected for the Commissioner-General of Selope III. He smiled faintly.

"Junior will have company, I see... Any others?"

Harper shook his head.

The intern went on, "This should be interesting. The young one seems to be in shock. I gave him two cc's of anthidar sulfate, and I see I'd better do the same for yours. Then... Well, I guess there's still nothing like serum albumen, is there? But you'd better help me strap them down. If they come to, there's a cell back aft we can put them in, until I can get some cages rigged up." He shot the stimulant into the flaccid arm of Harper's Yahoo.

"Whoever named these beasties knew his Swift," the young medico said. "You ever read that old book, *Gulliver's Travels*"?

Harper nodded.

"Old Swift went mad, didn't he? He hated humanity, they all seemed like Yahoos to him... In a way I don't blame him. I think that's why everybody despises these Primitives: they seem like caricatures of ourselves. Personally, I look forward to finding out a lot about them, their metabolism and so on... What's *your* interest?"

He asked the question casually, but shot a keen look as he did so. Harper shrugged. "I hardly know, exactly. It's not a scientific one, because I'm a businessman." He hesitated. "You ever hear or read about the Tasmanians?"

The intern shook his head. He thrust a needle into a vein in the younger Yahoo's arm, prepared to let the scrum flow in. "If they lived on Earth, I wouldn't know. Never was there. I'm a third generation Coulterboy, myself."

Harper said, "Tasmania is an island south of Australia. The natives were the most primitive people known on Earth. They were almost all wiped out by the settlers, but one of them succeeded in moving the survivors to a small island. And then a curious thing happened."

Looking up from the older Primitive, the intern asked what that was.

"The Tasmanians—the few that were left—decided that they'd had it. They refused to breed. And in a few more years they were all dead... I read about them when I was just a kid. Somehow, it moved me very much. Things like that *did*—the dodo, the great auk, the quagga, the Tasmanians. I've never been able to get it out of my mind. When I began hearing about the Yahoos, it seemed to me that they were like the old Tasmanians. Only there are no settlers on Barnumland."

The intern nodded. "But that won't help our hairy friends here a hell of a lot. Of course no one knows how many of them there are—or ever were. But I've been comparing the figures in the log as to how many females are caught and taken aboard." He looked directly at Harper. "And on every trip there are less by far."

Harper bowed his head. He nodded.

The intern's voice went on: "The thing is, Barnum's Phinet is no one's responsibility. If the Yahoos could be used for labor, they'd be exploited according to a careful system. But as it is, no one cares. If half of them die from being stungunned, no one cares. If the lighter crews don't bother to actually land the females—if any of the wretched creatures are still *alive* when the convicts are done—but just dump them out from twenty feet up, why, again: no one cares. Mr. Harper?"

Their eyes met. Harper said, "Yes?"

"Don't misunderstand me... I've got a career here. I'm not jeopardizing it to save the poor Yahoos—but if *you* are interested—if you think you've got any influence—and if you want to try to do anything—" He paused. "Why, now is the time to start. Because after another few stop-overs there aren't going to *be* any Yahoos. No more than there are any Tasmanians."

* * * *

Selope III was called "The Autumn Planet" by the poets.

At least, the P.R. picture-tapes always referred to it as "Selope III, The Autumn Planet of the poets," but no one knew who "the poets" were. It was true that the Commission Territory, at least, did have the climate of an almost-perpetual early New England November. Barnumland had been dry and warm. The Commissioner-General put the two Yahoos in a heated cage as large as the room Harper occupied at his company's Bachelor Executive Quarters.

"Here, boy," the C-G said, holding out a piece of fruit. He made a chirping noise. The two Yahoos huddled together in a far corner.

"They don't seem very bright," he said, sadly. "All my *other* animals eat out of my hand." He was very proud of his private zoo, the only one in the Territory. On Sundays he allowed the public to visit it.

Sighing, Harper repeated that the Yahoos were Primitives, not animals. But, seeing the C-G was still doubtful, he changed his tactics. He told the C-G about the great zoos on Earth, where the animals went loose in large enclosures rather than being caged up. The C-G nodded thoughtfully. Harper told him of the English dukes who—generation after ducal generation—preserved the last herd of wild White Cattle in a park on their estate.

The C-G stroked his chin. "Yes, yes," he said. "I see your point," he said. He sighed gustily. "Can't be done," he said.

"But why not, sir?" Harper cried.

It was simple. "No money. Who's to pay? The Exchequer-Commissioner is weeping blood trying to get the Budget through Council. If he adds a penny more—No, young fellow. I'll do what I can: I'll feed these two, here. But that's all I can do."

Trying to pull all the strings he could reach, Harper approached the Executive-Fiscal and the Procurator-General, the President-in-Council, the territorial Advocate, the Chairman of the Board of Travel. But no one could do anything. Barnum's Planet, it was carefully explained to him, remained No Man's Land only because no man presumed to give any orders concerning it. If any government did, this would be a Presumption of Authority. And then every other government would feel obliged to deny that presumption and issue a claim of its own.

There was a peace on now—a rather tense, uneasy one. And it wasn't going to be disturbed for Harper's Yahoos.

Human, were they? Perhaps. But who cared? As for Morality, Harper didn't even bother to mention the word. It would have meant as little as Chivalry.

Meanwhile, he was learning something of the Yahoos' language. Slowly and arduously, he gained their confidence. They would shyly take food from him. He persuaded the C-G to knock down a wall and enlarge their quarters. The official was a kindly old man, and he seemed to grow fond of the stooped, shaggy, splay-footed Primitives. And after a while he decided that they were smarter than animals.

"Put some clothes on 'em, Harper," he directed. "If they're people, let 'em start acting like people. They're too big to go around naked."

So, eventually, washed and dressed, Junior and Senior were introduced to Civilization via 3-D, and the program was taped and shown everywhere.

Would you like a cigarette, Junior? Here, let me light it for you. Give Junior a glass of water, Senior. Let's see you take off your slippers, fellows, and put them on again. And now do what I say in your own language...

But if Harper thought that might change public opinion, he thought wrong. Seals perform, too, don't they? And so do monkeys. They talk? Parrots talk better. And anyway, who cared to be bothered about animals *or* Primitives? They were okay for fun, but that was all.

And the reports from Barnumland showed fewer and fewer Yahoos each time.

Then one night two drunken crewmen climbed over the fence and went carousing in the C-G's zoo. Before they left, they broke the vapor-light tubes, and in the morning Junior and Senior were found dead from the poisonous fumes.

That was Sunday morning. By Sunday afternoon Harper was drunk, and getting drunker. The men who knocked on his door got no answer. They went in anyway. He was slouched, red-eyed, over the table.

"People," he muttered. "Tell you they were *human!*" he shouted.

"Yes, Mr. Harper, we know that," said a young man, pale, with close-cropped dark hair.

Harper peered at him, boozily. "Know you," he said. "Thir' gen'ration Coulterboy. Go 'way. Spoi' your c'reer. Whaffor. Smelly ol' Yahoo?"

The young medico nodded to his companion, who took a small flask from his pocket, opened it. They held it under Harper's nose by main force. He gasped and struggled, but they held on, and in a few minutes he was sober.

"That's rough stuff," he said, coughing and shaking his head. "But— thanks, Dr. Hill. Your ship in? Or are you stopping over?"

The former intern shrugged. "I've left the ships," he said.

"I don't have to worry about spoiling my new career. This is my superior, Dr. Anscomb."

Anscomb was also young, and, like most men from Coulter's System, pale. He said, "I understand you can speak the Yahoo's language."

Harper winced. "What good's that now? They're dead, poor little bastards."

Anscomb nodded. "I'm sorry about that, believe me. Those fumes are so quick... But there are still a few alive on Barnum's Planet who can be saved. The Joint Board for Research is interested. Are you?"

It had taken Harper fifteen years to work up to a room of this size and quality in Bachelor Executives' Quarters. He looked around it. He picked up the letter which had come yesterday. "...neglected your work and become a joke...unless you accept a transfer and reduction in grade..." He nodded slowly, putting down the letter. "I guess I've already made my choice. What are your plans...?"

* * * *

Harper, Hill, and Anscomb sat on a hummock on the north coast of Barnumland, just out of rock-throwing range of the gaunt escarpment of the cliff which rose before them. Behind them a tall fence had been erected. The only Yahoos still alive were "nesting" in the caves of the cliff. Harper spoke into the amplifier again. His voice was hoarse as he forced it into the clicks and moans of the Primitives' tongue.

Hill stirred restlessly. "Are you sure that means, '*Here is food. Here is water*'—and not, '*Come down and let us eat you*'? I think I can almost say it myself by now."

Shifting and stretching, Anscomb said, "It's been two days. Unless they've determined to commit race suicide a bit more abruptly than your ancient Tasmanians—"

He stopped as Harper's fingers closed tightly on his arm. There was a movement on the cliff. A shadow. A pebble clattered. Then a wrinkled face peered fearfully over a ledge. Slowly, and with many stops and hesitations, a figure came down the face of the cliff. It was an old she. Her withered and pendulous dugs flapped against her sagging belly as she made the final jump to the ground, and—her back to the wail of rock—faced them.

"Here is food," Harper repeated slowly. "Here is water." The old woman sighed. She plodded wearily across the ground, paused, shaking with fear, and then flung herself down at the food and the water.

"The Joint Board for Research has just won the first round," Hill said. Anscomb nodded. He jerked his thumb upward. Hill looked.

Another head appeared at the cliff. Then another. And another. They watched. The crone got up, water dripping from her dewlaps. She turned to the cliff. "Come down," she cried. "Here is food and water. Do not die. Come down and eat and drink." Slowly, her tribes-people did so. There were thirty of them.

Harper asked, "Where are the others?"

The crone held out her dried and leathery breasts to him. "Where are those who have sucked? Where are those your brothers took away?" She uttered a single shrill wail; then was silent.

But she wept—and Harper wept with her.

"I'll guess we'll swing it all right," Hill said. Anscomb nodded. "Pity there's so few of them. I was afraid we'd have to use gas to get at them. Might have lost several that way."

Neither of them wept.

* * * *

For the first time since ships had come to their world, Yahoos *walked* aboard one. They came hesitantly and fearfully, but Harper had told them that they were going to a new home and they believed him. He told them that they were going to a place of much food and water, where no one would hunt them down. He continued to talk until the ship was on its way, and the last Primitive had fallen asleep under the dimmed-out vapor-tube lights. Then he staggered to his cabin and fell asleep himself. He slept for thirty hours.

He had something to eat when he awoke, then strolled down to the hold where the Primitives were. He grimaced, remembered his trip to the hold of the other ship to collect Senior, and the frenzied howling of the convicts awaiting the females. At the entrance to the hold he met Dr. Hill, greeted him.

"I'm afraid some of the Yahoos are sick," Hill said. "But Dr. Anscomb is treating them. The others have been moved to this compartment here."

Harper stared. "Sick? How can they be sick? What from? And how many?"

Dr. Hill said, "It appears to be Virulent Plague... Fifteen of them are down with it. You've *had* all six shots, haven't you? Good. Nothing to worry—"

Harper felt the cold steal over him. He stared at the pale young physician. "No one can enter or leave any system or planet without having had all six shots for Virulent Plague," he said, slowly. "So if we are all immune, how could the Primitives have gotten it? And how is it that only fifteen have it? Exactly half of them. What about the other fifteen, Dr. Hill? *Are they the control group for your experiment*?"

Dr. Hill looked at him calmly. "As a matter of fact, yes. I hope you'll be reasonable. Those were the only terms the Joint Board for Research would agree to. After all, not even convicts will volunteer for experiment in Virulent Plague." Harper nodded. He felt frozen. After a moment he asked, "Can Anscomb do anything to pull them through?"

Dr. Hill raised his eyebrows. "Perhaps. We've got something we wanted to try. And at any rate, the reports should provide additional data on the subject. We must take the long-range view."

Harper nodded. "I suppose you're right," he said.

By noon all fifteen were dead.

"Well, that means an uneven control group," Dr. Anscomb complained. "Seven against eight. Still, that's not *too* bad. And it can't be helped. We'll start tomorrow."

"Virulent Plague again?" Harper asked.

Anscomb and Hill shook their heads. "Dehydration," the latter said. "And after that, there's a new treatment for burns we're anxious to try... It's a shame, when you think of the Yahoos being killed off by the thousands, year after year, *uselessly*. Like the dodo. We came along just in time—thanks to you, Harper."

He gazed at them. "*Quis custodiet ipsos custodes*?" he asked. They looked at him, politely blank. "I'd forgotten. Doctors don't study Latin anymore, do they? An old proverb. It means: 'Who shall guard the guards themselves?'... Will you excuse me, Doctors?"

Harper let himself into the compartment. "I come," he greeted the fifteen.

"We see you," they responded. The old woman asked how their brothers and sisters were "in the other cave."

"They are well... Have you eaten, have you drunk? Yes? Then let us sleep," Harper said.

The old woman seemed doubtful. "Is it time? The light still shines." She pointed to it. Harper looked at her. She had been so afraid. But she had trusted him. Suddenly he bent over and kissed her. She gaped.

"Now the light goes out," Harper said. He slipped off a shoe and shattered the vapor tube. He groped in the dark for the air-switch, turned it off. Then he sat down. He had brought them here, and if they had to die, it was only fitting that he should share their fate. There no longer seemed any place for the helpless, or for those who cared about them.

"Now let us sleep," he said.

MR. STILWELL'S STAGE

**Originally published in T*he Magazine of Fantasy
& Science Fiction*, September 1957.**

This happened in the spring of 1940, in New York. The Depression was behind, the War (for us, at least) had not yet come. The violets were out, up at N.Y.U., and the bedding was being aired at windows down at Orchard Street—both sure signs of spring. The Wilkie boom was getting under way, and so was the No Foreign War Committee; the British Consulate was picketed by party-liners who bore placards reading THE YANKS ARE NOT COMING, and LET GOD SAVE THE KING.

In the morning Edward Bunsen of the Inventors' Enterprise Company had dealt with correspondence concerning some plans to be submitted to the Patent Office. In the evening he was due to meet one of the Company's chief backers at that gentleman's home to discuss Money. As a rule Bunsen—on behalf of I.E.C.'s investors—did not see people who came with inventions unless they had some sort of reference. Crackpots could take up all his time if he would let them, and then they were apt to make nuisances of themselves for long after; hanging around the office, telephoning, writing threatening letters, sometimes even instituting lawsuits. None of them had ever won, of course, because none of them had ever had a case—I.E.C. didn't operate on those lines—but it took up time and it used up money.

Still, you never knew: once the receptionist had turned away a wild and haggard man who had something in an old coffee can which he said would revolutionize the manufacture of saddle soap. He had gone, muttering and gesticulating, to another company—the receptionist *there* was A Sportsman's Daughter, and she got him a hearing, and his gunk was put on the market, and it *did* revolutionize the manufacture of saddle soap.

Those things could happen, they were among the hazards of the chase, but I.E.C. felt it was worth it. Their receptionists were well-trained.

Just after Bunsen came back from lunch (he had his own entrance and did not have to pass through the front office—he had his own phone, too, chiefly because of the former Mrs. Bunsen, who remained on good terms and had thought nothing of asking the switchboard girl if *she* knew if abortions were *really* legal in Cuba? and similar questions, indicative of her big heart and little sense) he flicked a switch on the office intercom box and was about to call his secretary when he heard the tinkle of music and the sound of happy laughter.

Bunsen was surprised rather than annoyed; it was spring, but this had never happened any other spring, nor anything like it. He went out to the front office, not to make a fuss, but just to see what was up.

All of them, every one of them, was crowded around something on the receptionist's desk. He was tall enough to look over their heads. He saw a sort of box, a miniature stage complete with curtains, and a dog who was dancing on it to the music of what sounded like an old-fashioned music box. The music box was nowhere to be seen, but *that* was nothing; what held Bunsen's attention was that the dog was on scale with the stage: it must have been about an inch long. While the young women *oh'd* and *ah'd* the dog suddenly stopped dancing and faced off stage while it went through the motions of barking. The tiny jaws worked rapidly, but there was no sound from the stage except the tinkle of the music box, even when the animal faced the crowd in front.

One of the girls turned around and saw Bunsen there; she tried to assume a deprecating expression, but couldn't keep it up. Breaking into a smile, she said, "Oh, Mr. Bun Sen, just look! It's so cute!"

They all turned around at this, and then the music stopped, abruptly. He couldn't see the stage anymore because Mrs. Wimpold, the bookkeeper, was wedged in front of it like a piece of Roman siege-machinery, but he heard someone say, "Oh, please, Mr. Stilwell, turn it on again!" Bunsen moved forward and saw the man. He was fiftyish-looking and had a rather pursy jowly sort of face, and on it the look of a man who knows he has said or done something purposely funny, but prefers not to laugh at his own cleverness.

Bunsen felt that he knew—just from that one glance—a lot about Mr. Stilwell. Mr. Stilwell had never joined the I AM, but he had probably been a Rosicrucian. On deciding that the fiscal and social cosmogony of *The Saturday Evening Post* and *The Readers' Digest* was not, after all, the correct one, Mr. Stilwell had delved—not into Marxism, but into Technocracy and the descendants of the Greenback movement. He did not Drink, but when he *did* drink, he showed his lack of practice. Mr. Stilwell believed that there was A Lot *To* what was said by the practitioners of Mrs. Eddy's soothing science, but when he felt unwell he bought whatever nostrum was being currently touted on the radio because The Government wouldn't Let Them Get Away With It if They weren't telling the truth. And *Mrs.* Stilwell was certainly a fine wife to him, but by this time he was perhaps not quite so certain that he was going to Make Good and Show Them All.

Making a quick decision, Bunsen (who was almost never faced with the need for office discipline) decided not to make an issue of the thing. He broke one of his own rules.

"Will you come inside, please, Mr. Stilwell?" he asked. The man appeared to reflect on the matter. He looked as if he were about to say that he Didn't Mind If He Did, but what he actually said was, "Why, *yes*, sir. Just one moment."

He turned to the women and began to smile and bow in a manner which Bunsen mentally labeled Old Cunnel. By a steady flow of *Will you excuse me, miss?* and *I'm very sorry to bother you, ma'am*, and *Thank you, thank you very much*, he managed to clear away the crowd of women and get his stage back into a container. Then, still smiling and bowing and making courtly gestures with his hat, he followed Bunsen into the inner office.

Dealing as he did more with things than with people, Bunsen seldom found it necessary to be a bastard, but he expected nothing from Mr. Stilwell and was prepared to suggest he go visit the firm which had taken on the mad saddle-soap chemist. He gestured the man to a seat, where he faced Bunsen with the self-conscious pursy smile still on his face.

"Suppose you tell me a little something about your device," Bunsen suggested, sliding out a drawer where a watch lay, face up—drawer-sliding was so much more tactful than clock-watching.

"Well," Mr. Stilwell began—only, as he accompanied it with (so Bunsen thought) a pointless chuckle, it sounded more like "Weh-hell."

"I prefer to let my own work praise me in the gates, so to speak. May I, ah, *demonstrate* it?" He unpacked the stage and placed it on the desk. It was well-made, certainly. In between attempts to defeat inertia and start a perpetual motion, Stilwell had probably turned out some nifty birdhouses.

Bunsen asked, "What kind of wood is this?"

The inventor said, "Mahogany, sir. The *best.*" He touched a stud and the curtain rolled up. The interior of the stage was dark.

"Honduras? Or British Honduras?" Bunsen cared absolutely nothing about the origin of the mahogany; he was making talk to cover the concentration with which he stared at the darkness onstage. The model theater was standing in full light from the fluorescent fixtures over Bunsen's desk; there was no possible way the interior *could* be dark...but it was. Tentatively he extended a finger, Stilwell making no objection. No, there was no obstruction there to cut off the light. A slight tingling in his finger...but he may have imagined it. Across the far corner of his mind the phrase *darkness which could be felt* came and went before he could ponder it. Stilwell said nothing, had (perhaps) not noticed. He pressed another stud and then a third. The tinkle of the music box started again (probably in the base of the stage, Bunsen thought) and the little dog trotted out and began his dance once more. The tiny figure was outlined as if with a spotlight...

Only there *was* no spotlight.

Only the office lights and the darkness of the little stage and the minute area of light that accompanied the dog in his none-too-skilled dancings. Abruptly, Bunsen reached out his hand again. He met with nothing he could feel—unless there really was a tingle—but the image of the dog seemed to blur at the point where it touched his finger. Bunsen shivered a bit and shuddered a bit—the way he did when someone drew a shovel raspingly along a sidewalk. The papers on his desk dealt with a way to reduce the oil content in squeezed citrus juice; it seemed a hell of a long way from what he was now looking at.

"Ahhhh... Mr. Stilwell..."

"*Yessir*?"

Bunsen wanted a drink from the water cooler, decided to skip it. He said, "Mmm...is there anything else? Or just the dog?"

Mr. Stilwell said, "Oh...anything can be arranged. Just *any*thing: like, um, lions and lion-tamers, elephants, the U.S. Marine Corps Band, opera, plays, tales of romance and revenge"—again, his silly chuckle—"only, as my means are rather, uh, *limited* right just now...weh-hell..."

"Just so... All right, Mr. Stilwell, I've seen enough."

Mr. Stilwell pressed studs. The music stopped. The light went out. The curtain went down with a tiny rustle. The two men looked at one another; Stilwell pleased and pompous, Bunsen poker-faced.

"What do you have in mind for your invention? For its uses, I mean?"

Mr. Stilwell pursed his ample lips, considered. "Weh-hell...home entertainment, for *one* thing; and store-window advertisement, maybe... You take this television they've been talking about, oh, for *years*, now"—he leaned over and became patronizingly confidential—"they haven't got it *yet*. And who knows *when* or if they will? Now, you take the Ancients, Mr. Bunsen—" Bunsen's face displayed uncertainty as to which ancients he was supposed to take, or where he was supposed to take them. Smiling blandly, Stilwell said, "That is to say, the *Wis*dom of the Ancients. Mu. Atlantis, Lemuria. The old legends of the talking mirror. Weh-hell. I'd better not digreh-hess. *Any* way: A chimera, is what I think this television is. But my stage is as good as any television could be, and it's *here*. A bird in the hand, you know," he said, with ponderous archness.

Bunsen nodded slowly. He said, "...I don't want to ask you just yet to explain the principle involved, or to show me any plans...but the decision as to whether I.E.C. takes this up or not doesn't depend entirely on me."

Stilwell rapidly bobbed his head. "I understand, sir. You have to consult with your associates, your principals. I understand, I expected nothing else. Now—suppose I leave this with you? To show them? And I'll inquire back in, oh, about a week? *All* right. Oh, about these buttons or switches. *Ver-y* simple: top to bottom: music, curtain, performance, end performance, down curtain, end music. Clear? *All* right."

Bunsen ran through them all, and Stilwell showed him how to pack the little stage away in its container. Then he bowed and weaved himself out. Before the door had closed Bunsen had begun to make up for lost time. The thing was to get the last drop of sweet juice out without releasing the first drop of bitter oil. The rind…

* * * *

Finally the day at the office closed. Bunsen had dinner at his usual small restaurant. Then he got in his car and began the ride up to Westchester. Nicholas Black lived there, the famous Nicky Black of years ago and Prohibition, that Experiment Noble In Purpose. Black was now "retired," richer than ever, respectable as any Federal government could wish, though his personal habits were in no way diminished by his retired way of life or advancing age. Nicholas Black was I.E.C.'s principal stockholder, and a good thing he had in it, too.

Driving through the Bronx, Bunsen idled with the idea of picking up Stilwell and taking him along. On impulse, he took a left turn and drove to the address given on the form filled out by the receptionist. It was a two-and-a-half-story wooden house in a street filled with such houses, all wooden and all shabby, and all long since divided up into flats. Some had store fronts built into them. Stilwell's house had a defeated-looking tree in the front yard and on it was a sign reading MRS. MUNGO, CORSETS. Bunsen ran his finger over the name plates at the door. Mungo, Goldberg, McCooey, Hart, and one was blank but in the frame was wedged a scrap of paper: *Joey—Gone to Aunt Irmas. Ma.*

Mr. Stilwell's name was Edgar. But this was the address. Perhaps he was only a roomer. Bunsen shrugged, rang the lowest bell, that of Mrs. Mungo. Since she was, in a way, a public character, she must expect the consequences.

As the answering buzz came, he pushed through the door, and saw another one open in the hallway inside. A smell of bacon smoke and boiling cabbage came out, followed by the head of a woman who was chewing something. "I'm looking for Mr. Stilwell, please." The head (it appeared to have been fashioned by an apprentice doll-maker; Bunsen caught himself looking closely at the hairline for signs of glue) was followed by a body. Mrs. Mungo evidently did not use her own products.

"Why he don't live here no more," she said, frowning and swallowing and coming forward.

Bunsen shrugged. "This is the address I was given." He was set to go; it didn't matter if Stilwell had given an old address, they weren't going to bond the man. People had their odd ways. But Mrs. Mungo was not anxious to withdraw. Doing some hasty dental work with her tongue, she surged up to the front door.

"No, they moved right after Louise had all that trouble."

Again Bunsen started to leave. He was not particularly interested in the Stilwell's domestic difficulties, but Mrs. Mungo had somehow wedged herself between him and the door. Short of trying a judo hold there seemed no alternative but to stay and listen.

"I presume you know them, so I'm not revealing anything, but—*Wasn't* that a *ter*rible thing? He took it like a gentleman, though, I must say. 'I forgive you, Louise,' he hollered—I could *hear* him, right-through-the-wall!" She pumped her head up and down. "'I forgive you, Louise,' he hollered. 'It's *my* fault—I cou'n't give you the things you deserve,' he said. Oh, he admitted *that* all right. He says, 'I forgive you' and she says back to him, oh, crying something awful, 'But I can't forgive my*self*,' she says. Sobbing, you know. And crying?… I'm sorry that I can't tell you where they went, but they didn't tell me." An aggrieved note came into her voice. "Although I sh'd think they *might* of, Louise and me being so close. After all, it was *me* who found her with her head by the gas oven, *Me*." She thumped the place where her bosom had once been. "I heard the lil dog whimpering and I climbed right-through-the-window and *if I hadn't*—"

But this was too much, far too much. Mrs. Mungo unwisely moved just enough to give him clearance, and Bunsen slithered through. "I'm very sorry to have bothered you," he said, sincerely enough, over his shoulder, and walked rapidly away, half-fearful that Mrs. Mungo would come pounding after and drag him back. What *had* Louise done? Dropped a half-pound of supermarket sliced bacon in her reticule, no doubt, and been picked up by the Pinkertons. Well, it wasn't any of his business. He drove off.

* * * *

Nicholas Black lived in a large well-kept house like any other, in a village full of large well-kept houses. An unobtrusive couple who performed all the domestic duties lived there with him. Black had no immediate family.

"Hello, Ed," he greeted Bunsen, and looked at the case he was carrying. "Should've had Carl give you a hand with that. Something to show me?"

"After the usual business, yes." Bunsen noticed, with some relief, as he looked around the well-furnished room, that tonight there were no traces of female guests he was not intended to meet. No long gloves on the couch, no expensive handbag on the chair, no fur stole. Once, some months before, he had been rather surprised to see a cheap brown pair of women's house-shoes somewhere about. Nicholas Black wasn't the sort to entertain women who wore cheap, brown house-shoes. Anyway, they weren't there when he had gotten ready to leave.

An hour passed, devoted to talk of figures and sums. Finally Bunsen packed away the papers and Black said, "Well, now for a drink and a look at whatever-it-is in the case here." Black never drank while there was talk of money. The drink was made and accepted and Bunsen drank half of it before he began to unpack the stage.

"This was made by some odd character who thinks that television is a chimera."

Black grunted. "I just wish *we'd* put some money into that chimera," he said. "It will be on the market before a lot of people expect it to."

He looked like a turtle from whose jaws a fish had just escaped. Bunsen had the stage ready. "What interests me most in this is the lighting." He pressed the UP CURTAIN STUD. "Or rather, the darkening…here, turn that lamp full on it…you see? Stage remains dark. Can't you imagine what uses might be made of a method of lighting just part of an area while the rest stays dark?"

Black nodded slowly and looked intently at the stage. Bunsen started the music and then pressed the third stud for the performance. "Never mind that dog," he said.

"What dog?" Black asked; but Bunsen didn't answer at once because he saw that there *was* no dog on the stage. Instead, a tiny man, dressed in green, was dancing—or rather, capering. Not a very young man, to judge from the figure. The face was masked.

"Robin Hood, I suppose that's what he's meant to be." A feathered cap was cocked on the man's head, he had a bow and quiver slung about him. "That's funny—there was a dog the last time… Well, he *said* it could show *any*thing… Now watch that lighting; d'you see?"

Black waved him aside impatiently, said, "Yeah, yeah." Suddenly, two figures were on the little stage.

"If that's Maid Marian, she's kind of pudgy for the role." Solemnly and awkwardly the two figures performed the dance. They bowed towards each other, removed their masks, and then bowed down stage. Bunsen leaned close, suddenly noticed that the woman was wearing a tiny pair of what seemed to be brown house-shoes. Then he looked up at their faces.

The words formed in Bunsen's mind, Why, that's *him*—the pursy jowly self-consciously clever smile was almost absent, though, from the tiny features: the face was taut with fear or hate, an edge of teeth gleamed—all in a second Bunsen turned from the stage to Black, but before he could say the words his mind had formed, he saw Black lunge forward in his chair, face scarlet.

"*Louise!*" cried Nicholas Black.

Everything happened so quickly. The tiny figure in the green dress covered her face with a tiny hand, and the man whipped off his bow and fitted it with an arrow he had plucked from over his shoulder. Bunsen afterwards was never sure if the arrow had been shot or not, because he dashed his hand at the stage and knocked it to the ground. Even before he heard it strike the floor he turned around and Black was slumped in the chair, eyes open, mouth open…

* * * *

"I told him, I don't *know* how many times, that he couldn't keep on, carry on, like he did—like he was a twenty-year-old," the doctor said, later, putting his stethoscope away. "But he'd laugh at me, or snarl at me as his mood might be, and he'd say, 'I take what I want and I do what I want.' Well, well…he went quickly, want to or *not*. Just fell over in his chair, you say? I'm not surprised."

It was morning before Bunsen finally got away. At his home, he set up the stage and pressed the studs. Nothing happened. Finally, he took a knife and a screwdriver and forced the base open. There was nothing in it—nothing, that is, that could have made it work. Nothing that could give any hint or explanation of how it *had* worked. There was a piece of amber, a crystal which might have come from an old radio set, a vial of quicksilver which must have shattered when he knocked the stage over, some long strands of faded blonde hair running through everything—odds and ends like that. Really nothing…

Bunsen's "private investigators" found no trace of the Stilwells. From whatever down-at-the-heels world they had come, it appeared that they had returned there once more—furnished rooms in old, shabby houses, with great new hopes for each new job ("Why, one of our men made $125 last week selling Watkins Products!"), lots and lots of solemn talk about The Wisdom Of The Ancients and, like a concealing fog or pall, the smell of bacon smoke and boiled cabbage…

Just what had occurred between them and Black might be conjectured, never proven.

And although Bunsen tried to repair the model stage, tried to fix it up with another vial of quicksilver and fit it all together again; although he often—when his door is locked—spends long periods pressing the studs, nothing ever happens. It is a long time now, and it begins to seem as if it never *could* have happened—though he knows it did. But Mr. Stilwells stage had played its single "tale of romance and revenge," and it has never given another performance.

MISS BUTTERMOUTH

**Originally published in *The Magazine of
Fantasy & Science Fiction*, May 1962.**

No, No coffee. I *mean* it. I give it up for the time being. Say, you see this piece in the paper here, doodling and scribbles reveal the unconscious mind? It all ties in with the no-coffee. I *mean* it. Call it a hunch.

What happen? I'll tell you what happen. Couple months ago I was broke, like usual, and I was waiting for a money-order from my brother. The only thing that come was a couple of pamphlets from someone I never heard of. So to kill the morning I go to the library. You ever see a magazine called the *Illustrated London Weekly*? It's mad, I just read it for chuckles. This time they had a big spread called "Interesting Discoveries In A North Syrian Tomb," or some hot-blooded title like that. All about some big shot named Ebed-Haddad, which they plant him, with a two-wheel Cadillac and a couple of hay-burners along. So I thought. I'll tell Haddad down at the lunch-room about it—family news from the Old Country, Haddad, from the land of the Sherbert and the shishkabob. But I forget to.

Next day, still no money. I got beans, I got bacon, but no coffee. Then noises coming through the wall give me notice that my neighbor, former Associate Professor Dudley Washburne, was at home, so I start to go and join him in a cup of *his* coffee. I bring along the pamphlets since I can't make no sense out of them and maybe he can. You ever hear of a outfit called the Mother Honeywell Foundation of Supernal Light? Don't laugh, it's what I mean serious.

So I take the whole works to the Prof. I tell him, Prof, the good neighbor policy demands you give me a cup of coffee. He says, I never touch the filthy stuff; it rots the striated tissue of the kidney and debilitates the gonads.

Sure. That's the way them professors talk. When he was at the University there was all this gizmadoo about swearing oaths, not swearing oaths, and a lot of people figured that was why he lost his job. But the simple truth is he just cannot resist breaking the tax stamps on liquor bottles, and once he gets them open, well… As for not swearing oaths, you should hear him some night when he's falling over the furniture. But he's all right, though, the Prof.

He poured me out a cup. Brother. After the second one I give him the letter the pamphlets come in and the pamphlets too, and I ask him: See what you can make out of this, Professor. Well, he moans and says, Have mercy on him at that hour of the morning, and so on. Then he looks up and says, Surely, no one can *really* be named Miss Buttermouth? Anyone with a handwriting like this, he says, could give a course in cryptography.

I tell him to give a look at the pamphlets. What does this here Etaoin Shrudlu mean, I ask him. He says, I can't tell you till you take the higher degrees, he says. It would be a violation of my fraternal oath, he says. Then he says: Hello, Hel-lo, What's this? This is pure Ugaritic, he says.

That clicked. That was the name in the limey magazine about this Syrian tomb. I ask him what gives, and he points to this line in the pamphlet right after Etaoin Shrudlu. *This* I *can't* pronounce. I got to write it out for you. Like this here: *Tilt sswm mrkhht...* I tell you, it's nothing to laugh. Listen.

After the Prof finishes shaking his head and pulling his lip and rubbing the back of his head, he tells me something about this Ugaritic. How it's one of them dead languages in the ancient east and they only started digging it up not long ago and very few people know it. Only—he says—this particular line don't fit into the pamphlet at all. What? Of course I ask him what does it mean. He says it means a three horse chariot. Or maybe even Three horses, one chariot.

Sounds like part of an inventory from a puny form tablet, he says. But what's it doing with the Mother Honeywell malarkey?

Well, like I say, none of this Mother Honeywell Supernal Light Foundation stuff makes any sense, so after I sop up some more coffee I make a polite farewell and took off for Louie's. Where I borrow a scratch sheet and there it is.

The third race. Three horses.

Country's Flag, number one. Abalsom, number two. Chariot, number three.

Three horses, one is Chariot! Almost I go wild. Then—very calm—I ask Louis how much of a bet can I put on the cuff. He don't say, This much and he don't say, That much. He just looks at me like I'm crazy and he says, It's Wednesday. Yeah, yeah, I should of remembered Louis don't give no credit on Wednesday, it's his unlucky day. So I sound out everybody else and I tell you I never saw such a bunch of dead wood in my life. I even ran next door to Haddad in the lunch-room and I tell him, Let me take ten: I got a horse with a Syrian name.

He says, What name? He says, Chariot? You call that a Syrian name? You trying to kid me? So I start to tell him all about this Ugaritic stuff, but it was absolutely nothing doing. He act as if I'm trying to insult him and he just keeps on saying, All us peoples are Christian peoples. And by the time I get him cooled off I look at the clock and I see it's too late to place a bet.

I go back to Louie's and I ask, Who won in the third? Chariot win in the third, they tell me... Naa. Don't ask me what he paid. I'd break into tears if I tell you.

So I go home and I grab them pamphlets and what I mean, I read them. It says where they have what they call an illumination every night in the Mother Honeywell Auditorium, so that's where I go and I make it my business to find out who sent me them pamphlets. Who is Miss Buttermouth, I ask. They show me. Who is it but this gray-hair old biddy with a mouth like a rabbit-trap. Her name is really Miss Butterworth, but I always think of her the other way.

She just copies names out of the phone book—and get this: She writes them pamphlets herself!

I tell her what a deep impression they make on me and I walk her home and we stay up half the night talking about the Supernal Light. I get hold of the pamphlet with the—yeah, that one. And I ask her about the, about what I write down for you, you know? She says, Depend on it, it must have a deep and mystical significance, but she can't explain it; when she writes it is just like she's in a trance. All kinds of emanations from the spirit world take control she says. And for some reason the printer claims her handwriting is hard to make out, she says. Then I kind of slide the conversation to see if she knows anything about this Ugaritic, but all she says is, Mother Honeywell has freed us from the dead hand of the past.

So there it is. Like I say, I'm just playing a hunch. I bring her boxes of vegetable nut loaf and jars of yogurt and every night we go for Illumination at the Auditorium. I practically memorize the damn scratch sheet every day just in case she should let drop a name of a horse. But you know what she's starting to talk lately? Marriage! She don't believe in passion, though, because it dissipates the vital energies, she says.

Meanwhile I dasn't eat no flesh or onions or use strong drink, tobacco or coffee. That's what she says, or coffee. All of them things dissipates the vital energies, she says. Sooner or later my hunch will pay off and I'll clean up, I tell you, I'll clean up.

But I don't know how long I can hold out. I just don't know.

LOVE CALLED THIS THING

Written with Laura Goforth

Originally published in *Galaxy Magazine*, April 1959.

Nan Peter Baker Four This Is Nan Peter Baker How do You Receive Me Over and now a word from Our Sponsor interviewed in his office the Commissioner said but Ruth I can explain everything there is nothing to explain David it's all too obvious I'm Bert Peel Officer and this is my brother Harry a cold front coming down from Canada and we've got to get word to the Fort colon congestion is absolutely unnecessary in men and women over forty at any one of the ninety-one offices of the Clinton National Bank and Trust...

"*Embarasse de richesse*," the French count had said when he looked at all the pretty girls on the high school swim team, and explained what it meant in English. Penny wasn't really in love with him; she only thought she was, after pretending she was, to make David jealous, which she certainly did. But after the count gently explained to her, she and David made up just in time for the Spring Prom, which made the distant observer very happy.

At least he thought it did. "What is happy?" he often asked himself. Maybe just pretend. *You never really loved me Rick it was just a pretense wasn't it?* Like the distant observer thinking of himself as "him" when, really, he knew now—had known long—he was only an "it." *It's about time we faced up to reality, Alison.* Yes. It was about time. *We can't go on like this.* No, certainly not. It was time.

In the beginning, there was no time. There was sight—here dark, there bright. He did not know then, of course—and how long had "then" lasted? Memory did not tell that the bright was stars. And there was sound—whispering, crackling, shrilling. *What do you mean, Professor, when you say that outer space is not a place of silence?* And then (he knew now that this "then" was about fifty years ago) there had begun a new kind of sound Not steady, but interrupted, and interrupted according to patterns. Awareness had stirred, gradually, and wonder. He knew later that this was "wireless." *CQ, CQ, CQ—SOS, SOS, SOS*

And then the other kinds of sounds, oh, very different. These were voices This was "radio." And music. It was too different; the distant observer knew distress without even knowing that it was distress. But he grew used to it—that is, distress ceased: but not wonder. Urgency came with the voices. What? *What*? He groped for meaning, not even knowing what meaning was.

* * * *

Presently there was another kind of sight, not just the dark and the stars any longer, but pictures—flickering, fading, dancing, clear, pictures upon pictures Gradually he learned selectivity—how to concentrate upon one, how to not-see, not-hear the others. Still later: how to see and hear all without confusion. How to match sound and sight. That things had names. What people were, who made the voices and the music. What meaning was.

About himself, he learned nothing directly. For a while, he had tried to speak to them, but it was apparent that nothing of him reached Earth. He had learned Earth, yes. And knew what this place was, where he was. An asteroid. How had he come to be there? This was in space. There were spaceships—he saw the scenes on television. Meteors were dangerous to spaceships. He knew meteors. Sometimes spaceships crashed. He scanned all his little world, but there was no spaceship, crashed or otherwise.

You've got to help me—I don't know who I am! But that was more easy, oh, so much more so—that one was a man, and there were many men. The sponsors (in this case, Muls, the creamy-smooth deodorant) were men, too. Everybody was very kind to this man. He had amnesia. What was odor? This the observer could not understand. But to have no memory, this he understood very well. This he shared with men.

Gradually he had come to share many things with men. They spoke different languages, but the one which came with the first pictures was English. English from America. Later on, there was English from England, there was French, Russian, Spanish, Japanese—but American was first and best. So much more interesting than the Red Army and the hydroelectric dams, these stories of real life. Of love and sadness and of happiness.

Kid, there ain't no problem in all this world you can't lick if you really try. Very well, the observer would try. *You never know what you can do till you try*. His first attempt at taking shape wasn't good. It didn't look much like a man. So he tried again and again. Each time he grew better at it. It was true, what the people said. It was all true, every word and picture of it. *There ain't no problem—*

And so when it came time for his favorite Wednesday evening program, the distant observer was ready. Summoning all his effort, husbanding
all his energy, he passed along the wave length as a man walks down a
street. There was a slight jar, a click. He realized that he could never undo
what had just been done. There was a new body now, a new metabolism.
The past is dead, David. We have to live for the future.

"And what is your name—my, you got up here but quick!" burbled
Keith Kane, the M.C. of Cash or Credit. "I've never known a volunteer
from our happy studio audience to manage it quite so suddenly. This is just
the warm-up, sir, so you needn't be nervous. Not that you need the reas-
surance—cool as a cucumber, isn't he, folks? Say, did you folks ever hear
the story about the little Sunday School boy who said that King Solomon
had three hundred wives and six hundred cucumbers? Wow! I'm *really*
naughty! You other folks who volunteered just take seats right there—"

The first lady volunteer was old and pretty. Well, maybe not so old.
But maybe like Mary Clay who realized that she was too old for young
David Webster and after she cried she accepted the fact and sent him back
to Madge Barkley whom he really loved all the while, only they had this
silly quarrel.

The lady smiled at him. He smiled back. *I—feel—GREAT!*

"—So that's the way the rules work, and now, folks, in just five seconds
we'll be on the air! Five—four—three—two—one—Good evening, all you
lovely people out there in TV Land! This is Keith Kane, bringing you the
great—the greater—the GREATEST quiz program ever: *Cash or Credit?*"

Now he felt his heart beating very fast. So that was what it was like!
And now he knew what was odor. But the lovely lady volunteer next to him
smelled, yes, that was sweet. But if it was Muls or Van Art Number Three,
this he would learn later.

"—just rinse and dry, folks, that's all there is to it: Clear-o, the all-
purpose *vegetable* detergent. And now whom have we here? What is your
name, sir?"

Here it was. And how terrible if he should break down and press his
hands to his head and sob, "I—I—don't—*know*!" But he did know; he had
it all ready. "Davis. My name is David Taylor." All the ones named David
were good. Oh, they had their troubles, but in the end everyone loved them.
And see: nice Keith Kane beaming. The lady, too.

"Well, David, what'll it be? Cash—or—Credit? You know the rules:
If you pick Cash, we spin this little wheel. If it comes up with a number,
you go on to answer—if you can, hah-ha—a question worth however many
thousand dollars follow that number. If it comes up blank—you're out.
Whereas, if you pick Credit, you take your place among the volunteers and

if any contestant makes a boo-boo, why, you step into *his* shoes and *he* is out. Soooo—?"

"Take the cash and let the credit go," said David.

Grinning from lobe to lobe, Keith Kane asked the same questions of the lady, whose name was Mrs. Conar, Mrs. Ethel-Mae Conar, a widow: and received the same answer. The audience applauded, the wheel was spun, and it came up 10.

"Ten—thousand—DOLLARS!" screamed Keith Kane. "That's what your first question is worth and here it *is*: What former President of the United States is associated with this tune, and what is the name of the tune, which refers to his State? Remember, you have thirty seconds to think it over…"

David and Mrs. Conar won two hundred and eighty-five thousand dollars in *cash* before the program was over, as well as a year's supply of Clear-o, and fifty shares of stock in a mink ranch; and the band played "The Stars and Stripes Forever" as Keith Kane counted out the money. Mrs. Conar had kissed him and kissed David and was now clasping his hands and sobbing that she didn't really believe it.

"Oh, it's true," David assured her. "It's all true; that's the funny part of it." (David Mackay said that, in *Matinee*, when he admitted his wife was an alcoholic.) Sight and sound and touch (kissing was pleasant; no wonder it was so much done) and smell and—and—what was the other? Taste. Keith Kane bawled at him the question of what he was going to do with all his money. David deliberated. What was it that Clem Clooten, on *Saddle-Galled*, had said, the time he broke the faro bank in Dogie City? Taste… yes: "I'm goin' out'n buy m'self a cup o' java…" The audience went *wild*.

* * * *

Java tasted. Taste was as exciting as the other four sensations. And sitting next to him on the counter-stool was Mrs. Ethel-Mae Conar, gazing at his distinguished profile. It was clean-cut. He gazed down at her. He was tall, of course.

He searched for the right words. It turned out to be singular. "Happy?" he asked.

She sighed, nodded. Then—"You're a rather strange young man," she said. "Do you know that?"

Certainly he knew it.

He leaned closer. "This is bigger than both of us," he said huskily. "Let me take you away from all this…"

"I certainly *will*," she said briskly, "right over to my place in the Surrey-Regis on Park Avenue"—that meant she was unhappy despite her money I—"where we can have a *decent* cup of coffee."

The counterman scowled at the bill David offered him. "Whatsis? Play-money? A five-hunnerd-dolla bill? Whuddya, wise guy?"

David arose slowly, buttoning his jacket, and leaned over. "If you're looking for trouble, buddy…" he said. But the guy chickened out. Anyway, Ethel-Mae had some change in her purse. "Taxi!" David called happily. He helped her in, sank back in the seat, and when the driver asked Where To, David said crisply, "Follow that cab!"

The driver (Herman Bogancz, the license read) half-turned, half-growled. Ethel-Mae laughed. "Oh, if you aren't—never mind, driver: the Surrey-Regis, on Park near—" But H. Bogancz muttered that he knew where the place was.

David gazed out the window excitedly. Everywhere, men and lights and women and automobiles. "Little Old New York," he murmured.

Suddenly she yelped, dug her fingers into his arm.

"Darling!" he exclaimed. "Are you all right? Is anything wrong?"

"No," she said. "Oh, no—"

"*Something* must be wrong," he insisted. "You can tell me, dear. I trust you. No matter what you've done—"

"What I've *done*?" she screamed. "I've just won a half share in $285,000 is what—"

He seized her, turned her facing him. "Are you out of your *mind*?" he gritted. And then, memory returning, he (released her "Yeah… Gee' that's right. Yeah, how *about* that? Do you know what this *means*? Ethel-Mae, we're *rich*! WE'RE RICH!"

The driver twisted his chin slightly to the right. "Do y' mind, mister? Not so loud with the decibels I gotta near condition."

David said, shocked, "If there's anything I can do—anything at all—if you need money—we'll get the best surgeon there is—"

Herman Bogancz shrugged. "My cousin Sidney is the best surgeon there is, and he says an operation wouldn't help."

"Then," said David, "there's nothing more that any of us can do—except wait—and pray—"

"—and wash it out three times a day with a boric acid solution," said Herman Bogancz.

* * * *

David didn't quite understand why Mrs. Conar made him apply for a room at the Surrey-Regis by himself while she went up to her room through the side entrance. In fact, he didn't understand at all. The clerk looked at him rather oddly when he explained this to him, and asked for a room near hers. He looked even odder when he saw the $500 bill. Once again David buttoned his jacket (it had been necessary to unbutton it first) and leaned over. "I hope," he said, "that I'm not going to have any trouble with you."

"Oh, dear me, no," said the clerk. "Not at all…my goodness, Mr. Taylor, but you really are tall, aren't you? Suite 516. Mrs. Conar's is Suite 521—that's the best I can do right just this very *minute*, and—"

Another gentleman materialized at David's elbow "Good evening, sir," he said suavely "I am Mr. Feltz, the manager, is everything all right?"

"The boy's not to blame," David said, gesturing toward the clerk. "Society is to blame—we're *all* to blame. It's these crazy, mixed-up times we live in."

Behind David's back, the clerk spread open the $500 bill for Mr. Feltz's inspection.

"How right you are, sir," said Mr. Feltz.

"About the gentleman's—Mr. Taylor's change, Mr. Feltz—?"

David turned, put his hand on the clerk's shoulder. The man flushed, sucked in his lower lip "That's for *you*, sonny. There is no such thing as a bad boy. I never met a man I didn't like."

"*Front!*" said the clerk, his voice tremulous.

Mr. Feltz handed the keys to 516 to the bellboy himself, urged Mr. Taylor to make his wants known immediately. As David walked toward the elevator, the manager turned to his subordinate. "The Rich," he said simply. The clerk nodded solemnly. "We know their ways," said Mr. Feltz. "Eh? Well, that's very generous of you, Robert—but, no, sixty-forty is good enough. He seems to have taken a liking to you. Send up flowers, the morning papers, a split of champagne. And include my card, Robert."

As soon as the bellboy had gone (rather like a satisfied customer on his way out of a high-class opium den, with a $500 bill clutched in his hot hand), David went down the corridor and knocked on the door of Suite 521. "Ethel-Mae?" he asked, his face close to the door. "Dearest? This is David. *Please* open. I can explain everything."

And, sure enough, her words as she opened the door and fell into his arms were, "There is nothing to explain!" Then she said, "It's just that you're so sweet—and naive. But that nasty little nance down at the desk wouldn't understand."

Since David didn't understand either, he made no comment, but covered her face with kisses. "Darling, I *love* you," he said. "Please believe me." And she said, But she did—she did. "Do you know what it's like to be alone—always alone—never to know love? Do you? *Do you*? No. Of course you don't—"

Her answer was exactly correct. "Hush, darling," she said. "Everything's going to be all right." He sighed, kissed her again. Then—

"Ethel-Mae? Ethel-Mae? Mrs. Conar? What-? Why are you—" But she didn't seem to hear him. Nothing he had ever heard on radio or seen on television prepared him for what was happening now. But—he decided after a moment or so—what was happening now was—though strange—not unpleasant. "This is wrong," he groaned happily. "It's all wrong. But I—I don't care. Do you hear, I don't *care*!"

* * * *

It was two in the morning before he stumbled back to his own room, and bed. At half-past two, he was awakened by the bellboy's father and mother (smuggled up on the service elevator) who had come all the way from Mulberry Street to kiss his hands. At three, he was half-awakened by a Scratching noise at his door. After a few minutes, he got up and—after approaching it as cautiously as the Sheriff of Hangtown on the program of the same name—threw it suddenly open.

A pretty girl with her red hair in a pony-tail uttered a little scream. Pencil and notebook fell to the floor. "Why—you—you're only a *child*!" he said, in a hushed voice.

"Mr. T-Taylor—" she began very nervously. "I saw you at the studio and I fol-followed you"—she gulped—"over here. But it took till now for me to get up nerve—"

"Why, you're frightened," he said, looking down at her. "Don't be frightened. You don't *ever* have to be frightened of *me*. Come in," he urged. "Please come in."

She picked up her notebook and followed him in obediently. Then, taking the seat he gestured to, she said, "And I'm not such a child, either. I'm a senior at Barnard. Journalism major. And I want a story from you, Mr. Taylor, before all the other reporters get here. Please, Mr. Taylor, *please*."

He looked at her admiringly. "That took guts," he said. "Where I come from, the men get separated from the boys mighty young. But—don't call me 'Mr. Taylor'—Mr. Taylor has gray hair at the temples. Call me David." She called him David. And she told him that her name was Pamela Novack. And he said that Pamela was a lovely name. She told him that she'd hated it as a child, but that lately—in fact, just this very minute—she'd gotten to like it a whole lot more. And they laughed. They laughed a whole lot.

Before they knew it, it was getting light.

"Oh, golly," Pamela sighed. "Oh, gee, have I got a story! In a way, it's so sad, and you having such an unhappy childhood, I mean; your mother dying from the brain tumor and your father being an alcoholic—"

He said that was all in the past. He said they had to start looking toward the future. She nodded soberly. Then she stretched and said she was hungry.

"Hey, how about that!" David laughed, catching sight of his face in the mirror. It was a nice face. He had done well in making it; it looked like all the Davids he had ever seen. "You know something? I'm hungry, too! I haven't had a bite to eat since that cup of coffee after the show. Would you like to have some breakfast? You *would*. Hot diggety!... Hello? I want Room Service, please."

The narcoleptic tones of the operator said, Not till ha'-pas'six. And then suddenly were clear and alert and saying, "Oh, Mr. *Taylor*? Pardon me—of course, Mr. Taylor—what would you like? Scrambled eggs and coffee and toast and gallons of orange juice. Yes, *sir*, Mr. Taylor."

Then, suddenly, the smile was gone from David's face. Anxiously, Pamela asked what the matter was. Scowling, he mimicked, "Yes, Mr. Taylor, certainly, Mr. Taylor'—it isn't me they like—nobody likes *me*—it's the money. Once you been in reform school, nobody has any use for you, the cops are always watching you, the nice girls don't want to have anything to do with you—"

Pamela was troubled. "Oh, you *mustn't* say that. I—I—well, I think *I'm* a nice girl—" she blushed suddenly, looked down—"and I—like you—David."

He got up and walked back and forth, rubbing his left arm with his right hand. He swung around and faced her. "You!" he jeered. "Whadda *you* know? You're just a fresh young kid—"

"I am not!" she snapped.

"A senior at Barnard! Whadda you know about life? You—"

He stopped. He had been enjoying the experience of emoting so much that the significance of the scene had escaped him. *They were quarreling*! That meant they were in love! Of course—Davids always quarreled with the girls they were really in love with.

He dropped down on one knee beside her and looked into her flushed, pretty face.

"Darling," he said, brokenly, taking her hands. "Trust me—I can't explain now—but just trust me—"

There was a sound from the door. They looked up. Ethel-Mae Conar stood there, holding her throat with both hands. After a moment, she said, "I must have hurt you very much, David, for you to have done—*this*—to me—to have forgotten. So quickly."

Exquisitely miserable, he shouted, "Leave me alone! Can't you leave me alone? Can't you understand that it's all over between us?" And then, his voice dropping, "Oh, Ethel-Mae, forgive me. I didn't mean to say that. I didn't mean it. I—I can explain."

Letting her hands drop resignedly, she said, "There's nothing to explain, David. I understand. It could never have worked out. I'm—I'm just—too *old* for you, David." She walked over, lifted his head (he had hung it, of course), placed her palms on his cheeks and kissed him gently on the forehead. Then she turned to Pamela and said softly, "Be good to him, my dear. And give him lots of love." She went out, her head high, a wistful smile on her lips, and the awareness that she had half of the $285,000, the year's supply of Clear-o (the *vegetable* detergent), and the fifty shares of stock in a mink ranch.

There was a moment's silence. Then, "Gosh," said Pamela. "Golly," she said.

David turned to her. "Darling, don't cry any more," he begged. "Everything's going to be all right from now on."

"I'm not crying," she said. Her eyes were shining. "The hell with the story and the journalism course and the hell with Barnard, too. With all your money," she said, falling into his welcoming arms, "we can get married and start a family right away. Kiss me," she said, "hold me tight, don't ever leave me!"

* * * *

Mr. and Mrs. David Taylor live in a fifteen-room house in Westport with two picture windows, three boxers, and three cars. They have two children and a third is on the way. They are as happy as any couple in Westport has a right to be in these crazy, mixed-up days. David is a highly successful writer of television scripts, with an unerring nose for what the public wants. It is perhaps unfortunate that his work brings him into contact with so many clever and attractive women. He is, of course, unfaithful to his wife with one of them at least twice a year (or at least once a year with two of them).

There used to be a time when a David would never do a thing like this to his wife. He would *almost* do it—and then, at the last moment, not. But TV is maturing. The Davids do it all the time. All the damned time.

"But how *could you?*" Pam Taylor weeps. "David, how *could* you?"

And young David Taylor, his face twisted with anguish, cries, "Don't you understand? Won't you even *try* to understand? *I'm sick! I need help!*"

Well. Naturally Pam is very sad that her husband is sick, sick, sick—but, after all, it's the thing to be, isn't it? And so she's happy she can help him and happily she drives the two of them down to Dr. Naumbourg. David is very sad that he's made his lovely wife unhappy, but he's happy that he's fulfilling his destiny as a David. Dr. Naumbourg always insists on both husbands *and* wives Going Into Therapy at the same time. Pamela's case is a common enough one, merely a routine phallic envy. Naumbourg gets them every day.

But in all the years since Vienna, Dr. N. has never had another patient whose womb-fantasy takes the form of being a Thing on an asteroid. And so, while all three of them are very happy, Dr. Naumbourg is perhaps the happiest of all.

JURY-RIG

Originally published in *Venture Science
Fiction Magazine*, November 1957.

Doc Damon and Judge Peltz were at it again.

"If you'd just for once—*once* is all I ask—just one single time read that
there where Harry Stack Sullivan says—" Judge Peltz pleaded.

A grimace and a wave of the hand. "Never mind that. Harry S. Sullivan
or John L. Sullivan, that's no concern of ours. I want to ask you one single,
simple question: Is he either a danger to himself or a danger to the com-
munity?" Doc Damon glared out of red-rimmed poached-egg eyes. "Hey?
Yea or nay?"

The judge shook his head rapidly.

"You'd think I dint *like* the fellow or something," he said, aggrievedly.
"You act as though I was being contemptible tords your own talents or
something," he said. "*No*. All I say, *is*…"

The peninsula sticks out from the Pacific coast just enough to hook
around and make a harbor. The town used to be a lumbering port—it still is
a lumbering town, but the timber goes out by rail or truck now. Sometimes
at night, though, down near the wharves, with the fog coming in gray and
soft and cool, and the brackish smell of the bay, and the scent of the wood,
and the sound of the seals ooping and yerping—sometimes it seems as if it
still *is* a port. Then the place isn't a town, it's a city, a small city, but a *port*
city; and the air smells of distant places, and the tall cylinder which burns
up the sawdust might be Stromboli if you see it from the right perspective.

But in the daytime, when you hear the rasp of the saw, and the rattle
and dull *bonk-bonk* of the flat-cars thudding together as they back and fill in
the yards, and you notice how many of the stores are boarded up shut, and if
you know anything about the lumber business—then you soon realize that
not such a hell of a lot of lumber is going out of the place anyway, by rail
or by truck, and you know the arrival of a ship is almost as infrequent as a
presidential election.

During the course of their argument Doc Damon and Judge Peltz had
passed slowly into the lumber yard, passed the big saw and the sheds where

the green timber was drying, crossed the tracks, and came at last to the sawdust burner.

"Hi, Elmer," the doctor said. A short man in clean overall a size too big for him looked up at them. "How are you today, Elmer?"

"Day, day," the man said, cheerfully—very cheerfully "Lololo. Pleasingness. My, yes. If have kreelth."

"*See*?" the judge hissed in his companion's ear. "Whad Itellya? *Neologisms!*"

The doctor pulled away with a testy expression on his face He put the tip of his little finger in his ear and moved it vigorously. "Damn it, Al, I wish you wouldn't—What? Yes, yes, I'm *quite* familiar with the phenomenon. It don't mean a thing—except that he hasn't got all his marbles. Which is by no means news."

Judge Peltz's mouth set, then unset, in his horse-long face. "It's a schizoid characteristic," he said, doggedly. "Sullivan points out—"

The doctor waved to a passing workman. Then he said, "Listen. Do I try to teach you law?"

Elmer beamed at them. "Nice day, hey? Nice town, nice sawdust—" He picked up a handful of the stuff (before the burners were installed the sawdust seemed likely to engulf the town);, he sifted it lovingly through his fingers, "—nice people. One day—gren-a-mun-dun." He seemed just the merest bit regretful. The judge cleared his throat.

"Uh—tellus, Elmer—what does 'gren-a-mun-dun' mean? Hmm? Tell us?"

The doctor snorted. Elmer considered, rubbed his chin, raised his eyebrows. "Gren-a-mun-dun? It's like...um...cupra. But not for all the time cupra." And he beamed, turned back to his task of burning up sawdust.

"I trust that you are satisfied, Alfred?" the doctor asked. The day was warm, but now and then a cool breeze came up from the bay, and the sound of the seals with it.

The judge said, well, he wasn't. From his pocket he took a small notebook and a pencil.

"'Gren-a-mun-dun'," he muttered, writing. "I gottem all down here. And some day I'm writing to a member of the medical profession whose mind isn't closed to all the progress that's been made in recent years... Kreelth...tal-a-wax-na...esterral... I gottem all noted down here. Sometimes he just repeats the old ones, but today he used two more: Gren-a-mun-dun and cupra."

Damon shook his head. "Elmer is happy," he said. "The company is happy with him. He has not an enemy in the world. What do you want, Alfred?"

Elmer puttered around the base of the tall metal sawdust-burner with a few tools. "Kreelth," he muttered.

Judge Alfred Peltz said he wanted to know two things. "One: Is there any chance he might ever become *dangerous*? Two: Is there a chance he can be *helped*?"

The doctor rubbed his rufous eyes. He groaned. "Never let well enough alone, will you? Just like my damned old uncle, Freddy Damon. Thought the sailing men were a bad influence on the town. Wouldn't rest until he'd got the railroad in. The day they drove the last spike, what happened? Drunken, gandy-dancer sets fire to a box-car, burns up half the town—*including*—" he poked his finger in the judge's sternum—"my damned old uncle, Freddy Damon… Ha-pastwo," he said, abruptly. "I got to get back to my office. You drove me here, now you drive me back."

They started off. Doc half-turned. "Slong, Elmer. Begood."

"Gren-a-mun-dun," Elmer muttered, absent-mindedly, scraping a bolt.

* * * *

When the lease of Pighafetti the ship-chandler ran out, he didn't even bother to hold a Going Out Of Business sale. What stock was left in the shop stayed there. Most of it still remained when Tom Wong moved in because *his* lease had run out. Shipping and fishing might be shot to hell, but folks still had to eat. Knowing the value of the picturesque, Tom had simply redistributed the stuff; and so nets and coils of line and glass globes and ships' lanterns and a lot of similar equipage hung from the walls and ceilings.

"Yeah, I guess that's right, Judge," Tom observed. They were sitting at a table under an eel-trap. "Now when I was a kid, my father used to take me to an old Chinese man who stuck needles into me—gold needles, silver needles. Oh, it *worked*—but nowadays I see to it that my kids get penicillin, because, like you say, we gotta Move With The Times… How about trying today's Special? Curried shrimp." At the judge's nod, he signaled to his wife.

Judge Peltz put a cigarette in his mouth, groped around for a match. On the table by the ashtray with a pregnant dragon coiled around it was a book of paper matches, imprinted *Tom Wong's Waterfront Inn*; but the judge liked kitchen matches. He brought out the entire contents of his coat-pocket, not being able to disentangle the match, and dumped them on the table: a piece of fishing line, the pencil stubs, a glueless postage stamp, a few matches, and his little notebook. He pulled a match loose, lit his cigarette. The notebook reminded him—

"Now, it's an odd thing, Tom," he said, "how some people can't see the forest for the trees. I suppose you must meet up with people in the restaurant business world who are perfectly content to go right on doing just like they did thirty years ago?"

Tom nodded vigorously. His eyeglasses flashed. "Boy, don't I just!" he agreed. "Judge, those very words describe my wife's Uncle Ong, who's got that lunchroom over at the county seat. When I put in the dishwashing machine the salesman offered me a special price if I'd get *two*. Well, gee, I mean—so I asked her uncle, How's about it? But no—he's used to having the dishes washed by hand and he didn't see any reason to change. Get's in these hoboes and winos and odd-ball characters and by and by they *leave* him, so you'd think—But no. I said, Ah, come *on*, Uncle Ong, don't be an old stick-in-the-mud. So he started cussing me out in Chinese and yelling not to forget the Eight Virtues and that kind of stuff.

The judge, who had hoped for a single "Yes" only, listened. The moment Tom stopped he said, "Well, there you are. It's very sad. And how'd it be if the whole country was like that? Now, you take psychiatry, for example. What strides have been made in it! What marvelous recent discoveries!"

Old Ong's nephew said, "Boy, you bet!"

Growing enthusiastic, the Judge went on, "Now, you take for instance, I was reading some while back an article in the *Reader's Digest*—"

"That's a great magazine. I read it all the time. It's terrific."

"And it was describing the work of the late Dr. Harry Stack Sullivan of whom I'm sure you've heard." Wong made a noncommittal, encouraging noise. "You know much about the schizoid personality, Tom?" the judge asked.

The restaurateur wiggled in a fit of embarrassment. "Well, um, *no*, Judge. Y'see. The Business keeps me pretty busy, except for Sunday morning and I like to sleep late then if I get the chance. I was saying to my wife only last week, Judge, 'Priscilla,' I says, 'Can't you keep those kids quiet just—'"

Pushing the curried shrimp to one side and speaking rather loudly, Judge Alfred Peltz said, "This type of personality suffers from what you call a profound disassociation of ideas, I think. They retreat from Reality. See? They use Neologisms—what I mean, words that nobody knows what they mean, like—" He opened the little notebook. "Kreelth."

Tom Wong smiled. He chuckled "Kreelth," he repeated. "What kind of people did you say they were, Judge? I mean, where do they come from? Because that's what this simple-minded guy that washes dishes in my wife's Uncle Ong's lunchroom says all the time. Every time they bring him a pile of dirty dishes he says it."

* * * *

Old Mr. Woodrow Ong shook his head and waved his hand when Judge Peltz and Doc Damon came into his lunchroom.

"Closed up," he announced "Too late. Closed up. Oh. Judge. Hello, Judge." He glanced at the clock, sighed, struggled with his Confucian respect for the figure of the Magistrate. "Sandwich?" he suggested, feebly "Cup coffee?" He sighed again, surrendered. "Appoo pie, boo-berry, coconut custard, lemon mo-ang—"

The swinging doors of the kitchen opened and a man about Elmer's age and size came out, rolling down his sleeves. "Dishes finish," he said, and then saw the two newcomers. He took in a deep, resigned breath. "Kreelth," he said softly.

Judge Peltz looked triumphantly at Doc Damon. He consulted his little notebook. "Lololo," he said, tentatively. The dishwasher smiled. He chuckled at "gren-a-mun-dun" and "cupra". When the judge stumbled over "tal-a-wax-na," he corrected him happily.

"Fantastic!" said the judge. "Identical neologisms!" For once the doctor listened without demur.

"All right. Bring him along with us. Let's get the two of them together and see—whatever it is," Doc Damon said.

Old Mr. Ong watched them get into the car. He shrugged. Then he locked up, turned out all lights but one. An unfamiliar clicking noise in the kitchen drew his attention. He traced it to the garbage disposal unit, lifted out the mechanism. Its inward parts were a mystery to him, always had been. The devil-device clicked once again as he looked at it warily. A little parti-colored disk fell out of it, then another. They dropped to the floor. The cat strolled over, sniffed, licked, then began to eat.

Mr. Ong shrugged. He replaced the mechanism. "Let well enough alone" had always been his motto. The garbage disposal unit clicked one last time, then went silent as the last of the garbage emerged in the form of something resembling a Necco wafer, or a poker chip. Mr. Ong took a can of cold beer from the ice-box and went upstairs to watch Charlie Chan on the Late, Late Movie.

* * * *

Jack Girard, the manager of the lumber yard, was agreeable though puzzled. He leaned out of the car window and said to the watchman, "The four of us are going up to the sawdust-burner for a while. Tib—in case muh wife calls nasks."

The judge asked, "How come they *burn* the sawdust, Jack, instead of making a lot of whatchacallits?"

Girard shrugged. "Company Policy is Burn It So that's what we do. We burn it."

The judge's forehead, ridged and bumpy with thought, suddenly cleared.

"'By-Products!' That's what they call it, the stuff you can make from sawdust. How come your company don't convert all this good sawdust into By-Products, huh, Girard?"

"Such as what?" The doctor took over the task of answering from the foreman who—faced with the fearful thought of questioning Company Policy—shook his head, aghast.

"Ohhhh…" The judge, trying to recall what he had in mind, rolled the syllable *and* his eyes…stuff with names like Butyn Mephlutyn, or Bophane Hyperstannis, or *Something* like that…"

The yellow glare of a single lamp mingled with the red glare of the tall burner itself. Girard hopped out and held the door open for the others. "I still don't know what you intend to try and prove," Doc Damon complained, as he bent his head and slid out. "I'm not sure, myself," the judge admitted. "Okay, Joe, here we are—" The dishwasher (his Social Security card listed his name as Joe Jones), humming tunelessly to himself, got out and looked around. Girard strolled over to the burner. He examined a piece of piping on the side and frowned.

"What's *this*?" he asked.

Doc Damon said, indifferently, that it was part of the sawdust-burner.

The manager said the hell it *was*. "Elmer!" he called. "Hey, Elmer?"

Over their heads a voice called out cheerfully. "Lololo!" Their eyes swung up to see the short figure in overalls coming down the rungs set in the side of the cylinder. In a moment he was on the ground. "I just fix the wagmal," he said. "Takes much kreelth—much kreelth."

The dishwasher stepped forward. He said, "Lololo." He and Elmer exchanged wide smiles, spoke together rapidly. Then Girard tapped the piping.

"Who put this on here, Elmer?"

"I."

"*You*? Well, how *come*?"

"Tal-a-wax-na. Of course, not *best* kind tal-a-wax-na, but—" he shrugged. "It be okay for long enough."

Girard gaped. The doctor said, "Oh, here we go again. Look, now, Jack: the machine still burns sawdust, don't it? So what do you care if old Elmer sticks a hootenanny on it? You'll be as bad as old Judge Peltz here if you keep on reading the *Reader's Digest* and all."

Joe Jones, the dishwasher, walked around the base of the burner. Reappearing, he felt the pipe, nodded in a satisfied sort of way.

A sudden thought struck Elmer. "Klommerkaw?" he asked. "You get klommerkaw ready?"

Joe nodded, held up the shopping bag he had brought with him from the kitchen of Ong's Eats. He reached in his other hand, brought it out filled with little parti-colored disks.

"Some new kind of Necco wafers?" hazarded Doc Damon. "Poker chips to while away the hours? Nope—no cards... Well, whadda ya know?" His voice faded into a surprised silence as the dishwasher broke one in half, gave part to Elmer. They put the halves in their mouths, chewed ruminatively, swallowed.

"Very good klommerkaw," said Elmer. "Plenty, too."

"Now, look-a-here," Girard protested, "I'm responsabull to thuh owners for all this here e-quipment, and I gotta know what is that pipe *for*?"

Joe Jones looked at him. "Kreelth," he said. There was just a slight touch of reproach in his voice. "Do not be un-kreelth." He put his hand on the piping and directed his next remark to Elmer. "Wagmal fix? Estanrel?"

Elmer said, "Wagmal just now fix good."

Jones gave the piping a light twist—a gentle tug, really—his hand moved so quickly, so oddly. "Estanrel," he said.

Girard said, "*Uh*."

The side of the sawdust-burner opened where no opening had been.

"Obbertaw," said Elmer, firmly, holding back. Joe Jones went inside. So did Elmer. For a moment Jones' face looked at them. He smiled.

"Cupra," he said. "Cupra."

"But not cupra for all the time." Elmer explained. "Only gren-a-mun-dun. We come back. Have a kreelth, you see we come back some time to nice town, nice people, nice sawdust."

And the opening closed. The red glare of the burning sawdust turned yellow. The whoofing noise of the draft turned shrill. A sudden gust of cool wind came from the bay. And then, with a subdued, polite sort of swish, the sawdust burner separated itself from the ground and went up...

* * * *

They had a rather bad first five minutes of it. Finally, with the help of the *spiritus frumenti* in Doctor Damon's bag, the three men began slowly to recover.

"The way *I* see it"—Doc Damon was the first to say anything besides "Jesus", and "Gimme that bottle"—"the way *I* see it: those two fellas must've been sort of ship-wrecked here. Probably way, *way* back in the woods there's a twisted mass of metal somebody will come across one of these days."

The judge said, "Ohboyohboyohboy."

Girard said, "Gimme that bottle."

"So they did what any experienced mariner would do—they improvised—fixed up what you might call a jury-rigged vessel... At least, Elmer did. Guess he was the Chief Engineer. Maybe Joe Jones was the purser or supercargo."

"All *I* have to say," the judge announced firmly, "is that it never happened and if either of you say it *did* I'll do my damndest to see to it that you get indicted, prosecuted, convicted, and *severely* sentenced, for barratry, simony, unlawful usurpation...and anything else I can get away with," he concluded.

"How'm I gunna explain why were a sawdust-burner short?" Girard moaned.

"Condemned as a health menace," Doc Damon said, crisply. "No, no, Alfred. I won't say a word. But sooner or later everyone will know. They'll be *back*. Don't you *know* that? They'll be back for some more nice sawdust, because it looks like they have a way to get a By-Product out of sawdust to beat all By-Products. That Butyn Merphlutyn, or Bophane Hyperstannis, must be powerful stuff, *yes-sir*."

Judge Peltz asked, "And in the meantime we just *wait*? Isn't there something we can *do*, now that we know?"

Doc Damon said, "Well... If you hear of any other happy morons with neologistic tendencies, we might pay them a visit. You never know... And until then, and meantime: have kreelth."

* * * *

Sometimes at night, when the fog makes the slates of the sidewalk wet and glistening, or even when the cold wind blows up and clears the sky and shows the burning white stars, at such times the place isn't a town, it's a city—though a small one—it's a *port* city, and the air smells of distant places.

I DID NOT HEAR YOU, SIR

Originally published in *The Magazine of Fantasy & Science Fiction*, February 1958.

Bloodgood Bixbee knew nothing about art, but he knew what he didn't like: What he didn't like, he said—loudly and with much profane redundancy—was Bein' Played For A Sucker...See?

Milo Anderson saw, all right; he knew he should never have sold Bixbee the unauthenticated Wilson Peale, anymore than he should have collected in advance the five percent of the contract which he could never negotiate. But there were so few people left in the capital whom he could still expect to swindle...and he needed the money. He had counted too much on Bixbee's not being able to admit participation in an illegal deal, and it certainly wasn't the moral aspect of not telling the rich lumberman about the cloud on the picture's title which worried him. In fact, nothing about Bixbee had worried him at the time—for who, back in Qualliupp, Washington, would know a Wilson Peale from a citron peel?—all that concerned him had been getting the check to the bank in time. And then to the phone...

Checks, checks, telephones, telephones, and...

Damn them all, with their greedy open hands and yapping mouths.

> Big crooks have littler crooks to bite 'um
> And so on down, ad infinitum.

Wasn't Bloodgood Bixbee a crook, stealing lumber rights and ravishing the forests with a ruthless hand? Sure he was. And then following the classic pattern of trying to set himself up as a man of culture, with Genuine Oil Paintings on his walls. How the *Hell* did he find out, anyway? Was it possible that even Qualliupp had in it someone like Edmond Hart Ransome, from whom Milo had gotten the picture? No, impossible. The whole State of Washington was too new to interest old E.H.R., who seldom concerned himself with anything later than the end of the 1700's.

Anderson ran over in his mind the list of those with whom he had done business. Some one of them—there had to be at least *one*—would be in a mood to help him now, to advance money against future cooperation.

He dialed an unlisted number, tried to swallow. A man's voice, very quiet and cautious: "Yes?"

"Ovlomov?" He must not seem too—

"Who is this?" the voice inquired. A man with whom Mr. Ovlomov had done business? Didn't he know that Mr. Ovlomov had returned only that day to his homeland? He should follow the newspapers—No, no—he, the one speaking, was not interested in Ovlomov's contacts. Nor would it be of any use to call again: the number was being discontinued: Ovlomov was indiscreet.

So that way—the way of being a tenth-rate spy pretending to be a third-rate one—was out, and he was no closer to being clear of his snarl of checks and phone calls: people he was blackmailing (but only able to get small sums from), people who were blackmailing *him* (and getting large sums). For a while he had had an easy stretch, living at old Ransome's place.

The lease was up in a few days—another problem.

It wasn't as if the painting wasn't his; Ransome had left it to him, it was clear enough in his will. That was the devilish part of it—before simply stating "and all the rest of my property now located in my apartment," the old man had "left" him, had specifically named, every single article Milo had stolen from him. He had *known*. "And this bequest I make for a reason well known to my secretary, the said Milo Anderson." Rubbing it in. *Always* rubbing it in. "*Fast horses and slow women, eh, Mr. Anderson?*" That sort of thing.

Perhaps it would have been better not to have meddled with the old man's medicine bottles—but it was *so* easy—and so soon after the doctor had called; no trouble about a death certificate... *All the rest of my property...for a reason well known to the said Milo Anderson.*

But little enough property was left in the apartment by now.

By now everything was coming all at once. Bloodgood Bixbee wanting his money back and raving raw head and bloody bones if he didn't get it. Big Patsy the bookmaker wanting the markers to be made good, wanting it right away, not threatening but promising. And Mrs. Pritchard, her voice like half-melted margarine: "Carried you on the books a long time, Milo—been good to you—we all've been good to you. Now we have to get the money because the Syndicate goes over the books tomorrow, and you know what *that* means, Milo."

And he knew, oh, he *knew* all right. Even before the phone rang and the voice—an ordinary coarse unlettered unviolent sort of voice, saying its say as the cabbie might ask Where To or the laundryman announce the bill—Anderson: Get it ready, get the money ready, we'll pick it up (by now the voice a bit bored with so many routine calls) as soon after midnight as we get around there...

Milo Anderson's eye ran hopelessly around the apartment. Over the mantelpiece (or over where the marble had been before he'd sold it) was the faded place where the alleged Wilson Peale had hung before going to take its place over the silent hi-fi set in the Bloodgood Bixbee place in Qualliupp (who'd bother with hi-fi when the TV offered such quality fare?). The cabinet of old coins had stood over there—the Pine Tree shillings, the "York" pieces, halfreales, the dismes: all sold by now, and sold well, but the money long ago (it seemed long ago) spent... Big Patsy, Mrs. Pritchard, and all the others... Edward Hart Ransome's place had been stuffed with the treasures of the late 1700's, but almost everything had been sold or pawned by now except for a few pieces of essential furniture. These had been already priced and would bring only a fraction of what was needed.

Milo Anderson was not more fearful than most men, perhaps he was a degree less fearful. But there were too many things piling up just now. Everybody was putting the screws on him and there was nobody he could squeeze in turn—not *now*—not *tonight*... Like a hungry man who opens and reopens icebox and pantry: there must be *some* food left, only let me look once more: Milo roamed the shadowy apartment, looking and peering and hoping and fearing, something to sell, something overlooked, *something*...

With sweat cold on his back and with kneecaps articulating far from firmly, he pawed among the discards the dealers had left. Bellows, woodcarders, trivets ("Three for a quarter on the Boston Post Road," the dealer said.), apple-corers and nutmeg graters, new model spinning wheels...and *this* damned thing. Whatever *it* was. The dealer had simply laughed. Milo was about to kick it. He groaned, sighed heavily, listlessly began to examine it.

Basic design was a cabinet, smallish box, done—he peered closer—in curly cherrywood, a favorite wood of the period. It stood on four legs and on *one* side was a little wheel and on the *other* side, just sticking out, was a curved copper or brass...funnel, was it? He twisted the metal horn, it moved under pressure. He turned the wheel. Nothing happened, and this was, of course, wrong: for no Colonial craftsman would have spent time making a device which didn't *do* anything. He spun the wheel again, and a bell tinkled inside.

Well, yes—a box had to have an inside. Why hadn't he looked inside? People (he pushed a stubborn peg) were always hiding money inside of... There. The panel slid open easily enough. The bell tinkled again, a tiny silver bell on a silver loop in an upper corner. A small black horn (calf? bison?) hung on a thong. Copper wires led from the small end of the horn, and parchment, like a tiny drumhead, covered the wide end. Wedged firmly behind a glass panel were two glass jars lined with metal foil.

The thing to do was to get a hammer and—the bell rang a third time. Death, he thought, was waiting, and here *he* was, playing with an antique toy. He seized the horn, was about to tear it loose, then he put it to his ear instead. At once he dropped it and jumped.

"Your conversant, Sir?" That was what the horn had said in his ear. Or was it, "You're conversant…?" What was the apparatus supposed to be, a music box with vox humana, a primitive phonograph, a… No, if it resembled any piece of equipment he was familiar with, it was the telephone. Without stopping to rationalize his action in turning eagerly to anything which could divert him from his trouble, he thought, Let's see: Buffalo horn to ear, speak into…mm…copper tube (funnel, trumpet) on outside. Feeling a bit foolish, he said—what else *could* he say but: "Hello?"

The odd voice in his ear repeated what it had said before. Milo asked, "Conversant with *what?"*

"With *whom,* Sir," the voice corrected him; and then, as he remained baffled and silent: "I do not hear you, Sir. Pray consult the compendium, Sir, for the cypher of the conversant desired… Servant, Sir."

"Hello? Hello? Hey!" He even whistled shrilly, but there was no reply.

Putting the horn down he began pressing and poking around the box, and dislodged something from a narrow space under the shelf where the odd jars were. It was a small thin leather-bound book. He opened it. Obviously laid paper, linen-rag, age-yellowed and "foxed": brown-flecked… names, numbers…turn to the front…

THE COMPENDIUM OF THE NAMES, RESIDENCES, & CYPHERS OF THE HONORABLE & WORTHY PATRONS OF THE MAG- NETICKAL INTELLIGENCE ENGINE.

Assuming—nd a crazy-mad assumption it was, but here the thing stood in front of him—assuming that the telephone, or some long-forgotten precursor of it, *had* been invented in those days… But how could it still be working? Or was this some quirk of a few other off-beat antiquarians like old Ransome, to have their own odd-ball Bell System? Or was he simply out of his senses and imagining it all? Oh, well. He turned the page.

> EXORDIUM. *The Artificers of this Device have spared neither Pains nor Oeconomy to obtain the primest Materials and Workmanship, the Cabinetmaking being that of Mr. D. Phyfe, the Leyden-jars and other Magnetick Parts are the Manufactory of Dr. B. Franklin, Mr. P. Revere*

has fabrickated the Copper and Brass, and Mr. Meyer Meyers the Pewter and Silver.

SUBMONITION. The Cypher of each Patron is listed Alphabetick- ally. Spin the Wheel and on perceiving the Tintinnabulation of the Bell, Inform the Engineer of the Cypher of the Conversant desired, caveat. It is absolutely inhibited to tamper with the Leyden-jars.

Still dubious, but certainly curious, so much so that he even forgot his own danger, Anderson looked through the book. Almost automatically his finger stopped at *Washington, Geo., Gent. Planter, Mt. Vernon.* He spun the wheel. The bell tinkled. He put the small horn to his ear.

"Your conversant, Sir?"

This time he was prepared. He cleared his throat and said, "Patriot 1-7-7-0."

"Your servant, Sir." Somewhere away another little bell began to tinkle.

"Say—Engineer?" Milo ventured.

"Servant, Sir."

"Um...what's your name?"

"There are no names, Sir."

Trrrinnggg...trrrinnggg...

"Well, uh, what time are you in—or where are you?"

"There is neither time nor place, Sir. And it is not permitted to hold non-pertinent discourse whilst the engine is in use, Sir."

Trrrinnggg...

Suddenly the parchment crackled and a deep voice boomed from the horn: "Ah heah you, Seh!" Milo swallowed.

"Mr. Washington?" Surely not yet General in 1770.

"Yes, Seh—*and* no thanks to you, Seh! What do you mean by it, you damned horse-leecher? Sellin me these *con* founded artifized denticles—! Why, a wind-broken, bog-spavined *stal*lion couldn't get 'em comftable in his mouth!" The false teeth were heard clacking and grinding. The Patriot's voice rose. "Haven't ett a decent piece of butcher's meat in *days!* Live on syllabub and sugar-tiddy! Plague take your flimsy British crafts—give me honest Colonial works, say I!" The outraged voice rang in Milo's ear, then died away.

Mistaken for a quack dentist! Perhaps the only crime he never had com- mitted. Milo wanted to call back, found he'd forgotten the number—the "cypher," rather—but the place where it had been was blank. He shivered. The engineer's voice responded to his signal. "What is George Washing- ton's cypher?" Milo demanded.

"That intelligence is not available, Sir. Pray consult—"

"But it's no longer in the compendium!"

"Cyphers not in the compendium do not exist… Your servant, Sir."

* * * *

Well, so much for the Father of His Country. Anderson had discovered a hitherto-overlooked cause of the American Revolution, but a lot of good it did him. Once again, he realized his position. There was no one he could turn to—not in the present, anyway. Not knowing what else *to* do, he turned once more to the past. Spun the wheel, opened the little book.

"Your conversant, Sir?"

"Printing house 1-7-7-1…)

Trrrinnggg… The voice was brisk, still retaining after all the years a trace of the Boston twang.

"We must all hang together or we shall surely hang separately… What's your need, neighbor? The colonies should and will unite, but meanwhile the day's work goes on."

"Benjamin Franklin, I presume?"

"That same, my friend. Job-printing? Nice new line of chapbooks for your pleasure and instruction? Latest number of *Poor Richard's Almanack? Bay Psalm Book?* Biblical Concordance? Hey?"

"No, no…)

The voice dropped a notch, became confidential. "Just on hand by the last vessel to arrive in port, a French novel in three volumes…no? Make you a special price for *Fanny Hill!*"

"Dr. Franklin"—Milo grew anxious—"I need your help. I appreciate— I appeal to you—a Fellow American—" he stumbled.

The voice grew wary, then a trifle amused. "Nay, nay, I'm too old a tomcod to be taken with such bait as that. None of your Tory tricks. If you're working for Sir William Johnson, now, tell him—"

"But—"

"Tell him I'm a loyal subject of the King until he proves otherwise. I do but propose a continental union against French Lewis, the Dons, and the savage Enjians—though if Providence doesn't take most of these off our hands by rum and pox—"

Milo cried, "My life's in terrible danger!"

"Sell you a nice ephemeris—you can cast your horoscope and thus see the hazards you must needs discountenance… Stove? Sell you a Franklin st—"

* * * *

Of course, the cypher had vanished from the book and from his memory. It was plain he was allowed but one call to each name. And time was running short: it grew close to midnight and he could expect to hear from the Syndicate about the money he owed Mrs. Pritchard—if Bloodgood Bixbee and his friends, or Big Patsy and *his* friends didn't arrive first.

Well, no help from the Continentals: Try the Tories. Try the line he'd first used to approach Ovlomov: spin the wheel and hear the bell ring...
"Sir?"

"Slaughter 1-7-7-7...Hello?"

"I hear you, Sir." Cold, this voice, and smooth as an adder's skin.

"Sir Henry Hamilton? I'm a loyal subject of the King and I have information to sell...) He held his face close to the brazen mouthpiece. By now he had no slightest doubt but that it was all real: he would connive, he would—

"Oh, demn the loyal subjects of the King. I buy no information; I buy *hair,* Sir! *That's* how I make rebels into loyal subjects of the King, Sir! I buy their sculps! Have you some'at to sell, fellow? I pay top prices to encourage the trade—for the sculps of male Yenkees, two-pun-ten—female Yenkees, two-pun-even—infant Yenkees and disaffected Injians, ten shillin."

"Help me—help me get through to where you are—Sir Henry—I'll do—"

The Tory agent's voice grew cautionary. "Though, mind," he said; "mind they be well-cured, for if there's one thing I can*not* abide, d'ye hear, Sir," he said with fastidious distaste, "it's a mouldy stinking sculp. *Fah!"*

"You can find out how, some way, there must be a way I can come over—"

The voice grew fainter. "Hair; not the whole head: just the *haiiirrr...*)

It died away altogether and while Milo watched the name faded from the page.

* * * *

One after the other he called them up. And one after the other, though they did not know who he really was, they knew at once that he was a rogue and a scoundrel. He could not make them understand, could not find out how to get from his time and place to theirs. Voices traveled it, why not bodies? Desperately he riffled the pages of his compendium. Another name leaped at him. *This* man would not repulse him. He spun the wheel.

"Your conversant, Sir?"

"Tammany 1-7-8-9. And hurry!"

"...Servant, Sir."

Trrrinnggg...

A babble of voices...laughter...the sound of a fiddler...

Milo's voice trembled. "Colonel Aaron Burr?"

The colonel's voice was soft as cream. "That same, Sir." Lay the cards on the table. "Colonel Burr, I'm a thief, a swindler, a blackmailer, and a traitor."

The colonel chuckled. "Ecawd, but withal an honest knave... Nay, babe, nay, my poppet, don't jump so when I—"

"I need your help. I need it now!"

"Ah, not tonight, me lad. Burr might sell his soul for gold, but he'd not move outside the door even to *save* his soul when a pretty wench is on his knee—Why so flushed, my sweet tapstress? Bodice tight? Let me loose it... Nay, don't slap my fingers. You know you love me...)

Was there a single name left in the book? (Only a few minutes to midnight.) Yes. One.

"Your conversant, Sir?" Milo licked dry lips. "West Point 1-7-8-0." This time no silver bell tinkled. Slowly and with abrupt bursts, as if blown by gusts of wind, he heard the sound of a ruffle of drums... A puff of yellow choking sulfurous smoke billowed from the coppery horn. Milo ducked his head.

"I hear you, Sir." The voice was infinitely weary, infinitely bitter.

Milo croaked, "General Benedict Arnold?" And he told the whole story. There was a silence, but he sensed the listener was still there. And finally—

"I *can* help you. Matter *can* pass the barrier of time and place. For the sake of my wounded leg at Saratoga, shattered and bloodied in the service of my native land, I will do my native land this last service." Milo babbled thanks. The bitter, weary voice spoke on. "For my treasons I received money, commissions for myself and sons, a pension for my wife. Dust, all dust and ashes... I ask in my will that I be buried in my Continental uniform—"

"But *me,* you said you'd help *me*—" And the clock hands almost—

"I shall do for you what I should have done for myself. My old trade, in Hartford-town, ere I turned to war, I learned—But it's too late now. I should have done it that night at West Point, before I wrote to poor Andre—" One of the Leyden jars shattered with a sharp crack, splitting the glass panel. He reeled from a blast of heat. Amid the dust and shards he saw a small round box.

"No!" he cried, pulling back. The clock began softly to strike the hour. An automobile drove up below, heavy feet tramped the hallway, stopped outside his door.

Without further hesitation he opened the box, thrust something into his mouth. He trembled, fell forward, grasping the wheel. The bell tinkled once. The pillbox lay to one side. "Ben dT Arnold, Hartford," the label said. "Licensed Apotheckary."

Fists beat at the door, feet kicked it, rough voices called out.

The bell tinkled once more in the cabinet. "Your conversant, Sir?" a voice asked faintly. It repeated the question.

"I do not hear you, Sir," it said, at length.

"I do not hear you...)

FAIR TRADE

Originally published in *The Magazine of Fantasy & Science Fiction*, July 1960.

Could it be they want to use it for a bird-cage, maybe?—But I better start at the beginning.

* * * *

We were cut off from civilization.

Sounds grim, doesn't it? Well, it wasn't—and isn't. Happens every winter, time after time. There are some deep snows in northern Idaho, and it seems like the deepest ones pick the only highway around here to settle on. We're just as pleased—in fact, most of us prefer it. Those that don't tend to move away.

Of course, it's kind of big for a bird-cage, but maybe they got big birds there.

Santiago, Idaho, was named back in the summer of '98. Some wanted to call it McKinley and others held out for Bryan, but the news that Commodore Schley and Admiral Sampson had sunk the Spanish fleet down in Cuba settled *that* question. Our town isn't a big place no matter how you figure it. From Etienne (Frenchy) Tremblay's gas station to Dora Moriarity's café isn't no more than half a mile. Of course it spreads out a bit on both sides, but no matter how you count the population it still don't add up to much over five hundred people.

Of all the folks in Santiago who welcome the big snows and the chance we have to be all by ourselves and really socialize, I guess Omar Kennicott is the most welcoming. Omar and me always got along good together. For one thing I figure every man's got the right to go his own way and I never try to drench a man with my personal opinion the way you'd drench a sheep for worms.

He *is* stubborn and I'll be the first to admit that, but that's his affair. So what if he's just about the only citizen in Santiago that doesn't have indoor plumbing? Folks just have to take that into account if they want to go visit with him. And if he never gets a haircut, all I have to say is, the day compulsory haircuts go into effect I'm heading up the Snake River and leaving no forwarding address.

Live and let live, is my motto.

One reason why Omar likes it when the snow settles deep in the Pass and the plows give up forty miles below in the foothills, one reason is that there are no strangers coming through to yell and hoot at him, "Buffalo Bill!" or "General Custer!" or such like that. Another reason is that he builds up a real big old blaze in both of his stoves up there at his place, and he puts his equipment together and he runs off some of the sweetest, smoothest moonshine a man has ever drunk.

But only when he can be *sure*, you understand, that nobody is sneaking up Route 37 from the Internal Revenue Office in Boise.

Which goes to explain why just about everybody in town, leave alone me, was so surprised when he turned up at the Firehouse Supper and Dance with those two fellows that nobody'd ever seen before.

Or maybe for a small chicken-coop—but do they have chickens? I tell you, it beats me...

Not that everybody didn't know exactly what affair was going on in the Grange Hall, but anyway, there was a big banner hanging up reading SANTIAGO VOLUNTEER F. D. BENEFIT BALL. Right under it was that placard with the blue eagle, cog in one claw and arrows in the other (We Do Our Part), that Frenchy Tremblay tacks up at every event. Folks got tired arguing with him long ago. He was naturalized in '33 and I guess that took its effect on him, and besides, *he* was Fire Chief this year.

The band was tuning up, the coffee was making, the deer meat you could smell it cooking away off, and the soup with dumplings, and in came Omar Kennicott and these two fellows. Each one carrying a gunnysack with what everybody knew right away was a jug in it.

As nothing and no one had been up from the outside in days and days, it had to stand to reason that these fellows must of been with Omar all this time. But nobody had ever seen him associating with one stranger, not to speak of two.

"Hi, there, Charley," he says to me. And I says to him, "Hi, there, Omar." And I kind of smiled at the two fellows and then at him, just to let him know I was agreeable to be introduced if he was and they were, but that I wasn't going to press the point. But not everybody has learned tact and politeness, and there was more than one I could mention, and not a million miles away either, that gawped and rubbernecked.

Frenchy Tremblay, I'm not speaking of *him*, now, he's got these easily excitable ways, he hustled up and said hello and then he asked, "Who your friends, Omar?" And beamed and smiled so you could hardly take offense, not even if your name was Omar Kennicott and a notorious hardnose.

"Oh, hello, Eighteen," he said, calling the Chief by his French name like he always does. "These two fellows come over to my place this morning and we been enjoying ourselves all day so much I figured we'd just come on over here and spread the fun around. I guess their car must of broke down. I loaned'm some clothes, as a matter of fact, they was in their underwear. Excuse me, ladies. I just state the facts. Near's I can make out, their names are Ivan and Nelson. I think they must be Swedes or Dutchmen or something. Can't talk English. Try'm on French."

This Ivan and Nelson were nice enough looking fellows and they had big long mustaches that reminded me of my Uncle Julius, who was one of the miners got blowed up by that Harry Orchard fellow before he was convicted and got religion. Tremblay tried out in his language, and Gleb Peterkov tried out in his, and Leo Etchevarria tried in both Spanish and Basque. But nobody got through. Ivan and Nelson just smiled and made funny motions with their hands.

Then Lex Muller, who more or less *is* the American Legion in Santiago, began to make a long face and scratch his head. "Their car broke down, Omar?" he asked. "Now, how could their *car* break down and they get to your place by this morning?—when *you* know and *I* know that no car has been within walking distance of here in a week?"

Omar said, maybe they come up by pogo-stick. But Lex kept right on going. "And how come they were in their underwear, Omar? Now, *you* and *I* know that they'd of frozen to death if they went more than a mile or two in this weather in their underwear. Now, it seems to me—"

But nobody was really interested in how it seemed to him, and the band broke into music just then and everybody began dancing. Ivan and Nelson didn't, but by the way they gathered around and looked on, they surely enjoyed it. In fact, after the first dance was over, they put on a little dance of their own for us. Never seen anything like it in my life, and I guess nobody else did, either. Funny? I want to tell you—had us in stitches, all right.

All but Lex Muller. He'd taken a kind of dislike to those two. Ivan and Nelson, somehow. When they got done he said, loud and grumpy. "That's a Russian-type dance, in my opinion, if ever I saw one."

Gleb Peterkov said, "That's because you never saw one."

And Dora Moriarity said, "Shame on you, picking on those poor fellows that are so far from their homes and can't even speak the language." And lots of others said, "Yeah, Lex, get off their backs."

Omar kind of muttered, but he lit on the gunnysacks and his face brightened and he began taking the jugs out and some of the men gathered around to watch. Expectant, you might say, and sort of swallowing. Omar had really thumped those corks in hard and there wasn't enough to give his fingers a grip, so he pulled a jackknife out.

Before he could more than get the blade half-open, one of the strangers, Ivan I think it was, he was a little bit shorter—he sort of stepped in front of Omar and said something cheerful in his own language. He had a thing in his own hand, it looked like a nail file, kind of. He made three swoops with it and it seemed like that nail-file (or whatever it was) just went *through* the necks of those jugs without stopping or clicking or anything. He handed Omar three chunks of bottle-necks with corks stuck in them, cut off just as smooth and clean and level as could be.

"*Hot damn*!" says Fire Chief Tremblay. "You *see* that? Do it again—"

"Oh, no," Omar protested, kind of huddling over the glassware. "Jugs ain't that easily come by!" He looked kind of sour for a minute. Then he remembered he was the host of these two fellows and he said, "Much obliged to you boys. Somebody got some cups?"

And then Lex Muller did a very funny thing. He took off his wrist-watch and held it out to Ivan and with his other hand he pointed to the thing like a nail-file. Ivan caught on right away and they swapped then and there. Well, wouldn't you know it, Tremblay said, "Me, I want one too," and he swapped *his* watch. And in another minute lots of men were saying, "Hey, I bet you them things're valuable," and took off their watches to swap. But Ivan and Nelson just laughed and patted their pockets as if to say, no more: sorry. So a couple of fellows offered to buy them but neither Lex nor Frenchy would sell.

This all left us kind of surprised, so we had a drink in silence when the cups came. Almost as if his mind was on something else, Frenchy Tremblay cut the handle off his cup. He looked at it lying there and he gave a whoop and he yelled, "Look, everybody, come look at this device which I have just traded off the *voyageur*! Ladies, gentlemens, come look!"

Turned out it could cut through wood, cloth, steel—anything.

Place was in an uproar.

I guess either Nelson wasn't used to Omar's brand of moonshine, or else he'd soaked up a lot of it real quick, because before anybody knew it he'd give out a couple of whoops of his own, and tore off his clothes. I mean he tore off Omar's clothes that he'd borrowed. His own, were on underneath. In a way I guess they did look like underwear, long sleeves and leggings, but you never saw underwear made from any material like that was—whatever that was—nor in such pretty designs.

First Nelson commenced jumping up and down and hollering a song. I guess it was a song. Then he jumped up and began turning tumblesaults and doing contortion tricks. At first everybody applauded and yelled him on. Then, all of a sudden, there wasn't a sound out of us because it had just hit us that it had been quite a few minutes since Nelson jumped, up in the air, and he hadn't come down yet...!

If they want it for a souvenir, it's a doggone funny one, is all I got to say.

The first one to speak was Dora Moriarity. "That's what drink will do to you," she said. And then another lady began to scream—"Eee-eee-eee!" and we all turned around and it was Miss Lemack.

Miss Lemack had only been in Santiago a few years. She was an artist-lady and some of the young fellows got real excited when she asked them to pose, but after it turned out that she made them keep their clothes on and you could hardly recognize yourself anyhow in her pictures, the excitement died down. She minded her own business and she ate these health-foods by mail from Los Angeles.

"I see it all now!" she yelled. "They've come at last! We'll have to notify the Federal Government!"

Nobody was used to paying much attention to Miss Lemack anyway, and these last words sure as Hell didn't meet with no enthusiastic reception. Lots of people in town have no great love for the Federal Government. Omar Kennicott was afraid they would smash his little still up. Brigham Kimball had never forgive them for putting his grandpa in jail for having three wives at once. Leo Etchevarria said, "Low tariff on wool" like they were dirty words—which I guess they are, to a sheepman. Tim Newberg and a couple other kids waiting to be drafted—well, not to enumerate, but as I say, nobody was smiling when I asked her. "Just what do you mean, Miss Lemack, that we have to notify the Federal Government because you see it all, that they've come at last? You don't mean these two fellows have come from Washington?"

"No, no: from Outer Space," she yells. "The clothes they wear—the disintegrator implements—the anti-gravity techniques—What more evidence do you want? I'll let *them* testify!" And she pulled out a big pad and a sharp pencil and she called Ivan over. Some of us gathered around and the rest (most of the people) just stayed looking at Nelson eight feet off the ground with his head where his head had no business being located.

"Look!" says Miss Lemack, drawing quickly—swish, swish, swish—"Look. Look." Well, I don't understand nothing about such things myself, but it seems she drew some kind of map of the Solar System and Ivan picked out the Earth right away. She gave him the pencil and he drew some kind of map of his own and it seems that—according to him—he and his partner come from somewhere in the bottom-most dribble of the Milky Way.

An antique, maybe? Could that be it? An antique? I just don't know...

Then he turned over a clean sheet of paper and began to draw some more. A big circle. No, it was a globe. Sort of cut away so's you could see the insides. Machinery. Two people, real iddy-biddy but you could see it was him and Nelson, what I mean, *clear?* Then he starts making a smooth sort of noise. The engines. Then he goes *bloong—bloong*. Engine trouble. Wobbly motions with his hand. Ker-*plunk*! The spaceship, I guess you can call it, makes a crash-landing in the snow not far from the outskirts of Santiago, Idaho. And the charming little Omar Kennicott residence.

"So *that's* where they come from," says Omar. "I thought they was Dutchmen. Or Swedes."

But Ivan isn't finished yet. He draws another spaceship. A great big one. Lots of people inside of it. He calls them up or sends them a radio message, something like that. They get the message. And (here he shows us with the watch) they'll be along to pick the two of'm up in a couple of hours.

"Well, I don't believe a word of it," says Dora Moriarity. "Stands to reason they couldn't mean what you think they mean. *My*, opinion, they're advertising one of them new foreign moving pictures, is what *I* think."

Some said one thing and some said another, but Lex Muller, he agreed with Miss Lemack a hundred percent. "Only we *can't* notify the Federal Government. We're cut off here; the phone lines are down like usual, and there isn't even a radio transmitter in the place… And in a few hours they'll be gone."

"Well, gosh. I'll sure miss'm," Omar said. "Even if they did just about ruin three good jugs."

Lex gave a kind of hiss. "We've got to make the most of the time we have," he said. "They may never come this way again in our time," he said. "Why, those, um, disintegrators, they may be mere toys, no more than jack-knives in comparison to what their civilization has invented."

I hated to admit it, but right is right. "Lex, you're right," I said.

"Of course I'm right," he said. "How come they stayed so warm in this freezing weather with those mere tights on? How come this other jay-bird can float in thuh air like that in defiance of the gravitational law? To say nothing of the secret of space travel itself, which you bet those Russkies would never let them escape without divulging."

Well, of course, we don't operate like that in this country, as me and one or two others pointed out to him. He didn't like it, but he put it in his craw when he saw the rest of us wouldn't stand for no rough stuff. Besides which (as Leo Etchevarria pointed out), how'd we know but what they might have some secret weapons stashed away in their pockets—or under their finger-nails, for all we knew?

"I got another plan," Lex said, then. "Primitive as we may be to them, still, we ought to have something they'd like to have. Even if only for a souvenir. The only way we can find out is to show them around. If they seem to like something, we'll *give* it to'm—then, when we get back to their outfit, we can ask something for a trade for whatever they got."

It seemed like a good idea. So as soon as Ivan got Nelson sobered up (and I surer than Hell wish I knew how he *did* that trick!), off we went. No one felt much like dancing anymore, anyhow.

Of course, look at it this way: What good's a Chinese back-scratcher or a kewpie-doll?

Well, we took those boys into one house after the other. We opened up all the stores. We showed them the newest things in hardware, automobiles, John Deere tractors, clothing, phonographs and records—they just like smiled politely. It seemed like they didn't want anything we want. Not a blessed thing.

And then there was this funny noise in the air. Like a million little bells ringing. And Ivan and Nelson perked right up and we all rushed out of doors. There it was, like a great big moon come down overhead, with another but smaller little moon—which I guess was the wrecked spaceship—just sticking to the side, sort of. It settled down behind Omar's cabin. And there was a lot of good-byes and handshaking and so on. A big door opened and sucked the small ship inside. A smaller door opened and a couple of men stood there, wearing them funny clothes, too.

They greeted Ivan and Nelson by name. That wasn't just how they said it, but near enough. And, after some quick, last minute business, off they went. And have never been back. At least, not back to Santiago, Idaho.

Lex Muller's scheme fell through, all right. As for the two nail-files, they stopped working after a few days. Ran out of fuel, I guess, or something.

The thing they gave Omar, though, *that's* still working. "Still" is a pretty good word for it, too. It's about as big as a beer-barrel. Omar opens one end and puts in corn, sugar, yeast—whatever he feels like; fruit, maybe—and closes it up again. Right out of th' other end, in no time at all, comes the best drinking liquor that has ever been enjoyed on the face of this backward old planet.

If you ask me, Omar has the best of that particular trade. He's made so much money he's put in indoor plumbing. But what gets me is, what on Earth—or anywhere else—did those fellows Ivan and Nelson want with what they took in trade? With the only single item they saw in town that they wanted.

It's not new. It sags to one side and it's real weather-beaten. And just about the *only* connection it's got with space travel is that little old crescent moon carved in the door.

For a curio-cabinet? For a specimen of native wood-craft? To keep potted plants in? Oh, I tell you, I've thought and I've thought and I've thought, and it's just driving me crazy.

FAED-OUT

Originally published in *The Magazine of Fantasy
& Science Fiction*, October 1963.

In an old brown house on Cheromoya in the foothills of the canyon-cut range which parts The Valley from L.A.—in short, in Hollywood—in between a Chiropractic College which had no charter and the premises of an unfrocked rabbi who now practiced as a marriage counselor, lived Philip Farnel, world-famed star of stage and screen. P. Farnel was a lovable and G-d fearing little man who was so far from chicanery in any form that he even mailed back to the General Telephone System the occasional dimes in extra change which came his way in coin-boxes. Nature, however, had endowed him with a ratty and evil face surmounted by a bulging skull sparsely adorned with hair and divided by a mouthful of irregular and jutting teeth. On the strength of the ancient and time-tested axiom, If Life Hands You A Lemon, Make Lemonade, Phil had sought and obtained work as a moving picture and theatrical villain.

Success on the peripatetic stage had been moderate and full of interest, but when in 1925, Philip Farnel first saw Hollywood, when he observed the great studios looming like cathedrals amid the orange-groves, when he looked upon the palaces of the great stars gleaming alabaster and graced with cypresses, roses, and bougainvillea, as the villas and latifundia of ancient Rome—seeing the great people themselves riding by like the wind in their great custom-made cars, red, white, mauve, cerise, pearl gray and shocking pink—he said a farewell to the footlights and the one-night stands and even the occasional parts in New York successes. He turned up at the office of a reputable agent with his stills and his scrap-book, and within a week he was playing a disreputable sidekick to Noah Beery in a motion picture involving saloons, stagecoaches, and kidnapped school-teachers.

He never had more than a secondary role in a Grade A picture, but he often was the lead scoundrel in B films—dishonest guardians, chain gang captains, corrupt politicians, the boss of the turpentine camp, the brains of the bank robbers. Between 1925 and 1950 Philip Farnel was employed in an average of three pictures a year. He was sober, diligent, amiable, dependable, and he had many friends and no enemies; he knew the great and mingled with them without being one of them, and it did not at any time occur to him to snub or be snide to cameramen or stage-carpenters or wardrobe people or yes-men or writers or script-girls. The wheel turned, those who were low in '25, in '35 were often high (and vice versa). Secure in his many friendships and his own well-deployed if modest talents, Farnel was always in work. In 1950 the wheel made its last turn for him—the television was abroad in the land, the handwriting was on the wall, the doom of the B pictures was sealed; in neither spectacles nor horror films was there a place for him.

He accepted the situation calmly and without railing. Farnel was frugal, though never niggardly. He had saved, he had invested, bought and sold. He continued, in his retirement, to do so. He now owned the old brown house on Cheromoya, which was subdivided into apartments; as well as the building occupied by the Chiropractic College and the premises of formerly Reverend Doctor Bernardson, the marriage counselor. He collected stamps and coins and science-fiction magazines and dealt commercially in all three as well, in a small but profitable way. He had thus enough money for his needs and pleasures and was in some hopes of obtaining more through the reruns of old films in which he had appeared and which were now appearing on TV, although at too late an hour for Philip Farnel to care to watch.

One beautiful June day when the smog had lifted and it was possible from the hills to see as far as Ingelwood or Culver City, Mr. Farnel, who had been shopping in the great supermarket on Hollywood Boulevard and was walking home (his one eccentricity), was hailed by a passing motorist whom he recognized with pleasure as Malcolm Morris, an old-time wardrobe man.

"Wait there for me, Phil, will you?" Morris called. "I'll park and come back." Farnel replied that he would meet Morris in the coffee-shop nearby, and the latter nodded and drove off.

Over coffee and sweet rolls the two old acquaintances chatted for a while, discussing various friends, living and dead, and then their eyes met full on for a second. Morris dropped his gaze to the tabletop and began to draw circles out of a little puddle there. It always gave Farnel a small but definite pleasure to encounter in real life, a cliché out of the movies, and so it was with a certain sober relish that he inquired, "What's on your mind, Mal?"

Mal gave a nervous laugh, hesitated, then said, awkwardly but doggedly, "Couple years ago, Phil, there was an incident in all tire papers of a man turned up alive after everybody, including his whole family and the law enforcement agencies, they had all believed him dead. He was out fishing, this man was out fishing and the boat was found overturned and eventually they turned up this body which was identified as his and buried as his and then, after I forget how many years, he turned up alive in another state and he had run off with this woman who worked for him and they were living as man and wife under an assumed name. And the real body belonged to somebody else and had no connection with the incident. He had faked the overturned boat so he could run away with the other woman without anyone looking for him."

Farnel nodded slowly. "I remember it now. Yes. Didn't the insurance company try to get back the life insurance money they'd paid the legal wife at the time? How did it finally turn out?"

Morris shrugged. "No idea," he said. "I just mentioned it as an example. What I mean is, Phil, do you believe that a similar incident could of been staged here in Hollywood? I mean, it is *possible*, isn't it?"

Philip Farnel considered the question as he sipped his coffee. "Whom did you have in mind?" he asked.

"Ohhh…" Morris hesitated, made some more circles, joined them to form figure-eights, pursed his mouth, and then dropped the dumb-show altogether by lifting his eyes to Farnel's and saying, rapidly and defiantly, "S. Maxwell Pierce."

"No," said Farnel, at once "Absolutely not."

"You don't think so?" There was a disappointed, almost pleading tone in Morris's voice. Then, challengingly, he demanded, "Why not? Why is it so impossible? Tell me that, Phil? I could tell you—"

Farnel cut in. "I don't care what you could tell me, Mal. I'll tell you why not. Sam Pierce didn't disappear on any fishing trip, he dropped dead in his home in Beverly Hills the day before Pearl Harbor. He was pronounced dead of a heart attack by his personal physician who had been attending him for his heart condition and for his ulcers, namely Dr. William Allen Albine, a man of the utmost integrity; that's why not."

Morris wasn't convinced. "He could of been bribed," he said.

"Dr. *Albine*? Are you out of your mind? You know better than that! Why, the man is incorruptable. Listen, Mal—*you* know, and *I* know, that a certain actress got down on her bended knees and offered him $10,000 to perform an illegal operation, and he refused, and she offered him fifteen and twenty and finally $25,000, because she trusted him and was afraid to trust anybody else—"

"I know, I know—"

"—and he not only refused but he talked with her the whole night long and he talked her out of it and she had the baby, the delight of her life, and she blesses the name of Dr. Albine every day of her life So—"

Morris said, "But that was a different situation." Farnel went on to point out that they had both attended the funeral services and had seen S. Maxwell Pierce laid out in his casket and that he, at least, Philip Farnel, had accompanied the body to its cremation. Morris's reply was, "It's possible it was a wax image or something. I don't *care*!" he concluded, with a defiant cry that was almost a shout.

Farnel threw up his hands "The doctor was bribed, the coroner was bribed, the undertaker was bribed, a wax model was made—Mal! For heaven's sake! What's put this extraordinary idea in your mind, the most ridiculous notion I've ever heard, a man of your age—"

Whereupon Malcolm Morris proceeded to tell him that on two successive days in the past week he, M.M., had seen S. Maxwell Pierce and that Pierce had spoken to him. What had he said? was Farnel's utterly skeptical question. Morris, pale, half-ashamed, half-distraught, looked at him squarely, and quoted, in a flat and hollow voice, "*Help. Help. Help. Help, Help.*"

Much puzzled, and not a little troubled at his old acquaintance's extraordinary and stubborn delusion, Philip Farnel resumed his walk home. The day continued beautiful, all the more so for the ever-increasing rarity of such days in and around Los Angeles, and by the time he reached his residence the weight upon his mind was almost lifted. He prepared a roast of beef and put it in the oven, set the temperature low, and then went to his office in the rear of the apartment, intending to deal with the day's commercial correspondence, when, acting upon a sudden impulse, he got into his automobile and drove to Beverly Hills.

At the rear of a spacious estate in that city, attending to the fruit trees espaliered against the stone wall, was a small and wiry man in a faded plaid shirt, baggy trousers, and a filthy felt hat. Philip Farnel approached him. "Doc!" he called. Dr. William Allen Albine turned, squinted, beamed, and advanced to meet him. "Well, well, well—Phil Farnel!" he exclaimed, greeting him heartily. "This *is* a surprise. And a very pleasant one, I hasten to add." The two men shook hands and walked along, chatting of this and that, and took seats in the patio, where an Oriental manservant presently brought them drinks. They toasted one another's health, sipped, and then exchanged a silent look.

After a moment Dr. Albine spoke. "I'm glad you came, Phil," he said. "A great many of my old friends and patients do drop in to see me, from time to time, even though I'm retired, and of course I keep busy—as, I know, do you. But if I'd been asked to name one individual out of all whom I'd be most glad to see today, I'd have named *you*, Phil; I'd have named *you*. And you'll never guess why." He looked at his visitor; and, although Farnel smiled his gratitude at the compliment, nonetheless a shiver passed down his spine.

"You knew the individual whom I'm about to name, Phil," Dr. Albine continued. "And you were his friend, just as I had the privilege of being. To us he was more than a mere figure of glamour, although far be it from me to deny the immense value of what he did in bringing that glamour into many otherwise drab lives—the public. But I mustn't make a speech. Anyway, I know you will receive what I'm going to tell you, respectfully."

He took another swallow of his drink without removing his eyes from the face of the guest, then removed the glass from his lips. "One of the advantages of being retired is that a fellow can catch up on his reading. That's just what I was doing last night, at about ten P.M. I was sitting in my living room with a glass of milk and an apple, and I had some reading matter with me. The lamp was on behind my shoulder, and the rest of the room was in darkness. I had finished looking through *Time Magazine* and after that I started browsing a bit in the current number of the Journal of the A.M.A.—man named Harrow has been doing some remarkable research at John Hopkins into those non-specific microorganisms which so often masquerade as—but I don't want to bore you, you're a layman. I must have dozed off, and I woke up with a start. But—you know how it is, I didn't at first realize that I was dreaming, I thought I was still awake…"

Dr. Albine told Mr. Farnel that he had looked up, in his dream, and saw S. Maxwell Pierce advancing slowly towards him with a perfectly silent tread.

"He had that gloomy expression upon his face which I'd seen there so often," the physician continued, sighing, and shaking his head regretfully. "And I was just going to say to him, 'Oh, come on, now, Sam, you old croaker, cheer up'—when suddenly it hit me: Great Scott! This man is dead! And at that moment he spoke to me."

Farnel said, "Don't tell me what he said, just tell me if I'm right. Okay, Doc?" The doctor, astonished, nodded his head. And Farnel repeated the words, "'*Help. Help. Help. Help. Help*!'" imitating as he best could the flat and hollow sound of them.

The color ebbed from Dr. Albine's face, then slowly it returned. He licked his lips. "My G-d, Phil," he whispered. "How did you know?"

"Because. You're the second person today who's told me the same thing, or almost the same thing. Mal Morris—you remember Mal Morris? A real old-time wardrobe man, used to be with Famous Players, used to be with old Jake Fox, then for years and years he was with C-S—a heavyset man with a ruddy face. One of the first people I got to know when I started work out here." And Farnel recapitulated the circumstances of his meeting with Malcolm Morris on Hollywood Boulevard. Doctor Albine listened, nodding slowly.

"Well, you know, Doc, some outfit has leased the old C-S Studio down on Santa Monica, it's been lying empty for years, and they have some sort of a deal whereby independent TV outfits can sublease parts of it to make their films, and part of the deal is that the people who took it over from C-S supply wardrobe. To the sub-leasers, I mean. Sub-*les*-sors. Anyway, Mal Morris was bringing some items out of storage for the shooting—it was a jungle serial, and he had a bunch of old-time pith helmets and stuff like that. You probably wouldn't remember, but coming from storage along the south end is an L-shaped corridor and Mal says that he noticed as he went down that the lights were flickering in one arm of the L and when he turned the corner coming back they were almost out and that's where—he says—he saw Sam Pierce. Coming towards him. And saying just what I had said. And the next afternoon the same thing happened, only over by where the old dressing-rooms used to be. So tell me, Doc, what do you think it means?"

At first, all that Doctor Albine, who had been physician, friend, and counselor to the great and near-great among the stars during the Golden Age of Hollywood, could do was shake his head. Then he muttered something to the effect of "extraordinary coincidence;" and then he sat silent for a space of time.

Philip Farnel broke the silence. "Doc," he asked, "what did Sam really die of?"

Albine's benign and wrinkled face turned savage behind his gold-rimmed spectacles. "Ill tell you what he died of," he said, almost snarling. "He died of over-work. Worn outworn out at thirty-nine! Isn't that a fine commentary on our so-called Modern Civilization? He died because he was paying alimony to two ex-wives and the only way he could keep up with the payments was to borrow from his agent and the only way he could pay back his agent was to make one picture after another, as fast as he could, with no time out for rest or recreation or leisure or the finer things in life. No wonder he had a heart affliction. No wonder he had an ulcerated stomach. I tell you, Phil, in California, a husband has no rights which an ex-wife is bound to respect, and in my opinion, it makes a mockery of our fine, old Anglo-Saxon legal system."

With these cutting words ringing in his ears, Philip Farnel reflected, not for the first time, upon the unhappy story of Doctor Albine's sole venture into matrimony; and he did not say a single word, but shook his head.

* * * *

Farnel drove back home, pensively, and found that his married sister, Mrs. Edna Carter, had arrived in time to rescue the roast from the oven (where he had completely forgotten about it), and had made sandwiches from it for herself and teen-age daughter, Linda. "You'd forget your head, if it wasn't on your shoulders, Philly," was her greeting to him. He kissed the two women, mumbled an excuse, and sat down to eat, for—truth to tell—the untoward incidents of the day and the walks, as well as the ride through the clear air, had combined to give him an appetite perhaps somewhat keener than usual.

After a while he said, "Edna, you remember Sam Pierce, don't you?"

His sister threw back her head and lifted one hand. "Do I remember!" she cried, rhetorically. "I will never forget him as long as I live! What a loss! What a tragedy! What a handsome man! One of the greatest actors of our day and age."

"Oh, come on, Mother," said Linda, in a scornful tone. "S. Maxwell Pierce was a *ham*—and you know it. He wasn't even an *honest* man, like Uncle Philly."

Mrs. Carter said, "You shut your mouth," and glared venomously at her child. "Just because he doesn't talk with his mouth closed and scratch himself—"

P. Farnel swallowed some roast beef. "Why do you call him a ham, honey?" he inquired. "Have you seen any of his pictures in recent years?"

Linda said that she had. *The Dark Of The Moon* was on the Late, Late Show. "What a bomb," she said. "Not just because he's Pre-Method, as Mommy seems to think I mean. I mean, some of these real old-timey actors, like Frank Sinatra, are a gas. But—S. Maxwell Pierce? Phooey. Strictly from Hamsville."

* * * *

It had been many years since Farnel had laid eyes on, Roger Shennan and he was far from sure that the latter would consent to see him. The ease with which the appointment was made, and the fact that it was set for the following morning, surprised him. Even more of a surprise, and a sad one, was the inactivity he saw on all sides as he entered the offices of Cahan-Sherman Productions in the so-called New Studio in Culver City. He remembered when both the newer and the older C-S studios were hives of industry, and although he had accepted that things were not with the silver screen as they once were, still, it was a surprise.

The second surprise was what the passing years had done to Rog Sherman. The Young Lion of Hollywood, he had been called, once upon a time. The account of how he had wrested control of the studio from Sam Cahan in the days when the latter was still holding back cautiously from total conversion to sound, flying his private biplane across the country and interviewing Mrs. Yetta Meredith—widow of Isidore Meredith, co-founder of the studio—and then immediately flying his biplane back again with her proxy in his pocket: this is the stuff from which legend is made.

But time had wrought many changes in the one-time Young Lion of Hollywood, and he now looked like a very old lion indeed, with hollowed eyes, hollowed cheeks, hollowed throat, and his nice leonine mane more scanty than otherwise. Little as Phil Farnel was prepared for this, even less was he prepared for the expression on Roger Sherman's face. The head of Cahan-Sherman Productions glared at him, baleful, menacing, and hostile. Farnel felt taken aback.

"I'm waiting," said the movie magnate. "I. Am. Waiting."

Realizing that the man's time was valuable and not to be lightly wasted, Farnel plunged right into his narrative. "It's about S. Maxwell Pierce, C.S.," he said.

"I'll bet it is," said Mr. Sherman. "I'll just bet it is." Then a flood of scarlet washed across his face and he all but lunged from his desk, pointing his finger and shaking his hand at the astonished visitor. "Well, let me tell you that you won't get away with it!" he shouted. "I promise you and your rotten friends that!" And then he sank back into his capacious chair and fumbled a capsule, a pill, and two tablets into his mouth, and reached with a trembling grasp for the carafe of water.

Without even recovering from his astonishment, Farnel pushed the jug within reach, and waited until the medicine had been swallowed. Then he said, "C.S., I do not understand."

"You understand, you understand all right," the tycoon mumbled. A few drops of water glistened on his chin, and he wiped them off on one of the famous linen handkerchiefs with the monograms woven into them especially for him at a factory in Northern Ireland. "Don't tell me you don't understand. What, you aren't in cahoots with them—the whole rotten bunch of them? Damley Mackenzie, Emile Ungar, Richard Rowe, Stella Smith. Sir Q. Fenton Stock, and all the others? I suppose it's just the powers of my imagination, I merely fancied I saw your name on the letter sent to me by that terrible shyster, Leonardo Del Bello? Ha!"

A faint glimmering of light came to Philip Farnel as he recognized the names of other player's more famous in past days than at present. "Please, C.S.," he pleaded. "Don't excite yourself. Why do you take it so personally? It's true, certainly, that I and others have engaged Mr. Del Bello to represent us in discussions—"

"'Discussions,'" sneered Mr. Sherman. "On the surface, discussion; yes. And behind my back, what? Extortion! That's what it is and you won't get away with it, and when I find out how you're doing it, believe me, my good man, you and all your fine friends will rot in the common jail. The William J. Burns Agency is on the track of your tricks right now, and so soon as they obtain conclusive evidence—the police! That's what. You forget with whom you have to contend. I wouldn't put up with it when the motion picture business was good and I certainly have no intention of submitting to it without a wink or a blink when the motion picture business is no business at all unless a man of my standing is prepared to become a mere hired lackey or errand boy for the Chase Manhattan Bank, the millions and billions of dollars which the so-called 'stars' they have nowadays are demanding before they'll consent or condescend to shoot a single frame, and then what happens? All the evil diseases of Egypt, from a hangover to a miscarriage, meanwhile the money is eaten up, while these temperamental cuties sulk in their tents like Alcibiades and watch television. Twentieth-Century, why *they* deserve such fortune and me not, I couldn't tell you, they strike oil on their lot, and part of the property goes for a high-class housing development. But does C-S strike oil? Do *you* strike oil? That's how C-S strikes oil, and who, may I ask, would be crazy enough to start or even to consider a high-class housing development in Culver City? No one. Meanwhile, the costs continue and the debts mount up and the little shtickle income from renting the old studio on Santa Monica wouldn't begin to cover it. So what happens? I rent a few of the old films to television as an experiment and a desperation, they catch on, an offer is made to me by N.B.S. for all the old films in our vaults, an adequate sum of money for the years of service and aggravation which I've given to The Industry, and it would enable me to settle with my creditors for one hundred cents on the dollar and end my career honorably and have a little peace and pleasure in the few years left to me by Our Father in Heaven, so then what happens?"

Barely pausing for breath and a fresh sip of water, the head of Cahan-Sherman continued, "I'll tell you what happens, as if you didn't know, you snake-in-the-grass. What happens. Every surviving motion picture performer who ever played a bit part in a C-S production hires that Leonardo Del Bello, a money-hungry conniver from the word Go, in the hopes that they'll be able to gouge from me a share in the money for the television sales and even the few rentals to the same medium. You know what this means, Mr. Philip Farnel?"

Farnel lowered his eyes from a photo-portrait of the late S. Maxwell Pierce which, among those of other stars both male and female, adorned the walls of Mr. Sherman's still-lavish office.

"Why, Mr. Sherman," he said, mildly, "it seems to me that all it means is that all of those who helped create a picture will be able to share in the profits. We were paid, true, don't get me wrong, I'm not complaining that we weren't paid well enough. Maybe some of us were really paid too much. But we were paid for moving pictures intended to be shown in moving picture theaters. Television opens up an entirely—"

A dangerous calm descended on the Lion of Hollywood. A faint smile began its tracings on his distinguished face. "My friend," he said, softly, "let me explain to you. You are proposing to open the dike in order to irrigate certain fields of land. You think the water will flow here, it will flow there, it will flow exactly where you want, and it can be arranged just that way. No. No, my friend. Not so. A flood is a flood. If the actors obtain a share of the proceeds from television sales and rentals, then everybody will obtain a share. The producer." He began to count on his fingers. "The director. The assistants. The cameraman. The music arranger. The costumer. The carpenter. The electrician, the wardrobe man, the make-up man, the script-girl, the salad-cook in the commissary, the guard at the gate. Everybody. Literally, ev-er-y-bod-y. So with everybody obtaining a share, what is left? *Bubkis*, that's what's left. Goat-droppings, I'm sorry you oblige me to use such a coarse expression. And C-S Productions dissolves into bankruptcy. So you can understand my position. But what," and here he began to shout again, "about *your* position? Sabotage! Espionage! Extortion! Terrorist tactics! And you have the nerve to come here and tell me that you're here about S. Maxwell Pierce, yet? Shame! Shame! Ghoul! Vampire! To use the form and the voice of your old friend, you're not ashamed?

"I'd just like to know how you did it! *Why* you did it, that's obvious—to blackmail me and to squeeze your rotten ransom money from our depleted coffers, it's obvious. One single picture we've got in production and it hasn't cost me enough heartache, that bitch, Myffanwydd Evans, no—two million dollars, a modest little sum at today's prices—*She Stoops To Conquer*, in modern dress—as if you didn't know, you terrible person—" The mogul's phrases came rapidly, abruptly, his chest heaved, "—and into at least half the scenes we've shot—you and your rotten crew—ruined! Ruined!—right over the scenes, like double exposure, that fink you hired to masquerade as S. Maxwell Pierce—comes walking, comes walking—and his voice all over the sound-track—'*Help. Help! Help! Help! Help!*'"

This time it was Philip Farnel's turn to reach, with trembling fingers, for the carafe of water.

* * * *

It was Louella Parson's column (confused beyond correction, but mentioning both Pierce and Farnel and spelling their names properly) that brought Doody Michaeljohn to the old brown house on Cheromoya. She sat in the living-room of his apartment, sun-tanned, healthy, and ill at ease.

"I suppose it's only natural that you were interested," he said, also a bit nervous. "Considering that you and Sam were such good friends—"

"He'd been keeping me for years, as well you know, bless you, Phil," she said. "'Good friends,' yes, I guess we were. He would've married me, too, if it hadn't been for Irma and Dorothy... At least that's what he always said, anyway. I don't know. I just don't know. I never did. However—" Her voice lost its uncertain note and became brisk. "This happened over a month ago..." She rummaged in her purse, brought out a piece of paper, unfolded it. "…but I didn't understand it at the time. Mrs. Mobery told me at the time—"

"Mrs. Who?" Philip Farnel squinted, leaned closer. The burden of the entire affair was now weighing down on him; he would very much have liked to be able to get back to his Burmese airmails, his rixdollars, his complete collection of Gernsback *Amazing*, his business block in Chatsworth, and the other familiar items which had occupied his time before all this. "Mrs. *Who*?"

"Mrs. Phyllis Mobery. She's a very well-known Sensitive, Phil. I got to know her at the Spiritual Science Church on Cahuenga Boulevard, in connection with our Friday Night Dutch Suppers, and Phil—I want to tell you—she is marvelous! Simply marvelous! There isn't a thing to which she can't turn her hand, what she's done for the bedridden and the shut-ins, she can sing, she can paint, she has a pilot's license and a black belt, and her work with handwriting has attracted world-wide attention."

Farnel felt himself utterly lost. All he could say was, "Go on."

"It was over a month ago, there were only the three of us, Mrs. Mobery, Laura Bender, and me, and it was at my place, Phil, you were never there, I had to give up the bungalow, Phil, it had too many memories. I live in a court in Boyle Heights now. Well, it was about eight o'clock, and suddenly it seemed to've gotten very quiet and I looked at Laura and she looked at me and then we both looked at Mrs. Mobery and we saw right away that she had slipped into Trance. So I very quickly put a pad of paper and two pencils right by her hands, the soft-lead Eberhard Faber Mongol 480, the kind she prefers, you know…"

Curious soft noises began to escape from the parted lips of the Sensitive, but her hearers, knowing that they would never develop into coherent speech, wasted no efforts listening to them, but watched her hands, instead—old hands, strong hands, capable with mahl-stick and brush, capable with the organ and the judo-hold, airplane controls and pots and pans—and now, submitting to things utterly removed from any of those others, hands grasping pad and pencils, hands…writing.

Farnel took the sheet of yellow paper handed to him, put on his glasses and began to read—or to try to read. He looked up. "Doody, are you trying to tell me that one person wrote all this?"

"Do you think I'd lie to you, Phil? Laura and I *saw* it. Of course, you have to understand that she was just the medium whereby those who have passed beyond communicated with us… Go on, Phil—"

"No, I—well, just let me read this…" His voice died away.

In a clear Spencerian hand at the top of the paper someone had written, *Mother Mother Mother Dearest Mothe*—and had broken off abruptly without even a trace of the final *r*. Immediately succeeding this an entirely different handwriting began—small, cramped, bearing down heavily, quite incomprehensible: Farnel, looking at it in dismay, was not even sure that it was English. He was certain only that it was very ugly and that, whatever it meant, it did not mean well. It vanished in a swirl of lines, as if there had been a struggle to seize the pencil. After that was a space of about an inch, followed by an address vigorously written—*Mrs. H. M. Stevenson 1327 Franklin Street Reissborough PA*—and the words, *Hi, Pipsqueek. "Hank and Bucky."* The bottom of the sheet was subscribed in a large, uneven and faltering script, *our Fideral Unon it mus an will be preasarved.* And over this, on the slant, was something else which Farnel could not make out.

He looked up, met her eager glance, shook his head. "Means nothing to me," he said. "I'm sorry."

Doodie Michaeljohn gave a wordless exclamation, tapped her finger excitedly on the yellow sheet, then clapped her hands to her forehead "Oh, of course! Phil! Take it—hold it upside down—and hold it up to a mirror. That one over there. Go *on*, Phil!"

Farnel obeyed. He saw reflected his own face, those irregular and ugly features which had been his misfortune as a boy and his fortune as a man. Many thoughts went rapidly through his mind, but he forced his glance down to the reflection of the paper. All the writing was reversed and incomprehensible, and then part of it jumped suddenly into almost-clarity. He tilted the paper until the slanting words were straight, then jumped, startled, his breath hissing. The woman came up behind him. "There," she said. "Now do you see?"

"Yes," he said. "I can see it now."

Doodie help help Doodie help help stop them or no peace for me darling D flix no Ive got to faed-out hel—

His quick and frightened respiration was the only sound for a second or two. Then Doodie said, "We called up, you know, that Mrs. Stevenson? And she said everybody else used to call her husband 'Henry' and she was the only one who called him 'Hank', and 'Bucky' was the name they had for their little child before it was born, only it didn't live, and she started to cry—"

"Doodie—"

"—but she managed to tell us that his nick-name for *her* was '*Pip*—'"

"Doodie—" That the Veil of Oblivion should be lifted to no better end that the exchange of domestic trivia or the proclamation of obsolete political slogans seemed suddenly intolerable to Farnel. "Doodie, this is Sam's *hand*writing!"

She seemed surprised at his surprise. Very quickly, she said, "Yes, of course it is, Phil. And I've finally figured out what it means, don't you see, Phil? I've figured out what it *means*. He wouldn't appear to *me*, Phil, he wouldn't want to even faintly take a chance of frightening me, so this is what he did, you see." She chuckled, faintly, fondly. "He never was much of a speller. 'F-a-e-d-o-u-t.' That's one mistake he always used to make. And he was probably in a hurry this time, too, because who knows how much time he had. If there's any such thing as Time as we know it, There... don't you see, Phil, Sam wasn't just a player, a mere mummer, Sam was an artist, Sam was an *actor*. He had oh such a tremendous talent, and he didn't use it in the movies, he *couldn't* use it in the movies. He was type-cast and he couldn't escape and he needed money, he always needed money, Inna and Dorothy and their alimony, and so he let the studio push him into one piece of tripe after another and that's the reason—"

She stopped abruptly. Looking away from Farnel, she said in a lower tone. "That's not the reason. It's not the whole reason. He loved the rich living and the big house he lived in and the big houses he visited in and the big cars he drove. He loved the fine, fancy clothes he was always buying and he loved the stupid crowds at the stupid premiers—every few months, another premiere for him because every few months there was another picture.

Philip Farnel looked at a photograph in a gold frame showing the beautiful features of S. Maxwell Pierce. The star's arm was around Farnel's shoulders and the latter was looking at him with an affectionate smile which made his face even more than usually ugly, devoid as it was of even the minor dignity of villainy. "He was always talking of going on the stage," Farnel recalled "'I'm going to throw it all up, Phil,' he used to say 'When this contract is up I'm going to tell the Studio where to go, and then, it's New York for me. I don't care what parts I have to take at first or how hard I've got to work. Sooner or later Broadway will give me the kind of part I want, and then, Phil, I'll be the happiest man alive.'"

Doodie Michaeljohn nodded. S. Maxwell Pierce had told her the same things, too; told them to her often—and often with tears. But he had never made the move, had never been able to bring himself to make the sacrifice, do the hard work required. Not that the screen was a snap, no. Sometimes he had to be up at five in the morning after only a few hours sleep, to be on the set at seven. But once on the set, what did he have to do? Nothing. He just had to stroll through his lines, show his dimples, flash his teeth, take the girl in his arms, and that was it.

"It was easier for you, Phil," Doodie said "Actors like you and Quentin Stock and Emile Ungar and lots of others. You looked on it as a job. You were round pegs and you fitted comfortably into round holes. But with Sam it was *different*. He knew that he was prostituting himself and he hated it but he went right on *doing* it. He used to talk about 'that one talent which is death to hide—'"

Farnel nodded. "I know… He used to call it 'the real Sin against the Holy Ghost…'"

And then Pierce had died, worn-out at thirty-nine, but at least—Doodie said—at least he was at peace, at rest. "Until they took his old pictures out of the vaults and dusted them off and began showing them on TV. Because, you know, after he died, his popularity faded awfully fast. The pictures dated so quickly, the War and all, and there were newer and younger handsome men to take his place, and the exhibitors just stopped booking his pictures and the distributors didn't even push them. But by now, you see, Phil, they're so old that they're *quaint*—isn't that a terrible thing, Phil? Isn't that *ter*rible? People look at those bits and pieces of Sam Pierce's heart and body and soul, that he killed himself making, and they smirk and titter and yawn and reach for another can of beer, because it's only midnight and they aren't sleepy enough to go to bed. It's just killing *time* to them, Phil. And it's just making money, for the studio. But do you know what it is to *Sam*, Phil? Why, you only have to read this desperate plea of his for help, Phil. Each time I read it, it's an arrow in my heart. *Doodie help help stop then*—that should be 'stop *them*' of course—stop the people who're showing his old films. *Flix no*—that's what he used to call the movies, the flics, flickers, you know, English slang, I don't know where he picked it up. Oh, Phil!"

She began to cry and he awkwardly put his arms around her and patted her. "That's what it means. That's why he's haunting people and the studios. It's why his face and his voice keep coming onto the prints and the sound-tracks of whatever it is they're making there, and why he shows up and appeals to all these people, Phil. Because… Phil…*as long as his old films keep on being shown, his soul won't be able to rest in peace…*"

* * * *

The matter was settled, for the time being, at least, without too much difficulty Roger Sherman, balancing television rentals for *Dark Of The Moon* (starring S. Maxwell Pierce) against the losses being sustained in the making of *She Stoops To Conquer* (starring Myffanwydd Evans), was persuaded to make the experiment. *Dark Of The Moon* was retired to the vaults once more, and, with that, the ghost of S. Maxwell Pierce walked no more.

How long it will last, of course, no one knows. After all, Pierce starred in close to thirty pictures, and appeared in many others made before he reached starhood. Sherman will not remain active in movie-making forever; and when he retires, the complete stock of C-S films passes out of his hands. Only his continuance for the present, plus the law-suit (for it finally came to that) filed by the surviving old movie stars for a share in the TV rights to the films they played in—only these two things continue to keep S. Maxwell Pierce off the video screen.

Philip Farnel awaits the future with patience, resignation, optimism, and—in this particular instance—no small measure of sadness.

He had held S. Maxwell Pierce to be his close and beloved friend He had, silently, silently, silently, and very deeply, too—envied S. Maxwell Pierce every atom of personal beauty and personal charm which Pierce had possessed and he, Farnel, had not. He had suffered in the great star's death, and this wound, which time had eventually healed, had been opened again. It had been opened afresh—or was this yet another wound?—and it still pained, and still it bled. For Pierce's shade, drawn from the Valley of Death, had sought out friends, had sought out enemies, had sought out casual acquaintances, and even strangers.

But it seemed to have forgotten, utterly forgotten, that it had ever known Philip Farnel.

DEATH OF A DAMNED GOOD MAN

Originally published in *Isaac Asimov's Science Fiction Magazine*, January, 1991.

Steuart had a poor memory for names. Lawson collected bugs and lizards and things. Hughes couldn't jump. There you have it all.

Lawson's broad old house had its single floor high off the ground on posts in order to catch the breeze in hot summers and avoid extra-high tides or storm-driven waves; and like other such houses the underneath had eventually been boarded up to "protect" (as it might be) such items as a couple of old dories or dinghies or skiffs, lots of broken traps and eel-pots, a couple of failed generators, a chancy heater, a kerosene refrigerator or two, several automobile engines, and God knows what else; I never looked. If this cut off some of the cool breezes it also cut off some of the cold winds, and if it didn't, there was probably a pile of coal, and a cord of wood. And various flotsam and jetsam.

A visit to Lawson's house was a visit to an antique state of amateur science, and the smells of kerosene, old lamps, old newspapers, old books, old socks, old birds, and other things musty and musky and presumably also old. A vast brass microscope held down a heap of yellow and dirty Smithsonian *Reports*. Skins of things moldered on the wall next to ancient calendars. Out of a small hole in a wooden box, once, poured a thing with a head like a bat, body like a cat, and hands like a bird-eating spider; it had orange fur: I forget *what* Lawson said it was. He spoke baby-talk to it, fed it bits of banana, and told me it could have cuddled up in a tea-cup when he first got it. "I'm a widely traveled man," he assured me. "I have a great interest in native dialects and customs and odd corners of the world. *Look* at this ceremonial mask," he invited in a hortatory voice which implied that you had better look; "I got that in Celebes; Sulawasi they call it now. *Look* at the wing-span on those butterflies. I fit twenty of its cocoons into a common matchbox." Something went *bump* underneath the house and Lawson banged on the floor with his foot and the noises stopped.

So might the house of John Bartram or Louis Agassiz have seemed, I thought; though minus of course the kerosene; did any living man or woman still know what whale-oil lamps smelled like? "For Christ's sake *feed* it," the old lady said, speaking for the first time, the holy name suddenly shocking from that sagging flowing old face. "All right, Aggie Brown," Lawson said, not bothered or in haste. I suppose the huge wooden ice-box had come once upon a time from an old restaurant, and when Lawson opened it a wave of cold and corruption came rolling out. I was tempted to use again Aggie's word of emphasis, but—

"For God's sake what *is* that, Laws?" is what I cried.

A faint simper as he dislodged some log-sized hunks of god-knows-what, ice crystals on the dark-red-and-blue-green; the simper never faltered. "That is horse-meat I buy wholesale from the mink ranch for my German Shepherd police guard-dogs, this neighborhood is not at all what it was," he fumbled with his foot and raised a small trap-door and thrust the frowzy flesh through it and slipped the bolt back all in a few seconds; the odors of the snake house at the zoo were added to everything else in that close fuggy air. A dead boa constrictor smells a lot like a dead fish. But whatever he had just fed was not dead. *That is not dead which does eternal lie, And with strange aeons even death may die*—who had said *that*? Philemon Holland's translation of Pliny's Natural History was surely not in verse, was it? Well, it wasn't Edgar Guest. The old lady flapped her skirts; they could have done with a washing, too. I said that I hadn't noticed any Shepherd dogs, Laws; and he said (I think he said) that he was "getting some more tomorrow."

Fact, fascination, curiosity, or not, I moved rapidly. "Well, I've got to be *going* now, Laws—"

The old woman was at my heels going down the stairs and I turned to ask if he were all there but she moved off in another direction as we went out the thick-wired gate which swung back on its weights with a heavy sound behind us. My mind provided me with a picture of an anaconda or a python and Lawson's voice assuring me that it had been no bigger than a garter snake when he had gotten it (but only my mind); then a gust of wind from the not-distant-sea slapped at my face and I realized that I was holding my breath. The air, when I breathed it in again, was salty and fresh. Do I contradict myself? Very well then, I contradict myself. I am vast, I contain multitudes.

My neighbor, Wilfred Steuart, was retired from I don't know what; asking him a question was a pleasure because, for one thing, he usually knew the answer, and, for another, he never, ever, insisted *on Why do you want to know?* before he answered. It seemed to him the most natural thing in the world that anyone would want to know anything. And he saw no reason why, if he knew, he should not say; not for him the sad scowl of suspicion: to the pure, all things are pure. "Her name is Agnes Overholt, used to be Agnes Brown. O-ver-holt? Ab-er-crom—" He tasted the syllables. "I got a poor memory for names. She and Art Lawson they used to be childhood sweet-hearts." They *did?* something cried out within me. Lawson, with the face of a withered monkey and non-too-well-scrubbed, either—and old Agnes, whose own face had loosened out of all confinement, and who perhaps was not fanatically clean, either: childhood sweethearts? *Rejoice, young man*…and young woman, too…*ere the evil days draw nigh*—that Preacher knew what he was talking about. Even if Lawson showed no signs of knowing that the evil days had drawn more than nigh. And *Hughes?*

Lew Hughes had gone to the same school. What did he do now? Hung around other people's houses, mostly. Didn't actually come *in*, just hung around. Thus informed, I realized that I did know that Lew Hughes was a dedicated loiterer, had known this for longer than I had known I knew. Grey-faced Lewis Hughes, obviously a man with a grievance; and what was it? A general grievance, you may be sure, against anyone any less unhappy and discontented than Lewis Hughes. But specifically because he had some physical ailment for which the United States in Congress Assembled refused to allow him a pension. "Something the matter with his bones or his muscles or his tendons. 'You can *walk*, can't you?' is what I asked him; 'Oh…yeah… I can *walk*…but I can't *jump*—' 'What do ya wanna *jump* for? You wanna be a delivery boy hopping on and off of wagons?' But he keeps on mooning and moaning that he just can't jump, and he calls it *My Condition* and he claims he got it sleeping in the wet trenches during the War and the Veterans won't give him a pension because it's not Service Connected…*they* claim…*he* claims, Yes it *is*…*they* say, then how come it took thirty years to find out? Also—"

Also, Hughes was jealous of Lawson on account of Aggie.

"On account of *Aggie*?"

Steuart said, "Why sure. Aggie goes to see Arty Lawson. She doesn't go to see Lew Hughes. *No*body goes to see Lew Hughes."

I supposed so; still…smelly old dirty addled old Art Lawson? profane, smelly old saggy old Aggie? and sullen old Hughes: *jealous*?

"Know what he says, Lew Hughes? Says that Lawson's got a buried treasure and that when Aggie comes to visit, Lawson digs it up and lets her look at it!" Mr. Steuart laughed. I laughed, too, I didn't know what *he* thought about, but *I* thought about the scene in the Quixote where Sancho Panza's wife confronts him on his return.

What did you bring me, husband?

I brought you some precious jewels, wife.

Show them to me! Show them to me right now!

I will show them to you at home, wife.

Lawson?

Aggie?

You never know.

Not my business.

And Steuart told me that at one time he and Lawson had been "in the Merchants Marine together. We sailed on a *couple* of ships together. All through the South Pacific. All through the East Indies. All through the West Indies, too."

Clem lived next door.

"I cleck *clams,*" intoned Clem, looking at me out of his intense and almost Indian-dark face. "I cleck *clams*. I cleck *oysters*. I cleck *mussels*. Believe me, I'm a citizen, and I *earn* my money," he said, bitterly; implications of aliens lolling on federally funded opium couches. "What's the matter a citizen can't own a machine-gun if he so desires? Because the East Coast Liberal Uhstablishment wants to dis*arm* the citizens! They think I doe know about them uh-legal orientals being smuggled in offa the boats in the dark a the moan, they think I doe'n observe them Lo-etians or whatever they are slipping and slapping around in the shadows, but I observe 'em!" said Clem, coming closer. I feared for my buttonholes. "I can *smell* 'em! They eat *fish*! They live on a fish-head and a handful of rice a day and that's how come a citizen can't compete with 'em!" I thought of asking if perhaps they ate oysters, mussels, or clams, but I desisted. Clem was widely known to possess a large number of items which the East Coast Liberal Establishment had not succeeded in outlawing; and I was by no means satisfied with my ability to move Faster Than a Speeding Bullet.

No indeed.

Luigi had the contract to remove garbage and he removed it at his own rate of speed in an ancient truck which no appeals to civic pride had ever persuaded him to replace. Luigi's truck was parked one day very nearly outside the small police station, but even if I hadn't been able to identify it I would have known he was inside the station. First I became aware of a high shrill sound as I approached, then I recognized it as a *voice*, then I realized *whose* voice, then I began to understand elements of what he was saying. *Can't jump he says I can't jump he says Oh my God I was driving along real slow to save my tires and I hear him* screaming *he was* screaming *and I seen him running and I seen this thing chasing him*; by this time I was inside and saw O'Dowd the Chief of the two-man police force leaning his heavy hands on Luigi's shoulders. *He was* running *and he was* screaming *and I lean over the seat and I hold the door open and I yell jump Lew jump up and he yells I can't jump he screams I* can't *I* can't *jump Oh my God oh my God and I slam the door shut*; and then Luigi began to stamp his feet upon the floor and though his voice stopped speaking words, articulate words, his voice did not stop and O'Dowd wrestled him back down into the chair and just then Dr. Stanyan the Health Officer came in walking very fast and in his hand was something I recognized from the War as a morphine syrette and then I saw something else I recognized from the War namely that Luigi was splashed with blood evidently emitted under pressure—

—and then Petey the other policeman took hold of me by the elbow and walked me rapidly to the door; and even when I heard Clem say almost in my ear, "It was a steel-jacketed bullet, I'm a citizen and I had a right—" I kept on going, I did not insist upon my own right as a citizen, but even when the noise of the door stopped slamming Luigi's voice kept on going on and then by and by it sank to a drone and I leaned against a tree and first I was very cold and then I was very sick.

Steuart made a gesture at home when he saw me and began to talk. "Well what a terrible thing, two men dead," he said. "I suppose it was one of those alligators that maybe come up out of the sewer—"

"—that wasn't no alligator and it didn't come up out of no sewer," said Clem.

Steuart yielded the point entirely, "Well, then probably Hughes was poking around looking for Art Lawson's buried treasure but I don't believe Art had any buried treasure; did it *get* out or did Hughes *let* it out, oh of course by accident? well maybe I suppose we'll never know. Art went quick, that's a blessing, he went just like *that*," Steuart snapped his fingers. "We were boys together, him always climbing the trees to get the birds' eggs and such things like that: and now he's *gone*."

Someone else was in the kitchen, Aggie had made tea and she poured it out and it was strong dark tea and she poured rum into it and it was strong dark rum and it was hot in the kitchen and perhaps that was sweat on her eroded old face and then again perhaps it wasn't.

Clem gulped without blowing hardly at all. He must have had a mouth of iron. "It probably come ashore with them aliens from the boats," he said. "What would a *citiz*en want with something like that? Of course it's all hushed up, your big moneyed interests, Safeway, 7-11, they doe want no bad publicity, here. *I* didn't want any reward," he said, *gulp*. "*I* didn't want any Carnegie Medal. I just wanted the skin, Jesus I could of made some lovely holsters out of that skin. But you think the Police and the Public Health they even let me have a piece of it? They're Relks," he said, bitterly, *gulp*. "The Chiefs a Nelk, the Doctor's a Nelk: all of them Melks they stick together. That's your East Coast Liberal Uhstablishment for you," he said.

"Oh will you shut the Hell up," said Aggie Brown. "Your goddamn grandfather he was no goddamn good either. Lew Hughes he was no goddamn good either."

"Sealed *coffin*," said Clem. Then he held up his cup for more.

"Arty Lawson and me we were in the Merchants Marine," Steuart said. "We went everywhere. Like, couple times we went all through the East Indias. Jamoke, where the good coffee comes from? Sullivan's that a great big island, *no* I can't spell it, I ain't got no memory for names, everywhere we went he come back aboard with like natural history samples: bugs: lizards: Monkeys, *l*emurs; he used to smuggle them ashore. Bali—"

"Did your ship call at Komodo?" I asked.

Steuart's lips moved, he was trying out the word. After a moment he shrugged. "It could very well be," he said. "I dunno for sure. Well, a sudden death. Art Lawson I mean, we all—"

"He was a damned good man," said Aggie Brown.

Steuart had a poor memory for names. Lawson collected bugs and lizards and things. Hughes couldn't jump. There you have it all.

WHERE DO YOU LIVE, QUEEN ESTHER?

Originally published in *Ellery Queen's Mystery Magazine*, **March 1961.**

Cold, cold, it was, in the room where she lodged, so far from her work. The young people complained of the winter, and those born to the country—icy cold, it was, to them. So how could a foreign woman bear it, and not a young one? She had tried to find another job not so far (none were near). *Oh, my, but a woman your age shouldn't be working*, the ladies said. *No, no, I couldn't, really*. Kindly indeed. Thank you, mistress.

There was said to be hot water sometimes in the communal bathroom down the hall—the water in the tap in her room was so cold it burned like fire: so strange: hot/cold—but it was always too late when she arrived back from work. Whither she was bound now. Bound indeed.

A long wait on the bare street corner for the bus. Icy winds and no doorway, even, to shelter from the winds. In the buses—for there were two, and another wait for the second—if not warm, then not so cold. And at the end, a walk for many blocks. The mistress not up yet.

Mistress... Queen Esther thought about Mrs. Raidy, the woman of the house. At first her was startled by the word—to she it mean, a woman live with a man and no marriage lines. But then her grew to like it, Mrs. Raidy did. Like to hear, too, mention of *the Master* and *the young Master*, his brother.

Both of them at table. "That second bus," Queen Esther said, unwrapping her head. "He late again. Me think, just to fret I."

"Oh, a few minutes don't matter. Don't worry about it," the master, Mr. Raidy, said. He never called the maid by name, nor did the mistress, but the boy—

As now, looking up with a white line of milk along his upper lip, he smiled and asked. "Where do you live, Queen Esther?" It was a game they played often. His brother—quick glance at the clock, checking his watch, head half turned to pick up sounds from upstairs, said that he wasn't to bother "her" with his silly question. A pout came over the boy's face, but yielded to her quick reply.

"Me live in the Carver Rooms on Fig Street, near Burr."

His smile broadened. "Fig! That's a fun-ny name for a street... But where do you live at home, Queen Esther? I know: Spahnish Mahn. And what you call a fig we call a bah-nah-nah. See, Freddy? *I* know."

The older one got up. "Be a goodboynow," he said, and vanished for the day.

The boy winked at her. "Queen Esther from Spanish Man, Santa Mari-anne, Bee-Double-You-Eye. But I really think it should be Spanish *Main*, Queen Esther." He put his head seriously to one side. "That's what they used to call the Caribbean Sea, you know."

And he fixed with his brooding, ugly little face her retreating back as she went down to the cellar to hang her coat and change her shoes.

"The sea surround we on three sides at Spanish Man," she said, return-ing.

"You should say, 'surrounds *us*,' Queen Esther... You have a very funny accent, and you aren't very pretty."

Looking up from her preparations for the second breakfast, she smiled. "True *for* you, me lad."

"But then, neither am I. I look like my father. I'm *his* brother, not *hers*, you know. Do you go swimming much when you live at home, Queen Esther?"

She put up a fresh pot of coffee to drip and plugged in the toaster and set some butter to brown as she beat the eggs; and she told him of how they swim at Spanish Man on Santa Marianna, surrounded on three sides by the sea. It was the least of the Lesser Antilles... She lived only part of her life in the land she worked in, the rest of the time—in fact, often at the same time—she heard, in the silence and cold of the mainland days and nights, the white surf beating on the white sands and the scuttling of the crabs beneath the breadfruit trees.

"I thought I would come down before you carried that heavy tray all the way upstairs," said the mistress, rubbing her troubled puffy eyes. Her name was Mrs. Eleanor Raidy—she was the master's wife—and her hair was teased up in curlers. She sat down with a grunt, sipped coffee, sighed. "What would I ever do without you?"

She surveyed the breakfast-in-progress. "I hope I'll be able to eat. And to retain. Some mornings..." she said darkly. Her eyes made the rounds once more. "There's no pineapple, I suppose?" she asked faintly. "Grated, with just a little powdered sugar? Don't go to any extra trouble," she added, as Queen Esther opened the icebox. "Rodney. *Rodney*? Why do I have to shout and—"

"Yes, El. What?"

"In *that* tone of voice? If it were for my pleasure, I'd say, Nothing. But I see your brother doesn't care if you eat or not. Half a bowl of—"

"I'm finished."

"You are not finished. Finish now."

"I'll be *late*, El. They're waiting for me."

"Then they'll wait. Rush out of here with an empty stomach and then fill up on some rubbish? No. Finish the cereal."

"But it's *cold*."

"Who let it get cold? I'm not too sure at all I ought to let you go. This Harvey is older than you and he pals around with girls older than he is. Or maybe they just fix themselves up to look—eat. Did you *hear* what I say? Eat. Most disgusting sight I ever saw, lipstick, and the *clothes*? Don't let me catch you near them. They'll probably be rotten with disease in a few years." Silently, Queen Esther grated pineapple. "I don't like the idea of your going down to the Museum without adult supervision. Who knows what can happen? Last week a boy your age was crushed to death by a truck. Did you have a—*look* at me, young man, when I'm talking to you— did you have a movement?"

"Yes."

"Ugh. If looks could kill. I don't believe you. Go upstairs and—Rod-*NEY*!"

But Rodney had burst into tears and threw down his spoon and rushed from the room. Even as Mrs. Raidy, her mouth open with Shock, tried to catch the maid's eye, he slammed the door behind him and ran down the front steps.

The morning was proceeding as usual.

"And his brother leaves it all to me," Mrs. Raidy said, pursuing a piece of pineapple with her tongue. She breathed heavily. "I have you to thank, in part, I may as well say since we are on the subject, for the fact that he wakes up screaming in the middle of the night. I warned you. Didn't I warn you?"

Queen Esther demurred, said she had never spoken of it to the young master since that one time of the warning.

"One time was enough. What was that word? That name? From the superstitious story you were telling him when I interrupted. Guppy?"

"Duppy, mistress." It was simply a tale from the old slave days, Queen Esther reflected. A cruel Creole lady who went to the fields one night to meet she lover, and met a duppy instead. The slaves all heard, but were affrighted to go out; and to this day the pile of stones near Petty Morne is called The Grave of Mistress-Serve-She-Well. Mistress Raidy had suddenly appeared at the door, as Queen Esther finished the tale, startling Master Rodney.

"Why do you tell the child such stories?" she had demanded, very angry. "See, he's scared to death."

"*You* scared me, El, sneaking up like that."

Queen Esther hastened to try to distract them.

"'Tis only a fancy of the old people. Me never fear no duppy——"

But she was not allowed to finish. The angry words scalded her. And she knew it was the end of any likelihood (never great) that she might be allowed to move her things into the little attic room, and save the hours of journeying through the cutting, searing cold.

Said the mistress, now, "Even the sound of it is stupid... He didn't eat much breakfast." She glanced casually out the window at the frost-white ground. "You noticed that, I suppose."

Over the sound of the running water Queen Esther said, Yes. She added detergent to the water. He never did eat much breakfast—but she didn't say this out.

"No idea why, I suppose? No? Nobody's been feeding him anything—that you know of? No spicy West Indian messes, no chicken and rice with bay leaves? Yes, yes, I know, not since that one time. All right. A word to the wise is sufficient." Mrs. Raidy arose. A grimace passed over her face. "Another day. And everything is left to me. Every single thing... Don't take all morning with those few dishes."

Chicken and rice, with bay leaves and peppercorns. Queen Esther, thinking about it now, relished the thought. Savory, yes. Old woman in the next yard at home in Spanish Man, her cook it in an iron caldron. Gran'dame Hephsibah, who had been born a slave and still said "wittles" and "vhiskey"... Very sage woman. But, now, what was wrong with chicken and rice? The boy made a good meal of it, too, before he sister-in-law had come back, unexpected and early. Then shouts and tears and then a dash to the bathroom. "You've made him sick with your nasty rubbish!" But, for true, it wasn't so.

Queen Esther was preparing to vacuum the rug on the second floor when the mistress appeared at the door of the room. She dabbed at her eyes. "You know, I'm not a religious person," she observed, "but I was just thinking: It's a blessing the Good Lord didn't see fit to give me a child. You know why? Because I would've thrown away my life on it just as I'm throwing it away on my father-in-law's child. Can you imagine such a thing? A man fifty-two years old, a widower, suddenly gets it into his head to take a wife half his age——" She rattled away, winding up, "And so now they're both dead, and who has to put up with the results of his being a nasty old goat? No... Look. See what your fine young gentleman had hidden under the cushion of his bedroom chair."

And she rifled the pages of a magazine. Queen Esther suppressed a smile. It was only natural, she wanted to say. Young gentlemen liked young ladies. Even up in this cold and frozen land—true, the boy was young. That's why it was natural he only looked—and only at pictures.

"Oh, there's very little gets past *me*, I can assure you. Wait. When he gets back. Museum trips. Dirty pictures. Friends from who knows where. No *more*!"

Queen Esther finished the hall rugs, dusted, started to go in to vacuum the guest room. Mrs. Raidy, she half observed in the mirror, was going downstairs. Just as the mistress passed out of sight, she threw a glance upward. Queen Esther only barely caught it. She frowned. A moment later a faint jar shook the boards beneath her feet. The cellar door. Bad on its hinges. Queen Esther started the vacuum cleaner; a sudden thought made her straighten up, reach for the switch. For a moment she stood without moving. Then she propped the cleaner, still buzzing, in a corner, and flitted down the steps.

There was, off the kitchen, a large broom closet, with a crack in the wall. Queen Esther peered through the crack. Diagonally below in the cellar was an old Victrola and on it the maid had draped her coat and overcoat and scarf; next to it were street shoes, not much less broken than the ones she wore around the house.

Mistress Raidy stood next to the gramophone, her head lifted, listening. The hum of the vacuum cleaner filtered through the house. With a quick nod of her head, tight-lipped in concentration, the mistress began going through the pockets of the worn garments. With little grunts of pleasurable vexation she pulled out a half-pint bottle of fortified wine, some pieces of cassava cake. "That's all we need. A drunken maid. Mice. Roaches. *Oh,* yes." A smudged hektographed postal card announcing the Grand Annual Festivity of the St. Kitts and Nevis Wesleyan Benevolent Union, a tattered copy of Lucky Tiger Dream Book, a worn envelope…

Here she paused to dislodge a cornerless photograph of Queen Esther's brother Samuel in his coffin and to comment, "As handsome as his sister." There were receipts for international postal orders to Samuel's daughter Ada—"Send my money to foreign countries." A change purse with little enough in it, and a flat cigarette tin. This she picked at with nervous fingers, chipping a nail. Clicking her tongue, she got it open, found, with loathing large upon her face—a tiny dried frog—a *frog*?—a—surely *not*!—

"Oh!" she said, in a thin, jerky, disgusted voice. "Uh. *Uh*!" She threw the tin away from her, but the thing was bound with a scarlet thread and this caught in her chipped fingernail.

"—out of this *house*!" she raged, flapping her wrist, "and never set foot in it again, with her *filthy*—ah!" The thread snapped, the thing flew off and landed in a far corner. She turned to go and had one unsteady foot on the first step when she heard the noise behind her.

Later on, when Queen Esther counted them, she reckoned it as twenty-five steps from the broom closet to the bottom of the cellar stairs. At that moment, though, they seemed to last forever as the screams mounted in intensity, each one seeming to overtake the one before it without time or space for breath between. But they ceased as the maid clattered down the steps, almost tripping over the woman crouched at the bottom.

Queen Esther spared she no glance, then, but faced the thing advancing. Her thrust she hand into she bosom. "Poo!" her spat. "You ugly old duppy! Me never fear no duppy, no, not me!"

And her pulled out the powerful obeah prepared for she long ago by Gran'dame Hephsibah, that sagest of old women half Ashanti, half Coromanti. The duppy growled and driveled and bared its worn-down stumps of filthy teeth, but retreated step by step as her came forward, chanting the words of power; till at last it was shriveled and bound once more in the scarlet thread and stowed safely away in the cigarette tin. *Ugly old duppy...!*

Mr. Raidy took the sudden death of his wife with stoical calm. His young brother very seldom has nightmares now, and eats heartily of the savory West Indian messes that Queen Esther prepares for all three of them. Hers is the little room in the attic; her chimney passes through one corner of it, and Queen Esther is warm, warm, warm.

ADVENTURES IN UNHISTORY: WHO FIRED THE PHOENIX?

Originally published in *Isaac Asimov's Science Fiction Magazine*, May, 1981.

In my heart a phoenix flame
Darts and scorches me all day...
Here it begins: the work of love breeding
Among red embers...

—Robert Graves

That strange, odd book, *The Secret Languages of Ireland*, by Drs. Sampson and Macalister, which the Syndics of the Cambridge University Press caused to be printed in 1937, contains a section on the slang or cant of the stonemasons of Dublin in the early 1800s, when these workmen still spoke Irish Gaelic amongst themselves; for the most, interesting only as urban survivals of a language already beginning to die out even in the countryside. But one sentence strikes me as being worth a citation, *"Do sheabhraigheas-saceápaire cuilene tnúthughad* [read —adh] *carrain ag Ealp O'Laoighre* (H) 'I saw [better, have seen] pigeons bringing fire to boil meat at Dublin'—apparently a crude piece of rustic irony invented for the purpose of snubbing a boaster." I hope to point out evidence of its meaning much more than that.

Before I begin to begin doing so, I will ask that we consider the year 1934, and, of a decade which began in the Great Depression and ended in the Second World War it may be said that no year was a good year. However. Let us take our scientifictional time and space scanner, and, peeping backwards, zoom in, briefly, on a few randomly sampled items. *Item*, a theologian in Rome studies St. Cyril on men's unbelief (Strictly, of course, *Item* would never have been used for the first "item" on a list, only for the second and successive ones. But usages change. And change and...). *Item*, a schoolboy in Australia observes a bird doing something odd with ants. *Item*, a newspaper reporter in England is reproved for bringing in a Silly Story.

Have these three items any connection, not for that year alone, and not even for that decade, but for any year and any decade? It is almost certainly true that anything in this psycho-material universe is connected with any other thing in this psycho-material universe: therefore, what are the connections which link these three items? Where shall we begin? Once again I quote Charles Fort, that intensely normal-looking man, who spent forty years collecting reports on the abnormal; and he said:

"One measures a circle beginning anywhere."

He might have added, "Though in doing so, one must avoid circular reasoning..."

What has any of this to do with the phoenix? And before even beginning to try to answer that very pertinent question, let us not forget the advice of Socrates: *Define your terms.* Let us begin, then, by asking, what is the phoenix? I have had some personal and slightly painful experience in not taking for granted that everyone knows at least something in the way of an answer, even if only via the byword, *to rise from one's ashes, like the phoenix*, for example. Some years ago I wrote a novel entitled *The Phoenix and The Mirror*, which was described by one critic as "baroque fantasy." Several years later I spoke with a young woman who had recently read it. Our conversation, it soon became clear, contained some elements of confusion; and, soon later, as we continued to converse, it became clearer that she had never heard of the legend of the phoenix, not even via the byword: no: she thought that I had made it all up. She flattered me. I hadn't.—Anyway, I hadn't made it *all* up. The book was writ by magic, but the book and its magic are not the subject of this lecture; let us begin, then, by reading an abridgement of one of the versions of this very old legend, that of Lactantius. Sometimes he is called "the Christian Cicero," a comparison which probably pleased Lactantius more than it might have Cicero; and sometimes it is said that Lactantius never even wrote the poem from which my very brief abstract is taken...and, if so, as to who did write it, why, I have no idea. *I* didn't.

> "There is a happy spot, retired in the first East, where is the grove of the sun, planted with many a tree. There is a fountain in the middle, clear, gentle, and abounding with sweet waters. This grove, these woods, a single bird, the phoenix, inhabits,—single, but it lives reproduced by its own death. It obeys Phoebus, son of Apollo, the sun god. And when the phoenix has accomplished the thousand years of her life, and the length of her days have become burdensome, in order that she may renew the age which has glided by, full of years, she directs her flight swift into Syria, to which Venus herself has given the name of Phoenicia; and through trackless deserts the phoenix seeks the retired groves, where a remote wood lies concealed in the glens. There she chooses a lofty palm, which derives

the name of "phoenix" from the bird, and where no hurtful living creature can break through, or slimy serpent, or any bird of prey. She builds for herself a nest, or a tomb, *for she dies that she might live.* Rich wood she heaps together, cinnamon and balsam, cassia and the fragrant acanthus, rich drops of the tearful frankincense, tender ears of spikenard, and the pleasing myrrh. Then amidst such various odors she yields up her life, nor fears the faith of so great a deposit. But her body, though destroyed by death, is hot, and the heat produces a flame; it conceives fire, it blazes, and is dissolved into burnt ashes. And from these ashes comes a worm and this increases vastly into an egg, from which the new phoenix, having burst its shell, shoots forth, *even as a caterpillar is wont to be changed into a butterfly.* Her color is like the brilliancy of the red pomegranate when ripe, such color as the red poppy produces in the fields beneath the redly-blushing sky. O bird of happy lot and fate, born from herself! Happy she who enters into no compact with Venus, goddess of love and matrimony. Death is Venus to her; her only pleasure is in death: so that she may be born, she desires first to die. She is an offspring to herself, her own father and son, her own heir, and always a foster-child of herself. She is herself indeed, but not the same, since she is herself and not herself, having gained eternal life by the blessing of death."

Well. Not without beauty, either of description or concept. A fable. Even fables may mean something; what does this one mean? Leaving aside mythology, can we submit this to a process of absolute rationalization and come up with something?... Something sensible, that is, and which we can believe? Try this: long ago someone saw a bird fly into a nest. Unknown to him, also in the nest was an egg about to hatch. Suddenly the bird died, the nest burst into flames, the heat of the fire hatched the egg, and—

Hmm. Not very satisfying, is it? Why does the bird suddenly die? "Natural causes?" *Oh.* Very well, the bird suddenly dies of natural causes. Happens all the time. Yes, but how does the nest suddenly burst into flames? "Spontaneous combustion?" Well... I suppose... And, since I am supposing, I suppose I might as well suppose that the heat of the fire lasted just long enough to hatch the already ready-to-hatch egg, and then went out. By natural causes. But... But what? "The newly-hatched hatchling" couldn't have had any feathers, let alone those as red as the pomegranate and the poppy? Newly-hatched birds *have* no feathers? Oh, very well, then; if you are going to spoil my nice rationalization with such comments, I will have to admit: that part of it couldn't be true. The passer-by must have made it up. (It is strange how reluctant we are to allow ancient and/or distant people with imagination enough to make up, simply make up a story. We make them up all the time, and often they don't mean a thing. Not a thing...)

But perhaps you are unwilling to admit this. Everything means something: the subconscious mind, for example...

Well, having brought the subconscious mind in, let us, since we have failed to rationalize this story, proceed to psychoanalyze it. It is an erection fantasy. It is an archetypal account of copulation and birth. Not *re*birth. Just *birth*. We know that "die" is a colloquial word for orgasm. And we have read Jorge Luis Borges' story, *The Sect of The Phoenix*, in which immortal life was granted to the members of the sect by virtue of their performing a somewhat squalid act, into the performance of which they may be initiated even by children or servants. And we may even know that Borges himself has said that the "secret of the sect of the phoenix" is, simply, copulation.

What more do we need?

We need, for one thing, a further examination of this legend, which has from ancient times taken such a hold upon the minds of mankind. Unlike such legends as those of the werewolf, or even of the mandrake, this one, that of the phoenix, seems at least to be and to have been completely harmless. But it may be nonetheless fascinating. It might lead us somewhere. It might lead us nowhere. Let us, at least, see. Let us, for example, see what the theologian in Rome saw when he read the writings of St. Cyril when he was reading it in Rome in the year 1934. St. Cyril wrote (long, *long* before that year), "*God knew men's unbelief and therefore provided this bird as evidence of the Resurrection.*" You see that no less an authority than one of the Fathers of the Church, far from dismissing it as a pagan fantasy, accepted the phoenix as an actuality. As had many, many others in authority done, both before and after Cyril. There were, of course, skeptics. For example:

Here is Herodotus, a most learned and well-travelled native of Asia Minor and of Greek descent, called, in case you didn't know, "The Father of History." Had he, in his travels, learned about it? He had visited Egypt and in particular Heliopolis, the City of the Sun, and wrote some comment on the Egyptian veneration of the goose. Yes, the goose. You and I might not, I think, care to venerate the goose, but we might, and then again, we might not, prefer it to venerating some other of the creatures of which the ancient Egyptians were so fond, say, the crocodile: it might certainly be safer, for one thing. And the Father of History goes on to say:

> There is another sacred bird named the phoenix. I have never seen it myself, except in pictures, for it is exceedingly rare, only appearing, according to the people of Heliopolis, once in five hundred years, when it is seen after the death of its parent. If the pictures are accurate its size and appearance are as follows: its plumage is partly red and partly gold, while in shape and size it is very much like an eagle. They tell a story about this bird…the phoenix is said to come from Arabia, carrying the parent bird encased in myrrh; it proceeds to the Temple of the Sun and there buries the body. In order to do this they say that it first forms a ball

as big as it can carry, then, hollowing out the ball, it inserts its dead parent, subsequently covering over the opening with fresh myrrh. The ball is then exactly the same weight as it was at first. The phoenix bears this ball to Egypt, all encased as I have said, and deposits it in the Temple of the Sun. Such is their myth about this bird.

I have left out a few words. I shall now tell them to you. Herodotus says, "*Personally, I find it incredible.*" And well he might. *He*, however, leaves something out, did you notice? Nothing said here about the phoenix being burned to ashes and then being reborn out of them. Well, Herodotus didn't have to tell us everything he saw and heard. After all, how much were they paying him? Now, I would point out a few things. For one, note that the funeral of the dead phoenix took place at the Temple of the Sun; note, too, the mention of it being encased in a ball. We all know that among the many, *many* creatures venerated by the Egyptians was the scarab, a large beetle, and the scarab is shown, time after time, rolling the sun like a ball across the sky: which is why it was sacred. But what so many of our books failed to say, is that the scarab—in entomology as distinct from mythology—the scarab-beetle is a *dung*-beetle. And I can tell you, for I have seen it myself, not in Egypt, but in the Holy Land, right next-door, I can tell you that what the scarab rolls along the earth is a *ball of dung*. It forms such a ball, I saw it done out of camel dung near the ruins of the Philistine city of Ascalon, and then it gets right up on its hind legs and it *rolls* it. It keeps on rolling it along.

And why does it do this? No myth or secret, the scarab doesn't care who knows: it rolls this round ball to a place of its choice and then lays its eggs next to it, in another and pear-shaped blob of the same stuff. And the warmth of the decomposing substance (like the warmth of the sun) helps the baby scarabs to hatch; also it provides a hot lunch without Federal subsidy.

So it seems that the ancient Egyptians seem to have given the phoenix some of the characteristics of the scarab; and, if we had never seen any scarabs ourselves we might well say that they were mythical, and that, personally, we found the story incredible: as in part, about rolling the sun, it is. They also seem to have tidied up the tale a bit. *Myrrh*, for example, is ever so much nicer than *manure*. Well, with the phoenix appearing in Egypt only every 500 years, people had lots of time to think about it, and to think of improvements. As it happens, 500 years after Herodotus, and on the other side of the Mediterranean, lived the Roman poet, Ovid, who wrote:

> *All these receive their birth from other things,*
> *But from himself the Phoenix only springs.*
> *Self-born, begotten by the parent flame*

In which he burned, another and the same.

So, if the poetic element of fire wasn't there in the legend in the time of Herodotus, it certainly was there by the time of Ovid. And it is this part of the legend which has endured. People tended to forget about the big ball of myrrh. They tended to forget the filial piety of the blessed bird, in bringing his father all the way to Egypt for a big funeral at the Temple of the Sun. What people did tend to remember was that the phoenix built a sort of special nest, somehow caused it to catch on fire, was burned to ashes—and, out of the ashes, was, somehow, born anew. It is after all a metaphor of supreme vividness and strength, and to it was added yet another element, that is, that not only did the phoenix—which by now was not seen as being dead when its nest caught fire, but as being alive—that not only did the phoenix somehow start the fire; the phoenix was thought of and depicted as *fanning the fire!* upon which fire it was consumed…only to rise again. So one is not altogether surprised to read, in one medieval *Bestiary*—a bestiary being a book of beasts, with each creature being described not exclusively in terms of natural science but in terms of metaphor and allegory as well; of religion, that is—one is not altogether surprised to read the following passage: *The Phoenix. Know this is its lot; it comes to death of its own free will, and from death it comes to life: hear what he signifies. Phoenix signifies Jesus, Son of Mary, that he had the power to die of his own will, and from death came to life…*

And yet, about two thousand years after Herodotus, that wise man of Norfolk (England, not Virginia), Sir Thomas Browne, M.D., did find it necessary to include these lines in his book, *Vulgar Errors of the Day*:

> That there is but one Phoenix in the world, which after many hundred years burneth itself, and from the ashes rises up another, is a conceit not new altogether popular, but of great Antiquity: not only delivered by humane authors, but frequently expressed by holy Writers; by Cyril, Epiphanius, and others. All which, notwithstanding, we cannot presume the existence of this Animal, nor dare we affirm there is any Phoenix in Nature. For, first, there wants herein the definite tests of things uncertain—that is, the sense of man. For though many writers have much enlarged hereon, there is not any ocular describer, or such as presumeth to confirm it upon aspection. Primitive Authors, from whom the stream of relations is derivative, deliver themselves dubiously, and either by a doubtful parenthesis, or a timorous conclusion, overthrow the whole relation. As for its unity or conceit that there should be but one in Nature, it seemeth not only repugnant unto Philosophy, but also Holy Scripture, which plainly affirms there went of every sort at least two into the Ark of Noah. Every fowle after his kind, every bird of every sort, they went into the Ark, and two of all flesh wherein there is breath of life. It infringeth

the Benediction of God concerning multiplication. God blessed them, saying Be fruitful and multiply and let fowls multiply in the earth, which terms are not applicable unto the Phoenix, whereof there is but one in the world, and no more living than at the first benediction. As for longevity that it liveth a thousand years or more, besides that from imperfect observations and rarity of appearances no confirmation can be made, there may probably be a mistake in the compute. For the tradition being very ancient, the conceit might have its original in times of shorter compute. For if we suppose our present calculation, the Phoenix now in nature will be the sixt from the Creation, and but in the middle of its years, and, if the Rabbine's prophecy succeed, it shall conclude its daies not in its own, but in the last and general flames.

A consoling thought.—Now, as this may be generally considered a Protestant view, and as we have already heard what might be generally considered a Catholic view, are there any Moslem and Jewish views? Indeed there are. The 1962 Encyclopedia Britannica tells us, "Among the Arabs the story of the Phoenix was confused with that of the salamander; and the samand or samandal," from whose feathers a fireproof cloth is woven—the salamander of course being able to *live in fires*, and not minding in the least being regarded as the source of asbestos—"the samand or samandal...is represented sometimes as a quadruped, sometimes as a bird." A *four*-legged phoenix! Allah-hu akbar!

Dr. Maurice Burton, the British natural historian, upon whose book *Phoenix Reborn* this Adventure depends almost (if not quite) in its entirety for reasons you will get to see; Dr. Burton says, "The Rabbins tell us that all the birds, save the phoenix, shared in the sin of Eve, and ate of the forbidden fruit. As a reward the phoenix was given, not immortality but this modified form of immutability."

Legend, we see, supported the fable of the phoenix; so did poetry; so did anyway the old time religion, although the new time religion and the new time science was doubtful. The French naturalist, Cuvier, early on in the 19th century, suggested that the phoenix was actually a pheasant... precisely, the golden pheasant. Certainly in ancient times the golden pheasant was not known outside of China, and its plumage in a way resembles that attributed to the phoenix. But if it was not known outside of China, how could it have become the subject of a legend most widely known in the near or middle east and the Mediterranean? Cuvier suggests that, well, somehow, one might have so to speak lost its way. It is a long way to lose, but there is nothing absolutely impossible in the suggestion. However, how often could this have happened? Cuvier seizes on this very point. It could not have happened often, he argues: hence the belief that the phoenix appeared only every five hundred (at the minimal calculation) years. I find this somewhat circular reasoning, personally. Still…let us for the argument agree that in the appearance of the crimson and golden pheasant lies the origin of the description of the phoenix. But how about the rest of it? There is, to be sure, a Chinese legend of the phoenix, but the comparison with "our" legend of the phoenix vanishes while you examine it. I know, because I once, briefly, lived in China, and it vanished while *I* was examining it. The fact is, alas, that European visitors in China, observing that the Chinese had a legend of a marvelous red bird, too, in effect cried, *"The phoenix!"* The Chinese used to be very polite to foreigners (when indeed they were not cutting them into very small pieces), and so, very politely, they decided that this must be the proper foreign word for their own legendary bird. But that is about all.

* * * *

T. H. White, better-known for his *The Once and Future King*, translated a *Bestiary*, and in his own commentary on the phoenix, says, very calmly and casually, that it was probably the purple heron, called *benu*. He casually and calmly fails to mention that *benu* is pronounced *veenee* in Modern Greek, and was perhaps so pronounced in some of the ancient Greek dialects, too: as for *x*, the Greeks often added it to foreign nouns ending in vowels to show that it was a *foreign* noun and hence not requiring to be grammatically declined as Greek nouns were: example, the Apocryphal Book of Jesus the Son of Sira*ch*. White was in his turn very probably repeating the suggestions made by other and earlier writers on the subject of this fantastic bird, the phoenix, which made itself a nest of spicy and pungent and aromatic plants and then, fire somehow being introduced into this nest, fanned the fire with its wing and perished in an ecstasy…only to rise from its ashes, reborn… "suggestions" which suggested that the bird in question was indeed a heron. What is the connection?

Here is one. The heron was known to make its nest in the tops of palm trees. So was the phoenix. In fact, and we should take note of this, in the old Greek the word for palm tree was the same as the word for phoenix. Remember that Lactantius says that the tree derives its name from the bird— but may it not be the other way around? Palm trees after all are common in hot countries, and even in those merely warm, whereas one thing which all writers insisted on about the phoenix is that it was not only uncommon, it was exceedingly rare. It does seem likelier that the rara avis took its name from the un-rare tree rather than vice versa. Shakespeare, in his poem, "The Phoenix and the Turtle," refers to *"…the bird of loudest lay,"* of song, that is, as in *The Lay of the Last Minstrel; "Let the bird of loudest lay / On the sole Arabian tree…*and so on. It is not meant to imply that there was only one tree in Arabia, but that, I think, the tree of the phoenix was unique, as was the bird. As to why the bird of *loudest* lay, or song, well, it was another part of the legend that the phoenix, as it died, sang a song of exceeding sweetness. And I suppose it must have sung loudly, as well as sweetly, because, as it proceeded from Arabia (or Phoenicia, which is adjacent) into Egypt it was accompanied by flocks of other birds: perhaps alerted by the song, as well as by the red-and-gold-glory of the bird's plumage.

Now it may not have escaped attention that there is at least some resemblance between the words phoenix and Phoenicia. The matter is complicated, and I shall proceed to complicate it still more. The Phoenicians did not call themselves Phoenicians, but many people are commonly called by names other than their original names for themselves: the Hungarians call themselves Magyar; the American Indians, for example, never thought of themselves as "Indians," and nowadays many of them prefer to call themselves "Native Americans," as though the rest of us were all born somewhere else...and, for that matter, as though the word "American" were a "Native American" word...which it is after all *not*. However, the ancient Greeks it was who called the coastal people of what is now Lebanon and Syria by the name of Phoenicians. It means The Red Ones, so to speak; from the Greek *phoinos* or *poinos*—remember the *Punic* Wars? They were the wars between Rome and Carthage, a Phoenician colonially-founded city in North Africa. And we are usually informed that this name of "Red Ones" was given because the Phoenicians were sunburned by their long voyages at sea, which they made to bring the Greeks not only the alphabet but such trade items as glassware and copper (which is, by the way, *red*) and the famous Phoenician Tyrian dye. Which is almost invariably referred to as "purple" dye: as a matter of fact its colors ranged quite a way along the spectrum, and included blue *and* red. "...*and red*..."

The phoenix was also red. But the purple heron was, well, *pur*ple. I have never seen a purple heron, but I have, in Sausalito, California, seen a blue heron. Several. They are a sort of blue-grey. And some authorities are insistent that it is a mistake to connect the *purple* heron with ancient Egyptian bird-worship. It was the *grey* heron, they say. However, there is no grey phoenix. I have cited T. H. White in his *The Book of Beasts*, now let me cite Richard Carrington, in his book, *Mermaids and Mastodons*. He begins by quoting our old and so well-read friend Pliny the Elder, who said that the body of the phoenix was "a deep *red purple*" and that on its head it had a "tuft and plume." Carrington points out that the purple heron does have anyway a *plume* on its head, indeed, and that it "was one of the symbols of the sun god at Heliopolis"—which, remember, was the very place whither the phoenix brought, in one version, the body of its father for burial. T. H. White seemed to see no further problem, and even Carrington glides away from the subject; but there is one obvious and even matter of fact objection, and that is that the heron, far from being seen only once in a thousand or even five hundred years, is seen all the time. Something seems to have been lost in translation. But I am not yet ready to leave Carrington.

"In prehistoric times," he says, "when men sought gods in the forces of nature, a bird deity was the obvious choice to symbolize the sky, for birds were the only creatures who naturally belonged to that element." One had not to be a theologian in order to take the tempting trail to either symbolism or allegory—which are, after all, brother and sister—in an attempt to, so to speak, lift the Veil of Isis…in other words, decide what these ancient stories really meant; and the most popular method was to declare any one of them "a nature myth." And of these, *the* most popular was to say that something, anything, was "a solar myth." Applying this to the phoenix, let us admit at once, or, anyway, almost at once, that the phoenix lends itself really very easily to definition as a solar myth. It *is* red and yellow, it *does* die and it *is* reborn—all, just like the sun. But to go back to the myth of the scarab, which none of these writers whom I have quoted seems to have done, the Egyptian myth of the scarab which rolled the great globe or ball of the sun across the sky, this is not as glamorous as the Greek myth which has Apollo driving the sun as a chariot across the sky. How natural to assume, as many of the ancients did assume, that it was from the iron shoes that shod the chariot-horses of the sun that there came sparks, and that it was these which ignited the funeral pyre of the phoenix. It seems, somehow, to make sense…almost…until we pause, and realize that, after all, there are no horses…up there in the sky. There are no stones up there in the sky, either, hence, of course, stones cannot fall from up there, down to *here*, to earth. Hence the wise men of former times were quite right to deny the existence of meteorites: and they did deny it, and went right on denying it, well into the 19th century. Thomas Jefferson denied it, and when a couple of members of the Harvard faculty announced all the evidence, Jefferson said, "I would rather believe that two Yankee professors have lied than believe that stones fall from the sky…" He was a great man. But here he was wrong. And, perhaps, if you think that what I mean to imply is that it was meteorites, "shooting- [or falling-] stars," which ignited the nest of the phoenix—well, perhaps you, too, may be wrong.

And when we consider the melody of the dying phoenix, this inevitably brings to mind the legend of the dying swan…and its "swan song"…and of course it was also said that swans it was that drew, sometimes, the chariot of the sun…and *not* horses. After all, a singing horse would be a bit much.

However, I am not yet finished, really, with the scarab. My typewriter made a mistake right at this point and wrote, for *scarab*, *acrabs*, and *acrab* is the Hebrew and perhaps the Arabic word for scorpion. I intend to do nothing whatsoever about this; I shall return, as I said I would, to the scarab, the insect of the sun. Insects lay eggs, and the eggs turn into cater-pillars or grubs or maggots, or, well, *worms*: and in the case of the phoenix the process was reversed: the worm turned, indeed: it turned into an egg, and the egg into another phoenix. If we know nothing of birds, would we believe that they produced eggs? If we knew nothing of eggs, would we believe that they produced birds? Down to the age of Shakespeare, a certain European goose was never known to produce an egg; its goslings were never seen by man, and the universal explanation was that it hatched at sea from a certain crustacean, hence its name of *barnacle goose*; evidently the young barnacle looked vaguely goose-like enough to support such a story. Not until very late in the 16th or very early in the 17th century was the im-mense and frozen archipelago called Spitzbergen, or Svalbard, discovered, or re-discovered. Men went there for whales, and they found the whales, but they also found something else, something seen more-or-less for the first time by the eyes of man, namely the perfectly normal nests and eggs of the so-called barnacle goose, there above the arctic circle. The argument *ab silentio* on which this almost nursery rhyme had been based was destroyed by the squawking of, may I say it?—Mother Goose…

But no voyage to what was then called "the East Greenland seas" de-stroyed in the slightest the mysterious veil, and perhaps it was the Veil of Isis, which hung in tantalizing gauzy drapes all round about the fable of the phoenix. The sign of the phoenix appeared in the elaboratorial MSS of the alchemists and hung over the doors of the apothecaries; the 17th century gave way to the 18th and the 18th to the 19th, the sign of the phoenix was employed even by, of all antic notions, fire insurance companies!—but the mystery of the phoenix remained unsolved.

* * * *

John James Audubon.

Everybody knows the name of Audubon. Not everybody knows, how-ever, that he once planned to go into the steamboat business on the Ohio River with a young English immigrant named Keats—a brother, as a matter of fact, of the poet Keats. The steamboats, however, so to speak never got off the ground; Audubon probably lost his money, Keats-in-America cer-tainly lost his money, and Keats-in-England wrote to him, "I am afraid that Mr. Audubon is not a very honest man." Winona McClintock, another and a later poet, wrote, "Keats had TB, Shelley drowned, Shakespeare lies in the cold, cold ground." Audubon, meanwhile, not much knowing what else to do, began to paint birds. Before long he had enough for a book, but before long, too, he realized, that there weren't enough customers for it in Amer-ica; he went to England (we may suppose he did not bother to call upon the Keats family for a subscription); he went to Scotland. In Edinburgh he called on, among other people, a prominent local surgeon. I quote from memory: "He came to me directly from his dissecting-room, with, the blood still wet upon his hands. His manner was most gentlemanly and agreeable and he promised to help me in my endeavors as most he could." The surgeon, I will now reveal to you, was a Dr. Knox; in fact, he was *the* Dr. Knox, and the source of the bodies in the dissecting-room (whose blood was still wet upon his hands) will not bear examination; so let us examine it. As bodies were essential to the study of medicine and surgery and as the only bodies available for the purpose were those of criminals who had been hanged, a supply which had begun to dry up anyway, a professional corps (shall we say) had grown up, of graverobbers. They sold their robbed bodies to the medical profession. And they were known, not as Dickens's Jerry Cruncher preferred to be known as, to wit, Agricultural Character, but as "resurrection-men!"—shades of the phoenix! Eh?

Times had been very hard in Ireland, and, God knows they must have been very hard for people to migrate thence to Scotland! We well know that most Irish people are the salt of the earth, descendants of kings and princes, pious, sober, and learned; however, two of them were not any of these things: one was named Burke and one was named Hare, and in order to make the rent on their shall we say studio apartment, called in the pawky Scots dialect a "but and ben," and located in Tanner's Close, I regret to say that they proceeded to murder the many guests who found hospitality with them, and whose delectable corpses they sold to—but surely you know the verse? I wants to make your flesh creep, I'll recite it to you:

> Up the Close and doon the stair,
> But and ben wi' Burke and Hare:
> Burke's the butcher, Hare's the thief,
> And Knox the boy who buys the beef.

From Keats at one end to Burke and Hare at the other, Audubon was certainly connected with a lot of *very* interesting people, one way or another. And, taking another way, let us consider what *else* he had been doing: he had been watching wild turkeys and what *they* had been doing. This was in the good old USA, in one of the eastern states, perhaps Kentucky; I now quote Maurice Burton, from whose book *Phoenix Reborn* I have quoted before: he says that Audubon "spoke of [the turkeys] rolling themselves in deserted ants' nests," and then he quotes Audubon for the reason:

...to clear their growing feathers of the loose scales and prevent ticks
and other vermin from attacking them, these insects being unable to bear
the odor of the earth in which ants have dwelt.

Well, this is interesting, this is *very* interesting, because, do you remember, one of the random samples which we took of the year 1934 showed "a schoolboy in Australia seeing a bird doing something odd with ants..."

This, however, lay a bit in the future of the year 1847, when Mr. Philip Henry Gosse published the book *Birds of Jamaica*. One of these birds is the Barbados blackbird, also called the tinkling grackle—I think that only the English could come up with a name like "the tinkling grackle"!—yet be that as it may: Gosse described how the birds would often go and gather limes bruised by falling off trees, then stand on one foot and rub the oozing fruit under the opposite wing; then switch to the other leg and apply the lime beneath the wing on the other side. Was the blackbird (or, if you *insist*, the tinkling grackle)—was the bird by any other name concerned with possible under-*wing* odor? Burton says, "This 'bathing' might go on for an hour, and was presumed to have as its aim the application of the aromatic juice of the lime to the feathers."

Odd.

Thirty years later came a report that "a tame crow...was seen deliberately to take its stand on an anthill and allow the ants to crawl over its plumage, seize parasites in their jaws and bear them away." This sounds a little like the accounts of the small birds which are alleged to roam freely upon the crocodile in order to pick things from its teeth. Burton says, referring to the bird accounts, "During the next sixty years there were a number of similar stories published in a variety of journals, scientific and otherwise, but no self-respecting ornithologist believed them. They were, in fact, treated, like the myth of the phoenix, as wholly fictitious."

The year is now 1934.

Peter Bradley, an Australian schoolboy, writes to a Melbourne newspaper to say that "he had noticed...starlings...picking up ants and stowing them away among their feathers;" and this letter is read by A. H. Chisholm, who is working on a book called *Bird Wonders of Australia*. Chisholm does not altogether believe the story, but, Pete being persistent, Chisholm is impressed enough to add a note about it to his book. (I now switch from the historical present to the past.) The note was read by Professor Erwin Stresemann, in Europe, who published it in a monthly magazine about birds: letters poured in, not just from schoolboys, either; and in a short time the practice was acknowledged not only to exist but to exist in many different kinds of birds. It was named *anting*. It still is called *anting*, although it is now clear that the birds which *ant* do not always use *ants*; but we will get to that.

The bird, as observed, evidently, hundreds of times by now, picks up an ant in its bill, and, spreading its wings, rapidly rubs the ant along (usually) the inside of its wings, which are widely extended: "In this position the

quills or primaries," i.e. the primary feathers, "of the wings are fanned."
A Canadian observer, the ornithologist Roy Ivor, is quoted as saying that
when the anting process is "at its height the birds seem to be afflicted with
an ecstasy…toppling on to one side, or in other ways losing their balance."
A similar report comes from Hoger Poulsen, whose observations at the
Copenhagen Zoo include those of "152 birds representing 85 species belonging to 24 families;" he reports that the birds sometimes rub the ants on
their tails and shoulders as well as wings, often becoming so absorbed in
the task as to lose balance and fall over. These observations include birds
in the wild as well as in captivity, and well might the question be asked,
"Did birds only start anting rather recently?" The obvious answer must be,
Certainly *not*; and to the next question, Then why was it not noticed before?
The answer, not so obvious to those who have not seen anting, is that it is
all done very quickly, far more quickly than it takes to describe it: probably
no trained ornithologist noticed it because none was looking for it; and,
such is the general attitude of specialists of all kinds, observations reported
by non-specialists (who *had* noticed it) were brushed aside. Stories of birds
applying ants to their feathers were regarded by ornithologists much as
herpetologists regarded (and regard) stories that snakes form themselves
into hoops and roll down hills, or suck the milk from cows' udders. Old
wives' tales, we call them.

* * * *

However, young Peter Bradley *was* wrong in believing that the birds
"stow" the ants in their feathers, they do not, they never let go of the ant
till they have finished rubbing it; then they either eat it or, simply drop it.

Furthermore, close observations show that the ants are not used to eat
the smaller parasitical insects, bird-mites or bird-lice, which are usually
found in plumage; and, in fact, in implying that young wild turkeys wallow in old ant nests because their parasites will drop off, not liking the
smell of ants, Audubon was also wrong. In which case, or cases, why do
the birds who ant, *ant*? I have said a bit before, that, although the name of
anting is applied to such behavior, not ants alone are used; we have seen
the custom of the Barbados blackbird (or *tinkling grackle*, if you prefer; I
do not) in using bruised limes for the purpose of rubbing its feathers. Are
any other items used? Oh you bet. Herewith a partial list: Pine needles,
pepperina berries, English walnuts, "lemon pulp, lemon juice, vinegar and
beer, orange juice, choke berries and sumac berries, cigar stumps, roaches,
shrimps, moths, mothballs, tobacco pipe ashes, chimney smoke, a smoldering log, apple pieces or apple peel, pansy blossoms, hot chocolate, soapy
dishwater, cigarettes…" Perhaps this list is long enough, although, probably, other items are also used. It is evident that although the practice of

anting may be innate or instinctive, the items used are fortuitous: that is, a bird may engage in anting with whatever it may chance to find around.

As I so often quote Maurice Burton as the prime source for this Adventure, I will say that I know of him only that he is an Englishman, a doctor of science, and the author of several books, including *Infancy in Animals, Animal Courtship, and Animal Legends,* as well as *Phoenix Reborn.* It is in connection with his pet birds Corbie, Jasper, and Niger, that he came to write the book which, brought to my attention by Professor Robert Maccubin of the College of William and Mary, inspired this Adventure. But before going into that, let us take our scientifictional time-and-space scanner, and zoom back to the year 1934.

Again.

A reporter on an English provincial newspaper is reproved for bringing in a Silly Story.

Silly Stories are most common in what newspapermen call The Silly Season, usually the Dog Days of August, but can turn up all around the year, any year, and may range from (I heard this one phoned in one night to the office of the old San Francisco *News-Call-Bulletin*), a phantom aeroplane crashing into the Golden Gate Bridge (there was no aeroplane and, hence, no crash: there was a bridge, though) to a cat reported to have walked 30 miles between its old home and its new (the cat had walked perhaps the three miles actual distance between the two houses, or, perhaps, had simply been away a long time on business of its own). Flying Saucer stories are usually Silly Stories, but not always. Stories of elephants being dragged underwater by giant sharks are invariably Silly Stories, with the added factor of originating too far away to be tracked down; stories of people who are 120 years old are almost invariably Silly Stories—as Randall Garrett once said to me, "People over 112 years old always have in common that they have no birth certificate." To which I might add, that if they do, it is almost certainly someone else's birth certificate.

This particular Silly Story was about a house which caught on fire because a bird had picked up a lit cigarette and carried it to its nest in the rain-gutter of the house in question. It was explained to the reporter that such stories, though not terribly uncommon, were terribly untrue, because birds do not pick up lit cigarettes, let alone carry them off to their nests; cigarettes being inedible. *See?*

I *hope* you see. Rocks do not fall from the sky, because...

Burton's theory is that anting is an extreme form of preening and that it is related to an extreme form of sun-bathing. The bird does it because it *feels good.* I might go as far out on a limb as any bird, and suggest that it may be remotely related to what in human beings is called fetishism...but I won't press this point. Bird-anting seems also related to aspects of bird-bathing;

in both instances the bird seems to go into an ecstasy…sometimes. And now I shall ask you to recall that Lactantius, in his poem on the phoenix, says that it bathes the day before it burns. I shall ask you also to recall how many of the substances (or items, rather) with which birds engage in anting are or might be considered "aromatic," or, anyway, strong-tasting or strong-smelling substances: Pine needles, pepperina berries, English walnuts, limes, lemons, vinegar, beer, orange juice, cigar butts, shrimps, mothballs, tobacco ashes, smoke, apple, hot chocolate, cigarettes… Add to the adjective *aromatic*, the adjective *spicy*, and something like a revelation occurs. *Of what did the phoenix build its nest?* According to all the old reports (and there are after all no new reports) it built it from such items as cassia, spikenard, cinnamon, balsam, frankincense and myrrh… In other words, out of substances aromatic to the smell and spicy (or pungent) to the taste. And, if balsam and frankincense and myrrh sound ever so much more romantic than tobacco, beer, vinegar, lemon, lime and orange, recollect that legend placed the phoenix in Arabia and that southern and southeastern Arabia was of old the chief source of frankincense and myrrh and that it lay along the trade-routes along which passed such other odoriferous items as cinnamon, cassia, spikenard, balsam; one employs what may be available, whether one is a phoenix, or not. As to the rather obvious matter that anting, whatever it may be and whatever motive it may have, is not, repeat *not*, nest-building, I can only reply, No it's *not*. Is it.

Birds…sometimes…go into what we term "an ecstasy" whilst anting with ants…they go into this ecstasy…sometimes…whilst bathing or preening…sometimes this happens when they have merely *seen* ants and this happens sometimes when they are applying a variety of other items to their bodies and sometimes when (though they make all the motions) they have absolutely nothing at all in their beaks; and in the state which we, perhaps anthropomorphically, term *ecstasy*, they tremble and extend their wings and make odd and curious movements and sometimes whilst doing this they fall down. Don't they? Yes they *do*.

* * * *

We human beings sort of regard the prime cause of ecstasy as sexual, but there are many other causes. However, *is* anting and its frequent resultant ecstatic state connected with sexual activity—among, that is, *birds*? Evidently it is…but not terribly closely. Some of the movements are similar to those observed in mating dances. But only *some*. So we must look for other cause or causes. And we must also remember that old Lactantius told us that the Phoenix bathed *before* it sat upon its magic nest and burned and died, whereas Burton and others tell us that birds who ant frequently bathe *after* they ant. Well, Lactantius and others got the order of the egg and the worm wrong, so another error in the matter of sequence need not astonish us. Onward. *Do* birds perform in this ecstatic manner whilst sunbathing?

*Some*times.

And *do* they bathe, afterwards?

*Some*times.

We do say…sometimes…of aromatic or spicy substances, certainly of pungent ones, that, if too "strong," they "*burn*." Pliny the Elder complained of the loss of currency to Rome in importing immense quantities of pepper from India, when the pepper's sole function was, he said, "to provide a slight burning sensation to the tongue." Perhaps something of the sort happens when a bird ants, perhaps the formic acid in the ants and the essential oils in the fruit rinds or whatever provides somewhat of a burning sensation which the bird finds intensely pleasurable. The same thing might be said of the heat of the sun whilst the bird is sunbathing. And the same thing might be said of the anting birds which pick up lit cigarette butts and apply them to themselves, or which ant in the smoke of smoldering logs or upon the tops of chimneys, or even in the steam of kettles. The common factor, is, then, *heat*.

However, what of the birds who go into wing-flapping ecstasies while preening after being rain-soaked when it is not hot, or whilst bathing in water on a cool day? Ah…there you have me. And there, I believe, you may have everybody else concerned in this whole complex subject. The picture, you see, is not complete. And, incomplete as I have shown it to you, there is nonetheless something left out. Something of intense importance.

Maurice Burton had a pet rook, a bird closely related to the crow, Corbie was its name. This family of birds has long been known to be rather intelligent, although it did not seem particularly intelligent of Corbie to dance in front of the fireplace when the logs were burning—so close that the fireplace had to be screened. Corbie was subsequently seen to turn on the electric heater for his pleasure and even to pick up wooden matches in one claw and peck them until they burst into flame. Then he would hold the matches one by one under his wing, and *ant*. Now, Corbie was not the only bird that Burton had, and one of the others was a bluejay named Jasper. A lit cigarette butt came within Jasper's reach one day: he played and toyed with it a moment, then, "*Jasper went into the full anting display in a most dramatic fashion. He brought his wings forward to their full extent, the wings curving inward in front of the body, so the tips almost met in front… The magnificent coloring of his wings was shown to the full and his whole pose was statuesque…this display lasted…less than a minute.*"

Remarkable. *To say the least.*

Now, as Dr. Burton is a scientist, he desired to obtain scientific evidence of these displays, and a photographer was on hand to do so. A second rook, named Niger, belonged to the Burtons, and—but let me bring in Burton's own words again. "A rook," he says, "is a moderately large bird with a glossy black plumage. When he 'ants,' this plumage is displayed more fully than at any other time. The effect is magnificent and spectacular. It is, therefore, quite unmistakable." However, Niger refused to ant....with ants, that is. And so the photographer, who was, as a matter of fact, Dr. Burton's daughter, remembering how other birds would ant with embers and matches and burning cigarettes, decided to try something else.

She set fire to a small pile of straw.

Niger "*Jumped onto the fire, spread his wings...snatched at the flame with his beak...it seemed incredible that a bird could stand among flames with the tongues licking up to his outstretched wings without sustaining injury... Niger became wildly excited, hopping around...snatched at the burning straw with his beak, at the same time bringing his wings forward... and the head constantly in movement snatching at the smoke, snatching at the flame, and passing the beak up and down inside the wings... Yet there was no sign of singeing and no smell of burnt feathers.*" I should imagine that the film which showed this must be one of the most fascinating ever made and I would rather see it than any Hollywood or "underground" film ever filmed. Did the film come out when it was sent to be developed? It certainly did, and it showed, in Burton's words, "the vigorous flailing of the wings, there was something seemingly miraculous...about the performance... [the bird] would wallow and gyrate over the flames," and saliva formed in its beak. Burton showed the film to the London Zoological Society, and the chairman said, after the showing ended, "Of course, *it is the answer to the phoenix legend.*"

After this, almost anything one could say would be an anti-climax.

We do not know *why* birds behave this way, but we know they *do*. We do not know *who* the people were who first saw and spoke of the bird which gathered aromatic plants to make use of them, but we know that they really *must* have seen this. We cannot say who first observed a bird in a burning nest, fanning the flames with its wings, but we can say that they actually *saw* such an incredible sight. And if they also saw the same bird, in ecstasy, falling over or falling down, and, the rest of it being hidden from them by smoke, if they thought that the bird had burned to death in the fire, why, one cannot blame them for thinking so.

Where did the bird, in ancient times, before the time of matches, obtain the fire? From another fire, it would seem. From *any* other fire, for any burning ember or piece of wood with one end glowing would do. And if the scene was not seen often, and if indeed it was seen extremely seldom, why then, how natural to believe that such a scene took place only every five hundred or a thousand years!

As for the *benu*, the blue heron, which nested in Egypt in the top of the *benu* palm tree, why, it seems possible that anyway the name of phoenix came from that, possibly from a purely homonymous resemblance. As for other possible connections, well...who knows? What bird, then, was it, which, so gorgeous of plumage, gave its physical appearance to the phoenix of legend? Phoenix red and gold and purple and blue and... Parrots have been suggested, and golden pheasants, and the bird of paradise and the blossom-headed parakeet of India and... It is useless, it is vain to ask what bird with even merely red and blue and gold plumage might have been the original phoenix...or so *I* think... *I* think that, surely, the name does not come from the bird, but from the blue-gold-red *fire* the bird began: it was the, so to speak, *plumes of fire*, which were *phoinikos*, or, glowing-red. For, after all, the phoenix is, above all, the *firebird*. It is the bird of fire. It is the fire of life.

www.ingramcontent.com/pod-product-compliance
Lightning Source LLC
Chambersburg PA
CBHW05073525O626
47155CB00005B/1783